CW00350010

THE MOCK MARRIAGE

Dorothy Mack

SAPERE
BOOKS

THE MOCK MARRIAGE

Published by Sapere Books.

20 Windermere Drive, Leeds, England, LS17 7UZ,
United Kingdom

saperebooks.com

ISBN: 978-1-913518-35-6

CHAPTER 1

"Egon! I say, Egon, over here!"

The preoccupied expression of the driver of a smart phaeton vanished as he glanced over his shoulder in the direction of the hail. In an admirably short count of seconds, he had identified the hailer and neatly manoeuvred his bays over to the kerb. The groom, who had been sitting beside him, jumped down and went to the horses' heads while the driver followed the erratic progress of the modishly attired young man who dashed across the street in a precipitate manner that evoked a colourful stream of invectives from the driver of a cart piled high with furniture as he narrowly averted a collision. Amusement lurked in the dark eyes of the phaeton's owner as he surveyed the smiling person of the intrepid and unconscious young man.

"Well, well, if it isn't my little cousin, all grown up and decked out like a Bond Street Beau. How are you, Geoffrey? Shouldn't you be at school at this season?"

Unabashed by the other's drawling patronage, the younger man eagerly wrung the hand extended down to him. "Thought I couldn't be mistaken in that dark phiz of yours even after all this time," he said with satisfaction. "It's good to see you, Egon. I'd heard you had sold out after Waterloo. Are you home for good?"

"You see before you a dedicated civilian, coz. May I drop you somewhere?"

"Thanks. I'm on my way to Jackson's, if that won't put you out?"

At an inviting gesture from his cousin, Geoffrey climbed up into the phaeton. The driver flipped a coin to his groom to pay for a hackney carriage and enjoined him to meet him at his lodgings.

While Egon concentrated on easing his spirited pair out into the traffic again, the young man took the opportunity to study the cousin he had not seen in five years, noting the deep vertical grooves in lean cheeks, the tiny lines fanning out from the outer corners of his eyes, and the hard line of the jaw. His skin, several shades darker than Geoffrey remembered, stretched more tautly over the fine bone structure and had acquired a weathered look like old leather.

"Well, what's the verdict?"

"Eh?" Geoffrey blinked at the harsh tones.

Dark eyes compelled blue ones. "You were staring at me as if you weren't sure you had the right man."

"I thought at first that you hadn't changed, Egon, but I was wrong. Was it very bad — Waterloo?"

"Bad enough."

"I'm glad you came out of it in one piece, anyway," the younger man said, awkward but determined, when he realized the subject had been dismissed.

"I share your joy at this happy outcome, cousin, which makes two of us at least."

Though dry, Egon's voice had lost some of its earlier harshness, and Geoffrey was encouraged by the slight softening in the dark glance that swung briefly in his direction. The disconcerting sense of distance from the person who had been his boyhood ideal lessened when Egon displayed his strong white teeth in a familiar teasing grin.

"Speaking of changes, I think I am the one who has had the greater shock. I left an untidy young whelp behind and return to find a polished Jack O' Dandy with … can that be an incipient moustache I see?"

Quick colour ran up under Geoffrey's stiff shirt points, but he resisted the urge to finger the fuzz on his upper lip, and replied with commendable nonchalance, "I just wondered how I'd look with a moustache."

"Would you care for a disinterested opinion?"

His passenger hooted. "You do not think I'm still green enough to come to you for a disinterested opinion, do you? I haven't forgotten the time when I was about thirteen that you and Jack had me convinced that I was growing a hump on my back." Casual mention of his brother's name had straightened the line of Egon's mouth, and Geoffrey hastened to retrieve his error. "You may spare the criticism of the moustache. I was planning to get rid of it in a few days in any case," he lied jauntily. "It itches."

Egon's lips twitched but he held his peace. Not until he had feathered a corner and passed an eccentrically weaving brewer's cart did he speak again, with a return to his first question. "Why aren't you up at Oxford?"

A snort of disgust greeted this. "Lord, Egon, have your wits gone begging or do you think time stood still while you were in the army? I finished with the High two years ago. Didn't Grandmother keep you posted on family affairs?"

"I have not been in correspondence with our revered grandparent since I left England."

There was nothing to be gleaned from the bald statement delivered in even tones, but Geoffrey turned impulsively to his cousin. "Lord, Egon, I'm sorry. I had no idea. I do vaguely remember that Grandmother was furious with you at the time

7

you joined the army, and I recall asking Jack about it. He said you had refused to marry the girl she had selected for you," he went on more slowly, aware that his cousin's eyes had narrowed.

"Did Jack have anything else to contribute on the subject?"

"I … I don't think so." Hearing the steel in the soft voice, Geoffrey blurted, "Are you angry with me for asking? How could I know what really happened? I was still at Eton when you went off to the Peninsula, and you never even came down to say goodbye. You just vanished until today."

"I'm sorry, Geoff," Egon said after a thrumming pause, laying his gloved hand on the younger man's knee for a second before looking straight ahead again. "That was a churlish way to behave. The thing was, I was pretty angry myself at that time, not with you, of course, and I was simply hell-bent on putting as much distance as possible between me and my loving family. I could have sent off a line to you now and then. I hope you won't hold my dereliction against me?"

The smile that flashed across the older man's face erased the lines put there by experiences his cousin could only guess at, and forcibly recalled to the latter's mind the picture of Egon he had kept in his memory. "Don't be a gudgeon," he protested gruffly. "It's not a question of holding a grudge." He hesitated, then rushed on, "Speaking of which, I hope you're not still nursing a grudge against the old lady. You'll find her greatly changed. Oh, she still has a tongue that can peel paint," he added when his cousin sent him a look of inquiry, "but she's very frail now, for all that indomitable will of hers. She walks with a stick and never leaves Belhaven these days. She'll be thrilled to see you, Egon. You were always her favourite."

8

Egon acknowledged the pleading and flattery in Geoffrey's voice with a faint smile, but anything he might have replied was lost as they came around the corner onto Bond Street. He needed all his attention for his driving as a sports curricle came bowling toward them on the wrong side of the road. The vehicle was being driven by a young woman clad all in black except for several white ostrich plumes depending from the wide brim of a hat that was no blacker than her hair. By her side sat a fashionably dressed gallant who lifted a languid hand toward the reins upon assessing the phaeton's proximity. The lady, far from being grateful, gave a proud toss of her head and refused to surrender the reins, setting her lips firmly as she sought to control the skittish pair of black horses and direct them back on a safe course.

By this time, Egon had made his own assessment of the situation. By dint of climbing the walkway with the two offside wheels, he managed to keep from tangling with the curricle's wheel as it shot past with scarcely a check and negotiated the corner, apparently with undeserved safety, for no subsequent sounds of a collision reached their ears.

"Who the devil was that lunatic?" he growled as he eased the phaeton back onto the roadway.

The answer to his rhetorical question came from an unexpected source.

"That," Geoffrey said on a sigh of near-reverence, "was the Iceberg."

"I beg your pardon? Are you acquainted with that female?" Thick black eyebrows climbed almost to his hairline as Egon assimilated the fatuous expression on his companion's good-looking countenance. "*What* did you call her?"

"Everyone calls her the Iceberg. Her name is Clairisse Deschamps. She is an actress at Drury Lane and the town's latest sensation. She has this incredible voice like … like honey over ice, and she dresses exclusively in black and white. She is the most beautiful creature —"

"And Mostyn's latest doxy, evidently," Egon said, ruthlessly shooting down this panegyric in full flight.

"*No!*" At his cousin's sardonic smile, Geoffrey flushed and qualified his vehement denial. "At least, not yet. That's why they call her the Iceberg. Scores of men have tried to make her accept a *carte blanche* in the last few months, but she has refused them all. Mostyn has been the most persistent pursuer of late. He is in the green room every night, reeking of that odious scent he douses himself with, elbowing more deserving men aside with that snide manner of his," he finished gloomily.

"By the look of that black curricle with the white interior and wheel spokes, and those all-black horses, I'd say the lady had made her choice already."

"Clairisse couldn't allow herself to be bought by that degenerate. Why, he must be forty if he's a day, and he's had more women in his keeping than I've had hot dinners. It's unthinkable!"

Had he ever been that young? Egon shifted his gaze to the busy street ahead of him, biting back the jeering comment trembling on his tongue. Geoff s emotion was real even if his inamorata's virtue existed only in his mind. His eventual disillusionment was inevitable, but it need not be at the hands of his cousin.

"Jackson's is just ahead. Before you get down, Geoff, let me give you my direction. I've taken rooms in York Street, St. James's. Are you free to have dinner with me tonight?"

"Well, I'd planned on going to the theatre to see Miss Deschamps, but perhaps you'd like to come with me and we can get something to eat after the play."

"Very well," Egon agreed without enthusiasm. He was averse to being numbered among the followers of the woman responsible for Geoff s smitten state, but it would not hurt to take Mademoiselle Deschamps's measure personally. Not that it was necessary to meet her to do this. She would be in the mould of countless others before her: greedy, grasping, and manipulative. Such women bartered their attractions while they lasted, to enrich themselves and revel in their power over young idiots like his cousin. Well, Geoff need not expect him to fawn over the creature. If he followed his instincts, he'd rather see her brought before a magistrate for public indecency than pander to her vanity in the least degree.

Uncharitable thoughts of Geoffrey's "Iceberg" occupied Egon's mind to the exclusion of all else during the short drive to his lodgings. Hazlett, his groom, was waiting in front of the red brick house to collect the phaeton when he pulled up. Inside the spacious set of rooms he had taken on his arrival in London a few weeks before, he was greeted by Henley, his former batman, who continued to take care of him in civilian life. He listened patiently to his servitor's caustic complaints against the tailor who had not had his master's new coat ready for the day promised and had compounded his crime by trying to come the high-and-mighty over a free citizen as good as any little weasel with a needle. Only when he had taken the time to soothe Henley's ruffled feelings did he inquire for the post that had accumulated in the six days of his absence from town.

An hour later, Egon was comfortably seated in an enveloping wing chair of time-softened leather positioned in front of the fireplace in his bedchamber. His slipper-clad feet rested on a large ottoman. A small coal fire took the late-afternoon chill off the room. A half-full bottle of burgundy and a half-empty glass of the same stood beside an oil lamp on the table at his right hand. To anyone glancing into the room, he would represent an idyllic picture of a man totally at his ease.

The reality was painfully different. A more discerning eye could not fail to discover the dark fury that radiated from the eyes fixed unseeingly on the fireplace. One long-fingered brown hand crushed a sheet of pressed paper in his lap. The other was curled into a fist atop an untidy pile of letters and cards, two of which had evidently slid off the arm of the chair and now lay on the carpet, ignored by the tense figure in the chair.

Over the next few minutes, Egon's jaw gradually relaxed and the fire died out of his eyes. He brought his gaze back to the letter in his right hand, unclenching his fingers as he did so. Mechanically he smoothed out the creases in the paper that was covered in a large slanting black script. God, even her handwriting was imperious! A grim smile flitted across his lips as he reread the offensive message. Recalling his young cousin's well-meant urging that he should shed the light of his presence on his frail old grandparent, he allowed black amusement to deepen the curl of his lips. How timely his meeting with Geoffrey had been.

He had before him an invitation, not to say summons, from this fragile being, couched in terms both presumptuous and insulting. He had not known his grandmother was even aware of his return from the Continent. Geoffrey said she no longer left Belhaven, but, acquainted with her questing mind from his earliest memories, he should have realized that she must still maintain an active correspondence with any number of old cronies scattered all over the kingdom, any one of whom might have been her intelligencer. Certainly she had addressed the envelope correctly. She had written as though the five-year gap in their dealings didn't exist, beginning without personal preliminaries to state in a business-like fashion that, with her eighty-third birthday rapidly approaching, she thought it high time that she made her will. Since she remained averse to supplying the wherewithal for anyone to pursue an irresponsible bachelor existence, her heir must be a married man. By a fortunate circumstance, the girl she had selected for her eldest grandson five years before was still unmarried and was at present visiting at Belhaven. Her lawyer would arrive two days before her birthday on the twenty-first instant. If her eldest grandson presented himself at his ancestral home on or before that date, it would be understood that he was now prepared to marry Miss Winward after an appropriate interval. She remained, et cetera. The letter was signed "Grace Stanton Hollister."

Egon stared at the arrogantly scrawled signature while memories and regrets invaded his generally well-ordered mind. He had made plans to go down to Sussex to see his grandmother before the meeting with Geoffrey today and his gentle persuasion. Nor had he needed his cousin's reminder that he was his grandmother's favourite. From the circumstance of losing his parents in a shipwreck when he was only nine, he had been reared at Belhaven and must always be grateful for the happy childhood his grandparents had provided for him despite their lingering grief at the loss of their only son. He had ridden and roamed over every foot of the estate in all seasons, alone or with his cousins, and had developed an abiding love for the place.

He had survived Eton and then Oxford with no more than the usual hectoring and homesickness, and had emerged a reasonably well-educated and stable character despite the temptations ever available to a wealthy young man. He had never been stinted in anything money could buy, but as he had examined his life during long boring stretches of inactivity in the army, he had concluded that his education had rather encouraged habits of idleness when one was not expected to earn one's own living. At the time, though, he had known only the one life and had blithely set out to enjoy his freedom after Oxford in the company of similarly situated young idlers. His grandparents — or, more accurately, his grandmother — held the purse strings, which kept him from drawing the bustle too outrageously. He did not fancy having to explain to Gran a second time how he had happened to spend all his quarter's allowance in three short weeks, especially since she held all forms of gambling in abhorrence.

There had been remarkably little friction between them until he fell in love. When he met Melissa Cady, his grandmother had been hinting for more than a year that it was time he looked about him for a suitable wife, hints he had laughingly parried in his frequent visits home. When Cupid's dart found him he was four-and-twenty, not much past Geoffrey's present age, and giddy with the joy of discovering the existence of such a perfect being. It never occurred to him that a girl who was sublimely beautiful, gay, and charming — in short, the epitome of all the feminine virtues — could still be unacceptable to his grandparents. She was the sister of a university acquaintance and the daughter of a small mill owner in Lancashire. Hugh Cady was a thoroughly good sort of chap, quite comfortable with the fact that his background was different from most of his fellow students'. He had been universally liked at Oxford, as much for his kindness and level-headed approach to life's vicissitudes as for the prodigious speed and strength he displayed on the sporting fields. Egon had been pleased to run into him again at the York races and was very willing to accept an invitation to go home with his former classmate for a few days.

The few days had stretched into a sennight, by the end of which time he had been head over heels in love with Hugh's beautiful sister. In a series of uncharacteristically impetuous acts, he secured her parents' consent and Melissa's acceptance of his offer, and arranged to drive south with Hugh and Melissa at once so that he could present his intended bride to his grandparents without loss of time.

The visit that followed had remained in his memory for the ensuing five years with a peculiar vividness. The first inkling that all was not as usual came when they arrived to find the house full of guests, a rare occurrence since his grandfather's health had deteriorated in recent years. When he escorted his guests into the main drawing room that afternoon, he was greeted with varying degrees of enthusiasm by most of his extended family, comprising his father's two sisters, their husbands, and a fair sprinkling of their combined progeny, including his cousin Jack, closest to him in age but not in affection. If the thought crossed his mind that he was witnessing an impromptu gathering to welcome his fiancée into the family, his grandmother quickly disabused him of that comfortable notion in a whispered aside when he went up to greet her. He was commanded to withhold any introduction of Melissa as his betrothed until they had spoken privately. The private talk, held in his grandmother's dressing room before dinner, had served to acquaint him with her flat refusal to accept a mill owner's daughter as her successor at Belhaven.

Admittedly, she could not prevent him from inheriting the baronetcy in due course, but Belhaven had descended through her family, and the money that maintained it was Stanton money, not a penny of which would go to him if he persisted in the betrothal.

It did not end there, of course. While the others put themselves out to entertain Hugh and his sister, he spent hours trying to argue his grandmother out of the prejudices of a lifetime. In her turn, Lady Hollister extolled the virtues of the daughter of a local family whom she had selected as a suitable bride for her heir. When they reached an impasse, he declared his intention of marrying Melissa without his grandparents' blessing, and his grandmother promptly made good her threat to stop his allowance. It was left to Melissa to administer the *coup de grâce*, however. When Egon acquainted her with the situation and assured her they could get along on the money his mother had left him if she was still prepared to go ahead with the marriage, she had demurred in the most reasonable fashion, urging patience on their part until his grandmother should come around to their way of thinking. No amount of explaining Lady Hollister's inflexible nature had served to convince her of the futility of this tactic. Relations between the affianced pair became progressively strained. Within another sennight she came to him, sweetly apologetic but seeking to be released from their betrothal because she had discovered that she had mistaken her heart and really wished to marry his cousin Jack instead.

From the vantage point of five years of experience, Egon still squirmed with embarrassment as he forced himself to recall the naive, trusting youth he had been in those days. When it was borne inescapably in upon him that his fond grandmother had actively connived to steer Melissa into Jack's arms in order to remove the major obstacle to gaining her objective of picking her successor, he had decamped, though not until delivering himself of angry and indiscriminate recriminations.

In a state compounded of pain at the betrayals, disgust at his own credulity, and outraged pride at being defeated on all fronts, he had joined the army in a suitably ridiculous gesture of defiance. And here he sat five years later, chastened and matured by the harsh realities of war and free to make a life for himself at last. He had hoped that time would have softened his grandmother's intransigence. He had written to her twice during his military service, seeking to heal the breach with one who had taken the place of a mother in his life — once from Spain when he learned of his grandfather's death, and again last year when he had debated about selling out after Napoleon's first abdication. She had replied to neither overture, but he had stubbornly clung to the hope that he could end the estrangement between them if they met face-to-face. It had taken some time to establish himself in London and see to the acquisition of a civilian wardrobe and suitable vehicles and horseflesh for this new life he would make. In the back of his mind he had determined to go down to Sussex after the party he had agreed to join for the first October race meeting at Newmarket.

His eyes dropped to the crumpled paper in his lap.

She had made it impossible for him to carry out his peace gesture. Why hadn't he gone straight to Sussex two weeks ago? If he had kept on driving south this afternoon, he'd be halfway there at this moment, in blissful ignorance of this damned letter, this arrogant attempt to re-establish the control she had exerted over the child and youth in the past.

Unlike him, his grandmother did not hope to re-establish the bond of affection that had existed between them for a score of years. She was driven by a consuming desire to pick the female who would follow in her footsteps at Belhaven. The really wicked irony was the possibility that the girl she had found wanting five years earlier could actually end up in her shoes if she decided to leave her fortune to Jack instead of to her son's only son. There was also his cousin Michael, who had married recently, and young Geoffrey, of course, as well as two male cousins still in school. Though it seemed unlikely that she'd see her fortune go completely out of the family to the husbands of her granddaughters, he would not rule out the possibility that she was capricious enough and autocratic enough to do even that.

Egon reached for the glass on the table beside him and finished the wine in a single gulp. His bitter thoughts must have tainted it, for he grimaced and shoved the glass back on the table.

He had thought his prolonged exposure to war's inhumanity had crushed his capacity for experiencing strong emotion, but he found himself getting increasingly angry as he prepared for his appointment with Geoffrey. The earlier pleasure in anticipating a reunion with his cousin had been submerged in his resentment of his grandmother's declaration of power. How dare she throw away all that had been valuable in their long relationship? She was in dire need of a salutary lesson on the evils of trying to manipulate the people who loved her.

It would require a heroic effort to conceal his foul temper when Geoffrey arrived to collect him for what he innocently expected to be a delightful evening of worshiping at the shrine of his goddess. Only a reanimated affection for the boy he had known prevented Egon from cancelling their plans outright, but he did not wish to counterfeit his reasons, and it was unfair to unload his burning resentment and sense of ill-usage on the lad.

Had he been less absorbed in his unsatisfactory musings, Egon might have realized that Henley, on entering to help his master dress for the evening, was absolutely taken aback at the alteration in his demeanour, and that the batman-turned-valet's mind was a seething mass of conjecture as to what had changed his even-tempered employer into a silent thundercloud as he bore the servant's ministrations with ill-concealed impatience. Not, perhaps, a particularly propitious beginning to a social evening.

CHAPTER 2

Miss Deschamps expelled a shaky breath. That had been a close-run thing. For a heart-stopping moment, she had been convinced that a collision was inevitable.

"Well done, my dear. You brushed through that little crisis with the aplomb of a professional driver."

She closed her lips on a sharp retort and composed her features into a serene assemblage before turning to her companion. "You give me too much credit, sir," she said politely. "It was the other driver's quick reflexes that saved the day. I fear your horses are a bit too strong for a woman to handle, though I do thank you for allowing me the pleasure of driving them for a bit. It has been an exhilarating experience." So saying, she extended her hands in their black gloves to return the ribbons to him, but he waved her off, folding his arms in front of his chest.

"Nonsense, my dear, I have complete confidence in your ability to control them. And they are not my horses. I bought them and this curricle for you, as you well know."

"And as you well know, my lord, it is impossible for me to accept such a magnificent gift."

"I know no such thing. You have only to say the word and they are yours. I am a wealthy man, Clairisse, and it is my pleasure to do things for you. You wound me to the quick by your continued refusal to accept my trifling offerings."

"They are not trifling, sir," she replied, struggling to keep her tone free of the impotent rage his persuasive words with their underlying hint of coercion always aroused in her. "Your generosity is boundless, and I am deeply touched, but my position is precarious and I do not desire to lose my reputation or my independence."

"Acquit me, I beg you, of the *bêtise* of being so crass as to attach strings to a gift. Have I not made it clear that your acceptance of this equipage and pair will put you under no obligation to me?"

Despairing of her ability to convince him that she was not engaged in a delicate negotiation to secure more advantageous terms as his prospective mistress, Miss Deschamps met his light blue eyes and said frankly, "Lord Mostyn, please believe me when I say that I consider the loss of my reputation too high a price to pay for the distinction of flaunting my own curricle and pair around town."

"My dear Clairisse, can you really be so naive as to believe that a woman in your precarious position, to borrow your own words, has any reputation to lose in the eyes of the world?"

The weight of his anger was apparent in the soft, sneering voice, but Miss Deschamps was not to be lured into retaliation. She concentrated all her attention on keeping her horses together, and there was nothing to be learned from the calm profile she presented to the aging exquisite beside her to show that his shaft had gone home with a vengeance. What was the good of being an actress if she could not disguise her humiliation and deny him the satisfaction of knowing he had hurt her? Not the least of the emotions churning beneath her elegant driving ensemble of black superfine at that moment was a malicious enjoyment of his frustration. Lord Mostyn wanted her on the basest level, and he had long been in the fortunate position of having all such desires gratified, generally by the expenditure of some trifling part of his enormous fortune. She would deny him this particular gratification with her last ounce of strength, but could she do it without ruining herself in the process?

From the gossip circulating about the theatre — and Lord Mostyn's career had been peppered with the type of escapades that fuel gossiping tongues — he was exercising an unusual amount of patience and restraint in his pursuit of her, though from her point of view the pursuit could more accurately be termed a persecution. Recently she had been trying to ignore a recurrent uncomfortable premonition that she was dancing along the thin crust of a somnolent volcano while clouds of steam rose around her.

"On our dignity, are we? I apologize if my words wounded you, my absurd child, but you have always given me to understand that you preferred the truth to empty flattery."

"And so I do, my lord. I am pleased that some of my words have remained in your mind."

This gentle speech was accompanied by a smile of singular brilliance that had the desired effect of reversing his irritation with her. The danger died out of his cold blue eyes and the habitual sneer was less evident about his thin lips. As she felt his thigh brush against hers on the bench, she hastily drew his attention to an approaching rider. "I believe Lord Pembroke is trying to attract your attention, sir."

"I rather think it is your attention he wishes to capture, my dear." The words were uttered in dry accents, but he did ease away from her a bit as he acknowledged Lord Pembroke's salute with a smiling bow.

Miss Deschamps was at pains to conceal her relief as she turned the curricle into Albemarle Street. "My hotel is just ahead, sir, so I will turn your horses over to you now," she said, passing the reins into his reluctant hands on the words.

"Let me come up for a few minutes."

"No, that wouldn't do, my lord. I must rest before getting ready for the performance tonight. I have already stayed out longer than I should."

"I'll let you go if you promise to come out for a late supper with me after the play."

"Thank you, my lord. If it will not inconvenience you to bring me home directly afterward, I shall be pleased to dine with you this evening. I have a singing lesson scheduled very early tomorrow morning, and Signora Fellini is a terror if I am not in good voice." Apparently he had not detected her hesitation while she sought a valid reason to refuse the invitation, for he was wearing a smug expression as she was assisted from the curricle by a passing porter in front of the hotel.

Miss Deschamps entered the Tremont Hotel and proceeded to walk rapidly through the hall past the public lounges where some few persons were engaged in conversation or sat writing at a couple of conveniently placed tables. Her footsteps never faltered until she had walked right out the other entrance on Dover Street, where she paused and glanced about her before heading directly for a hackney carriage standing across the street.

The jarvey touched his whip to his hat.

"I hope you have not been waiting long, Mr. Tippet?"

"Nay, ma'am. Yon lad told me four o'clock. Home, is it?"

"Yes, thank you, Mr. Tippet."

As she sank onto the worn corduroy seat of the hack, relief at having escaped from Lord Mostyn without noticeably nettling him gave way to what was becoming a chronic state of anxiety over the immediate future, specifically, the search for a way to refuse his lordship's inevitable offer of a *carte blanche* without drawing down upon her hapless head the spite and retaliation that gossip credited him with having exhibited in such situations in the past. The man was notorious in the theatre world for taking aspiring young actresses under his protection year after year and using his wealth and influence to advance their careers while his passion for their charms endured. Conversely, he was equally known for exercising his influence against those unwise enough to move on to other protectors before his ardour had cooled enough to render him impervious to any slights to his pride.

It was most unfortunate that Lord Mostyn's recent favour should light upon someone constitutionally averse to the practice of being kept by a lover, and her wretched misfortune that she could not seem to convince him of her determination to remain independent of any such liaison. Seven months ago, when she had made the momentous decision to pursue an acting career, she had taken elaborate precautions to shield her identity and keep herself aloof from this aspect of the world of the theatre. And these had answered very well until the advent of the arrogant Lord Mostyn, with his total disregard for the humanity of anyone who hindered him in the pursuit of his carnal pleasures. By then, her aloofness from the ancillary aspects of appearing on the public stage had earned her the sobriquet of "the Iceberg," but she had not minded that. Combined with her preference for an all-black-and-white wardrobe (originally arising from considerations of the strictest economy), it had lent her a spurious air of mystery. Originally she had rather encouraged the development of this aura surrounding her person, since it facilitated her efforts to stay outside theatrical circles, but now she could see that she had spun the very web in which she was trapped. Ignoring the existence of other young actresses, some more beautiful and all more amenable to his designs, the dangerous Lord Mostyn had settled his fancy on herself, to her current dismay and lively fear of future distress.

Miss Deschamps glanced out of the window, annoyed with herself for her craven, almost fatalistic attitude concerning her noble admirer's power to ruin her career. She was behaving like the veriest ninnyhammer, almost as though she possessed no mind and no will of her own. Naturally Lord Mostyn was not going to be pleased to have his advances rebuffed, but she had no intention of causing him any public embarrassment. He was a civilized man of the world who could shrug off the occasional thwarted desire. No one could waltz through life with never a check or a setback.

As the hack turned into Long Acre, Miss Deschamps sat up a little straighter and consciously smoothed out the wrinkles in her brow. They were nearly home, and it wouldn't do for Sadie to suspect that she was really worried over the developing situation. Sadie's own concern was evident in the glowering looks she had been sending Mostyn whenever he appeared at the theatre of late. Thinking of Sadie and Samuel, who had been her good angels, almost her family, since she had arrived in London eight months ago, she slumped a little under the weight of obligation of which she was increasingly conscious despite their generous and sincere disclaimers.

She had known Sadie from her earliest childhood, when the comely young girl had come to wait upon the nursery at Fountainwood. Warm-hearted and lively, Sadie had taken the shy, motherless child that she had been under her wing and provided her with a constant source of affection and the example of a cheery and commonsensical approach to life.

It had been a deadly wrench when Sadie had left twelve years ago to marry Samuel Mullins, an ambitious young man who was starting in partnership with a shopkeeper in London. Though she had been only ten at the time, she had never forgotten Sadie. It had been the most natural thing in the world to look her up when she came to town eight years later to make her bow to society under the aegis of her mother's elder sister.

The young couple had prospered, with Sadie working as a dresser at Drury Lane, while the shop increased in size and profits. The stolen hours she had spent in their snug little house chatting with Sadie and playing with the couple's small son had been her salvation during that unhappy period. Her aunt, a childless widow, was a sharp-tongued, critical individual who never let her unfortunate charge forget that she was performing a tiresome familial duty in trying to bring this most unpromising material into fashion. Her noninterest in her niece personally, plus a lack of natural taste or acquired sense of style, ensured that the girl in her charge would remain a nonentity. Initially grateful, though shy and awkward, she progressed under such tutelage to a mindless compliance, a rote performance of what was expected of her, that covered a seething rebelliousness that she could acknowledge only in Sadie's comforting presence. Since she was essentially dowerless, it was not to be wondered at that she confirmed her aunt's low expectations by making no conquests and receiving no offers. It had been a relief to both parties when she had gone back home to Northumberland at the end of her doomed season.

Miss Deschamps's eyes were on the passing scene as the hack made its way through the bustling area north of Covent Garden, but her thoughts had winged back to the series of tragic events that had eventually catapulted her onto the public stage, something that should have been unthinkable for Claire Yelland of Fountainwood, daughter of an old and once prominent northern family.

Her charmingly literate and impossibly improvident father had crowned a long career of financial speculation and gambling by going bankrupt with spectacular suddenness last year. In perhaps the only act of financial responsibility of his lifetime, he had arranged to apprentice his son to a merchant banker in London, though Jeremy, much like his impractical father in temperament, would have greatly preferred a pair of colours. For his daughter, in whom he had never taken much interest, he made no provision, being satisfied in his own mind that the curate's three-year courtship would eventually culminate in a marriage that would see her settled securely. Having made his arrangements, Mr. Yelland had locked himself inside the library that was no longer his, finished off the last of the good brandy set down by his father, and put a bullet into his head with more efficiency than he had previously demonstrated in a lifetime.

When the shock had diminished and Claire had dismissed the curate, who to his credit had nearly managed to conceal his gratitude at his honourable release, brother and sister set off for London on the public stagecoach, he to begin his banking career at nineteen, and she at one-and-twenty to accept the refuge offered, nay, insisted upon, by Mr. and Mrs. Samuel Mullins in their awkwardly expressed but heartfelt letter of condolence. She had been determined to accept temporary sanctuary just until she could find a way to earn her living.

Sadie had been equally determined that she should make her home with them until something better offered.

The first flush of optimism in her ability to become independent had survived being told, quite truthfully, that her educational qualifications were woefully inadequate for a position as a governess or teacher. She had been quite dashed down, however, to be told by a large confident matron, who had advertised for a social secretary, that she was unsuitable before she had even opened her mouth. Puzzled and chagrined, she had not been able to conceal her disappointment from the mousy little woman, evidently the present holder of the position, who had been ordered to see her out, for this lady had kindly advised her not to mind, that it had simply been a case of not engaging an attractive young woman in a household containing a susceptible youth. She had been able to laugh about it by the time she described her reception to Sadie, cheerfully predicting that there must be some ladies seeking secretarial assistance who were not encumbered by impressionable sons. Sadie's retort that those that didn't have impressionable sons most likely had susceptible husbands, she had treated as a joke, but the fact remained that she had not secured a position in a genteel family.

In her desire not to become a drain on the Mullins's resources, she had suggested putting her one real talent — the skill at stitchery that Sadie had imparted to her — to use by hiring herself out as a milliner's or dressmaker's assistant. This suggestion had met with strong opposition on the part of her old nursemaid, who flatly declared such menial labours to be beneath consideration for one of gentle birth. Since starvation or living off the generosity of friends seemed to be the alternatives to demeaning herself, Claire continued to argue, but to no avail. Sadie remained adamant on the subject of what was fitting employment for her former charge.

The idea of going on the stage had been born of desperation, and Claire had not dared mention it until she had worked out the answers to what she knew would be Sadie's violent objections. She had anticipated the necessity of concealing her identity, if for no other reason than to spare her aunt the humiliation of public disclosure. Much as she disliked the woman, she owed her this much for her unwilling sacrifice for her dead sister's child four years ago. Her brother-in-law's suicide had been enough of a scandal to face without adding to the disgrace. It would mean a new name for Claire and some basic alteration in her appearance. This would solve the most pressing problem of the instant loss of the status conferred on her by her birth that would result from performing in public. As far as her personal respectability was concerned, she would still be under the Mullinses's protection, though she proposed to adopt the pretence of living in a hotel to keep the connection from becoming known.

As expected, her plan had not been favourably received, but she had pointed out that the one area her sketchy education had not skimped was literature. Her father had dabbled in poetry all his life and had the classics at the tip of his tongue, delighting in producing fitting quotations from the ancients for all occasions. Claire had learned pages of dialogue and dozens of poems from earliest childhood. Her voice was an asset, or so she had been told, and surely she could learn the gestures and movements that constituted stage technique. By dint of prolonged and well-reasoned arguments, she had gradually prevailed over Sadie's instinctive disapproval. It was unfortunately true that no other work was likely to be nearly as remunerative. If she could put enough money aside, perhaps in a year or two she might be able to establish a home for herself and her brother, who was living in cheap lodgings while he pursued his training. Eventually Sadie had been persuaded to countenance the plan, keeping her reservations to herself and her eyes open for trouble.

Claire was still absorbed in the immediate past when the hackney came to a halt, and she gathered her poise about her before facing Sadie's searching inquiries. She paid Mr. Tippet and engaged his services for later that evening, her mouth twisting wryly at this reminder of her appointment with the detestable Lord Mostyn.

The modest yellow brick structure in front of her was similar to its immediate neighbours in having only two windows in its narrow facade, but it was solidly built and well-maintained. The oval-headed door on the right was encased in attractive moulding topped by a fanlight. The entrance-floor window repeated the oval heading, while the windows in the upper two stories were rectangular in shape. The railing and the window trim were freshly painted, and spotless lace curtains hung in smooth folds at the windows, a testimony to Sadie's housekeeping. Claire used her own key to enter and had already taken off her hat in her room on the second floor when footsteps on the stairs indicated that Sadie, generally down in the kitchen at this hour, had been keeping an ear out for her return.

"I am beginning to detest this wig," Claire announced with a small laugh as the other woman stood in the doorway watching her lift off the elaborate black headpiece and position it carefully on the wig stand on the pine dresser. "I think it has given me a permanent headache." She pulled out the pins anchoring her own tawny-coloured hair at the back of her head and shook it free, rotating her neck to relax tense muscles.

"It's the best quality to be had. Not even the most jealous bit player has ever suggested that it's not your own hair." Sadie was absently drying her hands on her apron as she studied her former nurseling from a pair of large hazel eyes that missed little.

"Thanks to you and your skill at styling it while I'm wearing it at the theatre." Claire gave another little laugh and tried to look unconcerned, but she should have known better than to try to deceive the person who knew her best.

"He offered you a *carte blanche*, didn't he? I knew it, I have been afraid of this for weeks. I —"

"No, no, truly, Sadie, he did not."

"But he will. It's just a matter of time. I know how he proceeds. I've observed him for five years. You must not go out with him again, Miss Claire."

"I'm afraid I promised to have dinner with him after the performance tonight," Claire admitted reluctantly, fiddling with the ostrich plumes on the hat she had laid on the dresser near the wig stand.

"You shouldn't have done that! You ought not to give him any encouragement."

"I would have refused, but he wanted to come into the hotel with me this afternoon, and when I said no, he got off some nonsense about not insisting if I went out with him after the performance. I was afraid he'd follow me inside and discover the truth, so I agreed to dine with him. It will be all right, Sadie. I've already told him I have to come straight home because of a fictive singing lesson tomorrow."

"That's not going to hold him off for long. I wouldn't put it past him to force his way into that hotel, and then the fat will be in the fire."

"No, Sadie, you worry unnecessarily. We may not like the man, but he's a gentleman, after all. I had again refused to accept the horses and curricle I told you about, and that put him in a touchy humour this afternoon."

"His type gets in a bad skin the minute they're crossed, gentleman or not, and I have my own opinion on that question. Millie Townsend, who he had in keeping most of last season, came into the theatre on two occasions with bruises on her arms that weren't made by no gentleman! Mark my words, Miss Claire, this one will turn ugly the minute he sees that you're not a-going to give him what he wants."

"Now, calm yourself, Sadie, he cannot very well create a scene in public," Claire said soothingly, knowing that Sadie's rare lapse in grammar was an indication of her agitation. "I promise that I won't accept any more invitations from Mostyn after tonight. I wish I had never agreed to go driving with him, but I had accepted invitations to drive with other gentlemen from time to time and he was so pressing. I'm beginning to regret that we did not create a husband for Miss Clairisse Deschamps when we were making up her history. It would have saved me from having anything to do with the men who haunt the theatres."

"Only if you could produce him every night, my love," Sadie said dryly. "An absent husband is deemed an invitation to most of the so-called gentlemen in the green room to play off their tricks."

"Oh, many are perfectly ordinary, harmless young men like that nice Geoffrey Blyden, the boy who sends me all the white roses. I do hope he is not spending all his allowance on those flowers."

"Not even a boy is harmless when what he wants could ruin a woman's reputation."

"According to Mostyn, a woman like me has no reputation to lose."

Claire regretted the bitter words the instant they left her tongue. She had not meant Sadie to know what small regard the earl held for her, despite his persistent attentions.

"What did I tell you? Please reconsider that supper appointment. He means no good by it. You've parried his advances too long and he's determined to bring you to heel."

"I'll try to plead a headache, Sadie, but I did promise. Actually, if I do not rest for a short while, the headache won't be a fabrication."

"Let me brush your hair for you, Miss Claire. That always soothes your nerves and smooths away the headache."

"I'd love it, Sadie, but should you not be in the kitchen at this hour?"

"Martha can handle the rest," the older woman said, coming up behind the dressing-table bench where the girl had dropped thankfully. She began to pull the brush through the thick shining tresses that fell several inches below Claire's shoulders. Neither spoke for a few moments, and Sadie could feel the relaxation in the neck muscles beneath her fingers.

"I haven't seen Timothy yet to thank him for sending Mr. Tippet over to the Tremont this afternoon," Claire murmured, sinking into a pleasant lethargy under the rhythmic brushstrokes.

"He's happy to oblige. You do much for him, turning over all those flower holders and trinkets that the men shower on you, for him to sell. It's too much for a child of ten."

"Nonsense, Sadie. Timothy knows the money he gets from selling those useless trifles is for his education. I do too little for any of you. You won't let me give you a penny for living here, and you help me make all my exotic wardrobe, and what's most important, you and Samuel and Timmy make me feel that I'm not alone in the world. Oh, I know I have Jeremy, but he's young and absorbed in his own life."

And he only comes here when he wants something from you, Sadie mentally finished as she slowed the pace of the brushstrokes. She produced a little chuckle to divert Claire's thoughts from her unsatisfactory brother. "That exotic wardrobe that started from our efforts to make your mourning clothes look more presentable when I took you to the theatre that first day to meet the manager. We were right to continue in that vein once he'd admitted it was the contrast between your yellowish eyes and fair skin and the black hair that captured his attention — that and your voice, of course. It has become your... What did that Lord Eppingly call your black-and-white wardrobe?"

"My signature. Clever of him and helpful to us. There are times when I fear it is the only thing about me that is responsible for my getting larger roles these days," Claire confessed. "I cannot claim to be a very good actress yet."

"Fustian. You are always adequate, and sometimes much better than that as you gain experience. You can't take a gently reared girl who's never faced an audience in her life and turn her into another Mrs. Siddons overnight. You're learning to move about the stage with ease, and you've always had the kind of voice that makes people curl up their toes and smile. You'll gain more confidence for the really dramatic roles in good time."

"You mean you don't think I'm quite ready to play Lady Macbeth yet, Sadie?" Laughter bubbled beneath Claire's words.

"Give it a month or two," came the calm reply.

If Lord Mostyn didn't see to it that she was blackballed from the theatre altogether. The fear that had lurked beneath the surface of Claire's mind ever since she had realized that she would not be able to prevent him from making her an illicit offer surfaced like a diver coming up for air, causing her spine to jerk upright. "Thank you, Sadie," she said breathlessly. "I am refreshed now and ready for a fast-paced comedy tonight, even if tragedy is still beyond my reach."

CHAPTER 3

Geoffrey, sans moustache, his cousin noted, arrived in good time to do full justice to the sandwiches Henley had put together to hold the two men until after the play. If he noticed that Egon actually ate little of what was placed in front of him, he did not comment on this oddity, being more interested in catching up on the five years that had passed since their last meeting. He peppered Egon with questions about his military experiences throughout their scanty repast, which his cousin good-naturedly addressed himself to, well aware that his answers were neither detailed nor graphic enough to satisfy the romantic inclinations of the questioner.

"Why did you stay in the military after the victory in the Peninsula, Egon? Did you have some inkling that it wasn't the end of Boney?"

Egon smiled briefly at the eagerly attentive young man facing him across the small round table Henley had set up before the fireplace in the sitting room. Geoffrey had always been an appealing lad, open-faced and openhearted, with no guile in him. He had inherited the Blyden fair colouring, as had his older brother, but whereas Jack's light blue eyes and regular features generally revealed nothing of his thought processes, Geoffrey's every reaction was there to be seen on his ingenuous countenance. It might be just a function of his youth, but Egon could not recall that Jack had been ingenuous at any age. He closed his mind against images of Jack Blyden and replied to Geoff s question.

"Loath though I am to disdain the implied compliment, I cannot take any credit for political prescience or an intimate knowledge of the workings of Bonaparte's mind. After years of silence following Grandfather's death, I wrote to Grandmother again after Napoleon's first abdication to let her know I was thinking of selling out. When she didn't reply, I decided my presence wasn't desired in Sussex and I stayed in." He shrugged, seeing but rejecting the sympathy in the other's honest eyes. "I couldn't stay away forever just to indulge the old lady's whims. She can send me to Coventry but she can no longer keep me out of England."

"Well, I for one am delighted to have you back. Grandmother will come around once you've made your peace with her." Seeing all expression suddenly wiped off his cousin's features, he added hastily, "How long have you been back? Why haven't I seen you before today?"

"I've been in England for more than a month, but it took some little time to find lodgings and set about turning myself into a civilian again. Until I met you today, I had been labouring under the delusion that my tailor had succeeded in bringing me up to the rig, but I now see I was quite wrong. I cannot possibly hope to compete with that creation." With one long-fingered hand, he indicated his cousin's pale pink waistcoat of watered silk.

Geoffrey grinned, refusing to take umbrage at still being the butt of his elder's teasing. "These waistcoats are all the crack among the younger men," he declared too innocently. "Naturally, one would not expect to find such distinction in the stodgier, the more settled members of society."

"*Touché!*" Egon gave a bark of laughter and pushed back his chair. "We'd best be off if we hope to find a hackney that will get us there in time for the start of the performance."

On the way to Covent Garden, they spoke of the changes that had taken place in the capital since Egon had last been there, and he described his recent sojourn in Newmarket, where he had seemed to possess the golden touch in picking winners. "I'm going to take it as a good omen that the years of being chronically purse-pinched are over."

"Purse-pinched!" Geoffrey looked startled. "But doesn't Grandmother…? Oh, I beg pardon! Not good form to inquire after a man's finances."

"Cawker!" Egon laughed at the younger man's discomfort. "I thought it was common knowledge in the family that our esteemed ancestress cut me off without the proverbial shilling when I refused to knuckle under to her matrimonial scheme."

"No, at least not to me. Of course, I was away at Eton at the time. Jack may have known, but he has never mentioned it to me."

"Oh, yes, Jack knew," Egon said coolly. "Fortunately, my mother's money came to me on my majority and provides me with an income of sorts, and I had my army pay. I also have the Hollister property now, where my parents lived when I was small. It's not worth a great deal; much of the land was sold off over the years, and the house has been allowed to run down, though I understand it has been rented until the last few years. Grandfather had damn-all to leave, but what he had came to me. I'd no idea he was virtually Grandmother's pensioner all these years, but it does explain why she always seemed the dominant partner. Of course, we all knew Belhaven was Stanton property originally."

"Actually I never knew any of the financial history of my mother's family except that Belhaven was my grandmother's originally. I've always assumed that it would go to you, since your father was their only son."

"She can leave it where she pleases," Egon said shortly, and something harsh in his tone had Geoffrey scrambling around for a change of subject.

"Speaking of Jack, I got a letter from him today asking me to go to Fribourg and Treyer and have them make up some of his special snuff mixture. I knew before I opened it that it would entail some inconvenience — Jack wouldn't put pen to paper unless he wanted something."

"Filthy habit, taking snuff."

"Any filthier than that pungent cigar smoke you blew at me tonight?"

"You have me there, coz. I picked up the habit in Spain, but I confess I wasn't thinking of the effect on the uninitiated when I smoked one at the table. I don't usually indulge in company, or even indoors, because Henley hates 'em too and makes my life miserable with his complaints, but this evening I felt a craving for a smoke."

"Grandmother has banned cigars from Belhaven. Michael smoked one at the dinner table last year — aping the soldiers, you know — after the ladies had retired, but she smelled it in the drawing room and kicked up a fuss. Poor Mike didn't dare show his face for months."

Egon smiled reminiscently. "I can picture her face while she dressed him down in her best lady-of-the-manor voice, soft as a summer breeze, but every syllable distinct and wintry."

"Mike had to get married to get back into her good graces."

The smile had departed from Egon's face. He made himself inquire, "How is Mike these days?"

"He seems to have grown very sober and staid overnight. You know what Mike was like, always ripe for a lark and damn the consequences. If that is what marriage does to a man, I'll have none of it, thank you."

"What is his bride like that she takes the joy out of his life?"

"I didn't mean to imply that it was Jessica's fault," Geoffrey backtracked hastily. "She seems a nice enough little thing, quiet as a mouse, actually, with no conversation to speak of."

"Poor Mike," his cousin echoed.

The men were silent for a moment, lost in their own thoughts, until Geoffrey bestirred himself. "If you are going down to Belhaven in the next week or so, I'll give Jack's snuff mixture to you to deliver."

"Jack is at Belhaven?"

"Not yet, but he mentioned in his note that he and Melissa were due to pay a visit soon, complete with infant."

Egon did not initiate any conversation until they reached the theatre precincts and joined the throng milling about the entrance. Since they were unencumbered by any ladies, they decided to watch the play from the pit, though perhaps strict accuracy would dictate that it be noted that only Mr. Blyden really watched the play. Sir Egon's eyes may have been directed toward the stage, but for the most part his attention was on his own thoughts, which were far from pleasant.

The news that his cousin Jack was expected at Belhaven with his family had been an unwelcome shock, though he supposed he might have expected it from the phrasing of his grandmother's letter. For all he knew to the contrary, she might be filling her house with her married grandchildren for this will-making event she had scheduled. The fact that Geoff apparently knew nothing about it would seem to indicate that the unmarried ones were not included in the summons, with the vital exception of himself. His appearance at Belhaven would be tantamount to a public surrender to her will. What a wicked, unyielding old tyrant she was!

The play was a revival of Sheridan's old hit *The Rivals*, an entertaining farce he remembered from play-reading sessions during the winter months of idleness in the Peninsula. Tonight it could not sustain his interest, though he was dimly cognizant of the appreciative snickers as Mrs. Malaprop got into her stride and the conniving venality of the servants was exposed. The production was more than competent; with a single exception, the actors snapped off their lines with effective timing and panache. The character of Julia, the one sensible female in the play — as opposed to one with sensibility — was poorly served by a young actress of superior physical attributes that were unfortunately allied with a nasal voice and a flat delivery. In contrast, Geoffrey's idol, Mademoiselle Deschamps, imbued the less sympathetic role of Lydia Languish with the charm of ingenuous conviction in her youthful and excessive romanticism. His cousin had been correct about the attraction of her voice; even raised to project from a stage, it possessed a seductively sweet quality that told only part of the story. Her movements about the stage were graceful and assured and revealed the lithe suppleness of a lovely body. Geoff's enslavement was less of a mystery to Egon by the end of the play, but more of a concern. He would not like to see his young cousin run afoul of the Earl of Mostyn, though there seemed little likelihood of that, judging by what they'd seen this afternoon. Mostyn must have the inside track to the lady's heart, or her favour at least.

By the time the performance concluded to generous applause and enthusiastic curtain calls for Miss Deschamps, Egon had to acknowledge that he could thank that dangerously attractive young woman for luring his bitter thoughts out of the unproductive circular path of recrimination that his grandmother's ultimatum had set in motion. When she was on the stage, his attention, albeit largely critical, remained away from his personal problem. He raised no objection when Geoff suggested going around to the green room to meet the lady who exercised such a fascination over him.

When they arrived, the green room was already filled to the point of discomfort with flowers and young men-about-town ogling the fair players. Mademoiselle Deschamps was surrounded by a considerable court, but she looked up with a smile when Geoffrey's fair head appeared in her line of vision. She slipped away with a smiling word of excuse to offer her hand to her young admirer, saying in her beautiful voice with a slight hint of huskiness, "How do you do, Mr. Blyden? I must thank you for the magnificent white roses you sent me. They are exquisite, but you should not be so extravagant."

Geoffrey disclaimed inarticulately, his colour heightened under the actress's smiling reproach. "Clairisse, I'd like you to meet my cousin, Sir Egon Hollister. Miss Deschamps, Egon."

Egon had been taking advantage of the couple's short exchange to subject the actress to a thorough survey. She looked younger close up, and he found himself revising his estimate downward from the mid-twenties he had assumed from her poised presence on the stage. She seemed smaller also, but that might have been because the actors with whom she was working were men of slight stature. Not beautiful, he decided, taking in the wide cheekbones from which her face narrowed to a rather pointed chin. She had masses of black ringlets ending in a fringe that reached nearly to her eyebrows, giving her face somewhat the shape of an inverted triangle. No, it was the striking combination of midnight hair and long eyes of pale amber-brown, thickly surrounded by long black lashes, that rendered her appearance so arresting, that and a complexion of creamy perfection that owed nothing to makeup, though her lips and cheeks were artfully reddened. She was giving him a direct look from those spectacular eyes as he bowed over her hand.

"*Enchanté, mademoiselle. Vous êtes française?*"

"*Mes parents seulement, monsieur. J'étais née en Angleterre.* I consider myself quite English," she went on with a faint smile, "having lived my entire life in England."

That didn't sound as if she were pretending to be a noble French émigrée, though the accent was flawless. "May I compliment you on a fine performance tonight, Miss Deschamps? You more than met the challenge of the role."

"Thank you, sir," she said simply.

"Yes, Clairisse, you were wonderful, far and away the star of the evening," Geoffrey put in eagerly.

Miss Deschamps's eyes twinkled as she teased, "You always say that, even the night I fell over a chair in the fourth act. How can I value your compliments when you ignore the greater merit of Mr. Roddenbury, whose superb craft makes Faulkland so believable, not to mention Mrs. Martin and Mr. Logan?"

"You seemed to accept Egon's opinion at face value," he grumbled.

"Ah, but your cousin does not approve of me, and that, you know, lends credence to his flattering opinion."

"Miss Deschamps, if I have given an impression of disapproval, I must beg your pardon —"

"No, no, sir," she interrupted, holding up a hand to stop his apology and giving him another of her direct looks. "It does not signify. You are concerned that I may pose a danger to your cousin. I shan't, but you cannot know that, of course."

"Stuff and nonsense," put in Geoffrey. "No one in the full possession of his senses could possibly disapprove of you. You are becoming fanciful. Will you come out to supper with us, Clairisse?"

"I am so sorry, but I have a previous engagement tonight."

"With me," a suave voice said, and three pairs of eyes took notice of Lord Mostyn, whose arrival at Miss Deschamps's side had gone unremarked in the noisy hum of a dozen conversations being carried on simultaneously. He took the actress's hand and placed it on his arm, covering it with his other hand as he bent a mocking glance at the unsuccessful petitioner.

Miss Deschamps withdrew her hand gently and extended it to Geoffrey. "Ask me to go driving with you sometime," she said with a gentle smile. "And thank you again for the roses, Mr. Blyden. Goodnight, Sir Egon." She turned to Lord Mostyn, who was holding a white velvet evening cape over his arm. "Shall we go, sir?"

The cousins could not help but note the proprietary manner in which the earl placed the cape around the actress's shoulders before they strolled out of the room.

"That old lecher! I'd like to darken his daylights," Geoffrey muttered in an angry undertone.

"He got there first," his cousin said flatly, "and if you'll accept a piece of advice, do not cross swords with Mostyn. Do not make the mistake of underestimating him because he affects the manner of a bored dandy. He has killed his man on more than one occasion and would feel no compunction at dispatching another who got in his way. Believe me, the game's not worth the candle."

They had been making their way toward the door as Egon spoke. Neither said anything else until they were out on the pavement, gulping in the crisp night air.

"She *cannot* like the man!" Geoffrey declared, an edge of pain in his voice. "Never mind that he reeks of musk and ambergris. He's an ugly customer."

"Let's walk," his cousin advised, taking his arm in a firm grip. "It will clear your head. Perhaps Miss Deschamps does not have an aversion to musk or ambergris."

"This is no joking matter." Geoffrey rounded on his cousin, causing a couple behind them to crash into him. When apologies had been exchanged, Egon again pulled his cousin forward as they crossed Bridges Street and headed into the market area.

"I beg your pardon if I seem not to attach quite the degree of seriousness to the matter as you, but it is Miss Deschamps's business, you must agree, with whom she chooses to associate."

"But she is too innocent to see the man for the debauched sadist that he is! You must admit his reputation is unsavoury in the extreme," he added when Egon's eyebrows soared at the strong words.

"Somehow, innocence is not a characteristic one generally associates with females in Miss Deschamps's profession," he began.

"You have only to look at her and listen to her to see that she is virtuous!" Geoffrey retorted hotly.

Egon maintained an unconvinced silence on this point as they veered past the end of the incredible clutter of building attached to the market stalls to walk across the centre of the square toward St. Paul's, looming darkly in the fitful light of a crescent moon that appeared and disappeared as clouds trailed across its face. The area was still well-peopled with returning theatregoers and carousers heading for the nearby taverns, with the occasional amorous couple weaving an unsteady path punctuated by halts to exchange embraces. That Geoff neither saw nor heard anything outside of his head was evident in his automatic avoidance of pitfalls in the uneven pavement and his frowning silence, which he broke at last to declare:

"I know that scoundrel is manoeuvring to make her his mistress. Someone should warn her about him before he ruins her life."

"If you feel so strongly about it, why not offer her a *carte blanche* yourself?" his cousin suggested. "She seemed well-disposed toward you."

"I would not so defile her!" Geoffrey gasped out, stopping under the shadow of the church to glare at his unsympathetic companion. "I'd make her an honest offer except that I won't come into my inheritance until I'm twenty-five, almost two years from now."

And thank God for that circumstance! Egon took care to keep his traitorous thoughts from appearing on his face as he resumed walking westward, leaving the actors' church behind. Obviously Geoffrey, who had evidently started late in the petticoat line, having been obsessed with sport in all forms when last he knew him, still placed women in two categories only. He did not yet recognize an element of lust in his infatuation for Miss Deschamps and consequently saw her as no different from the virginal young misses who paraded through Almack's each year. If he was to worship at her shrine, she must continue to appear as pure as the driven snow. Egon judged that he would be cured, though disillusioned, the moment the actress accepted Mostyn's terms or imposed her own on the earl.

His thoughts gravitated back to his own problem as he walked beside his troubled cousin, no longer listening to his bemoanings with more than half an ear. After a bit he hailed a hack and saw the dispirited youngster back to his lodgings, citing a late appointment with an old military comrade passing through town as a reason to eschew a visit to a tavern to help Geoff drown his sorrows.

It wasn't exactly a lie. An old friend of his was newly arrived in town and putting up at the Tremont Hotel. McHenry had sent a note around to his lodgings just before Geoff had arrived this evening. Not anxious to go home and start on his mental treadmill again, he decided to call upon his comrade-in-arms in a personal reply. If McHenry was out, he'd leave a note in his turn.

A half-hour later, having left a note with a sleepy batman, Egon started down the stairs from his friend's second-floor room at the Tremont. Suddenly he stopped, arrested in mid-step by a low but impassioned voice coming up from the stairwell below.

"Stop pulling me. I am not going anywhere with you!"

"Oh, yes you are, my dear. It is more than time that we came to an understanding. I am beginning to find all these preliminaries a trifle wearying. We are going up to your rooms, where we will not be disturbed."

"I told you I don't have rooms here anymore. I moved out today."

"No, my dear Clairisse, the truth is that you moved in today. When I left you here this afternoon, it occurred to me that you might not have been completely open with me, so I returned to make some inquiries. I was not altogether surprised to find that you were not registered, but I remedied that situation at the time. You now possess a fine suite of rooms on the second floor of this thoroughly respectable establishment."

"Well, it will do you no good." It seemed to Sir Egon, peering down over the rail in an unsuccessful attempt to see the speakers, that Miss Deschamps's voice shook with restrained passion. "Do not think you can make me your mistress by force, sir, any more than by raining costly gifts down upon my head. I refused the horses and carriage, I refused the bracelet, and I am refusing you now, once and forever. Let go of my arm this instant or I shall scream until I wake everyone in this place!"

"One squeak out of you and these fingers will choke off your air supply. Now, cease these melodramatic posturings and come along quietly. Do not make me hurt you; I should hate that."

Egon shook off the sense of shocked disbelief that had held him motionless and dashed down the stairs to the next flight, his footsteps making almost no sound on the carpeted treads. He was upon the couple struggling together in mid-flight before either party was aware of his presence.

Lord Mostyn's hat fell off as he was jerked backward by an ungentle hand on his upper arm. Before he could regain his balance, a powerful fist crashed into his jaw and sent him sprawling on the stairs.

Miss Deschamps had taken instant advantage of her release to run down the staircase, her white velvet cloak trailing soundlessly behind her like some ghostly vestment as she vanished around the landing between the first and ground floors. Egon stayed just long enough to ascertain that the earl was in no condition to offer immediate retaliation before following the fleeing female.

He almost caught up with her as she reached the door opening onto Dover Street. She slowed her flight to a hurried walk past the two men who had just entered the hotel, her face averted to avoid their curious stares. By the time he had dodged around the bemused men as they stopped to observe her exit, the door had closed behind her. Egon could only admire and deplore her fleetness of foot as he erupted out onto the pavement in time to see her vanish into a hackney carriage that had been standing across the street.

He cursed his luck as he watched it move off smartly, but as he replaced his hat at a more secure angle and set off toward Piccadilly and St. James's, it occurred to him that it had not been blind luck but foresight that had placed that hackney at that particular spot. The conversation, if such it could be called, that he had overheard between Miss Deschamps and Mostyn had implied that the lady had pretended to live at the Tremont. Obviously if her escorts returned her to the hotel she would need transportation to her actual residence, hence the waiting hack.

Egon's interest in Miss Deschamps was piqued as he walked back to his lodgings. Such elaborate precautions to preserve the sanctity of her residence from her admirers spoke of extraordinary caution and secrecy and perhaps of sad experience with previous protectors. She had certainly failed to take Mostyn's measure when she had led him on. What did she hope to gain by refusing his offer? Were her sights set on bigger game?

This, then, was the young innocent Geoffrey burned to introduce to his family as his wife! Egon bit back a harsh laugh at the thought of his grandmother's reaction to Miss Deschamps as her grandson's bride. If she had not considered Melissa Cady's background good enough for her heir, it was amusing to speculate on what she would make of an actress being brought into the family. It was merely a hypothetical exercise, of course. Thanks to the divine providence that sometimes protects idiots, Geoffrey was not going to marry Miss Deschamps.

Geoff had not even been invited to Belhaven for the upcoming epochal event. As his grandmother had said in her letter, her heir must be a married man. In an excess of generosity or conscience, she was permitting her eldest grandson to enter the running for what was actually his birthright as long as he was prepared to marry at his grandmother's dictation. The old tartar would have been well-served if he had come home from the Continent with a foreign bride, he thought savagely. That would have put a crimp in her plans for the disposal of the estate, for he had been groomed from childhood to take over at Belhaven until the fiasco five years ago that had wrenched him out of his grandmother's design. She must have changed a great deal in the intervening years if she now favoured Jack and the daughter of a mill owner to succeed her. Somehow this theory still had not gained credence with him.

No, this will-making ploy was her way of forcing him to do her bidding, and it was beyond what a man could accept and still retain his self-respect. Egon's footsteps slowed as he grappled with the beginnings of an idea, an idea so outrageous that his mind rejected it outright, only to have it resurface in the next moment in more fully defined form. By the time he reached his doorway, the brooding look that had sat on his countenance most of the evening had been replaced by an expression of controlled excitement.

CHAPTER 4

Claire had stopped shaking by the time Mr. Tippet deposited her in front of the Mullinses' house, but her gratitude at being rescued from a nasty situation had given way to a smothering sensation of impending disaster. Her defiance of Lord Mostyn tonight had put an end to any faint hope of being able to refuse him in a manner that would not cause him to lose face. And if it should become known that he had been struck down like a common felon, he would lay his humiliation at her door. The man was known for his vindictiveness, and she must expect him to try to revenge himself on her in some fashion. She bit her lip fiercely to keep back a moan as she alighted from the hackney. Her thanks to Mr. Tippet that evening were uttered with a fervour that left the jarvey puzzled but pleased.

Would a gentleman think tonight's little drama a good story to spread around the clubs? That worry accompanied her to the doorstep. She had recognized her rescuer in the instant between his pulling Mostyn away from her and delivering the blow that had knocked the earl off his feet. A little more thought made her dismiss the slim hope that the victim might not have seen enough to identify his assailant. The two men had had a good look at each other in the green room tonight, even if they had been previously unacquainted. It covered her with shame to realize that she had fled without even thanking Sir Egon, but at the time, her own escape had been uppermost in her mind. He had come after her and, not knowing his intentions, she had blindly obeyed her instincts to head for safety.

Sadie met Claire at the front door, having been too nervous to support the idea of sleep until she saw her chick safely home. By the end of Claire's spare description of her evening with Lord Mostyn and its violent climax, the older woman was clasping her hands together, her fine eyes staring out of a colourless face beneath the utilitarian cotton nightcap tied under her quivering chin. When she spoke, however, it was with the composure that descends when the most dreaded possibility has actually come to pass, ending all suspense.

"Mostyn is a worse scoundrel than even I feared, which, I can tell you, is a thing I never thought to say of anyone." Reading the distress in Claire's eyes despite her stoic stance, she added in the crooning tones used to comfort children in the nursery, "Never mind, my pretty, it's over now. He doesn't know where you live and there's no one who will tell him, for no one at the theatre is aware of the connection between us. You need never be alone with him again. In fact, until this blows over, you had best keep away from the green room entirely. A headache will do for a night or two, and then we'll see. Samuel will escort you home each night. Now, you come along upstairs with me and we'll take off that wig and brush your hair out for you. That always relaxes you and makes you ready for sleep."

Mrs. Mullins was sliding her arm about Claire's waist as she spoke, and she urged her gently up the stairs. The girl went willingly, immeasurably comforted by the older woman's presence, though she protested with a shaky little laugh, "You need not treat me as though I were on the brink of the vapours, Sadie, for I promise you I am no such thing. It is just that, now that the unpleasant incident is over, I feel so ... so besmirched somehow, as if —"

"Now, Miss Claire, that is nonsensical and you know it! Your behaviour has always been just as it should be, and you have no call to reproach yourself because others have prurient notions and can't recognize a born lady when they see one. On their own heads and consciences be it."

They had reached Claire's room by this time, and Sadie bustled her onto the dressing-table bench while she hung the velvet cloak on a hook. Her covert attention never left the drooping figure staring blindly into the mirror while she performed this small task, and she kept up a soft stream of encouraging chatter as she returned to stand behind the seated girl. Claire had not made a move to take off the wig, but Sadie forbore to scold as she removed it herself. Seeing the pinched look on the girl's wan face as she sat with her own hair scraped to the back of her head, a virulent hatred of Lord Mostyn welled up in the dresser's ample bosom under the cherished brown velvet wrapper Claire had presented to her before she had gone back to Northumberland after her unsuccessful season. The earl was the author of her nursling's present distress, and Sadie would have relished taking a stick to him personally for inculcating feelings of unworthiness in her angel.

"Miss Claire," she said briskly, and was rewarded by an arousal out of this disturbing state as the girl blinked and turned toward the voice of authority. "I set the kettle on the hearth an hour ago and I am going to pour water into the washbasin. You'll feel much better after you wash your face and hands."

"You were right, as usual, Sadie," Claire said five minutes later. "I feel refreshed and normal again." She seated herself and began to pull the pins out of her hair. "I beg pardon if I seemed to be exhibiting die-away airs just now, but the more I think back on what transpired tonight, the more tainted I feel."

"Then don't think about it," Sadie advised bluntly, brushing out the confined tresses of tawny silk with strong strokes.

"I don't know quite why I should have been so badly affected," Claire went on as if she had not heard this eminently practical advice. "It isn't as though I were unaware that actresses are considered to have loose morals and are held in low esteem by the upper classes, and perhaps not just the upper classes either. I must have deluded myself into thinking that the general opprobrium wouldn't extend to me if my behaviour remained ladylike and circumspect. Well, I know better now, and I shan't make that mistake again."

"Now, give over this self-pitying talk, Miss Claire, right now. Nobody likes a whiner."

Claire tried to look indignant, but after a second her lips twitched and she said in a meek little-girl voice, "Yes, Sadie, you know best."

"Well, I think so," Mrs. Mullins concurred, refusing to be diverted. "You are not responsible for that man's defects of character, and nothing you did caused him to act in that unprincipled manner. The best thing to do is put it behind you."

"Yes, but will I be allowed to do this? I shudder to contemplate what must be Sir Egon Hollister's opinion of me after this episode."

"His opinion means less than nothing."

Claire disagreed, but forbore to argue, since she could not seem to come up with a satisfactory explanation for just why Sir Egon's opinion of her should matter. She hesitantly voiced one of her primary concerns in the wake of the distasteful incident. "Sadie, do you think he — Sir Egon — would spread the tale around the clubs? I know Lord Mostyn is not very well-liked, and he might think it a good story with which to regale his acquaintances."

"A true gentleman would not bandy a lady's name about even to give someone like Mostyn his comeuppance."

Claire was silent, not wholly reassured by Sadie's decisiveness. What did she know of Sir Egon Hollister beyond the fact that he was young Mr. Blyden's cousin and was possessed of a fine pair of dark brown eyes whose softness was belied by the rest of his features? She had read disapproval in those eyes before she had spoken a word to him, and had guessed at the reason; in fact, some demon of contrariness had prompted her to charge him with it. Would he consider it necessary to protect the fair name of an actress? The question nagged at her, but Sadie's ministrations were having the desired effect of making her sleepy, and shortly thereafter Claire persuaded her that she would sleep like a baby, with the help of a manufactured yawn.

If Claire's rest was not quite so perfect as she claimed the next morning, at least her appearance at the breakfast table passed Sadie's eagle-eyed scrutiny. Gone were the drooping posture and woebegone attitude of the previous night. Her head was carried proudly, her eyes were clear, and her smile was at the ready. The effort it cost to project this image was known only to herself, though Mrs. Mullins had her own opinion on that subject. Claire was wearing her prettiest daytime cotton gown in a deep raspberry pink that they had just made up as a welcome change from the everlasting black and white of her public wardrobe. She had brushed her long hair back and confined it at the nape with a matching ribbon. It would have taken a very discerning eye indeed to detect Miss Clairisse Deschamps in the smooth-haired girl with the widow's peak that rendered her face heart-shaped when her forehead was not concealed by the long black fringe. The contrast between creamy fair skin and jet-black hair that was Miss Deschamps's most outstanding feature was gone, but Miss Yelland's leonine colouring was saved from being a monochrome by the thick dark lashes that were quite natural and rather startling in connection with her hair. Her brows, though not so dark as Miss Deschamps's, were several shades darker than her hair and did their part to assure that blandness could not be associated with fairness in her case.

She wished everyone a smiling good morning and professed herself hungry for more than her usual thin slices of bread and butter with her coffee. Under Sadie's sceptical eye, she consumed half of a bowl of porridge and maintained her share of the family conversation. Initially Mrs. Mullins had planned that Claire should have her meals alone in the parlour, claiming it was not fitting for a quality-bred girl to share their simple table, but Claire would have none of it, though she had had to threaten to leave and find a room of her own before Sadie had capitulated.

Claire's determinedly cheerful portrayal lasted through the morning until noontime when she sustained a visit from her brother. Her quick smile of welcome when Sadie ushered the young man into the parlour faded before the door closed behind him.

"Jeremy, what is it? Are you ill? You look dreadful!"

"No, that is, I have a head cold, but nothing to signify. It's much worse than that." Her brother's voice, hoarsened from his cold, shook slightly and the hand that laid his narrow-brimmed beaver hat on the nearest table was not quite steady either. By now Claire was a little disturbed and she urged him to sit down.

No one could have failed to discern the resemblance between brother and sister. Mr. Jeremy Yelland was a tall, well-set-up youth with his sister's colouring taken one or two shades darker, and his eyes were a more definite brown, though fringed with the same black lashes. As he moved reluctantly over to perch on the edge of a rather spindly chair with a padded oval back in a carved frame, he displayed a profile that was a masculine version of his sister's with decided cheekbones and a straight narrow nose just a bit too long to be considered classical. A little more chin would have improved him, but he would pass anywhere for a good-looking young man. His eyes were fixed on his sister's face with a painful intensity compounded of shame and desperation, and he seemed to be having trouble speaking after that first outburst.

"Jeremy, tell me what is troubling you," Claire urged in a calm voice that did not betray her mounting concern.

"I … I have lost a large sum of money. If I do not return it before the end of the week, I'll be ruined." Having dropped his bombshell, he shifted his gaze from his sister's shocked face, looking about the room while his mouth worked uncontrollably, his lips pulling in tightly and relaxing by turns.

"How did you lose this money?"

His eyes met hers for an instant, then darted away. "Playing faro," he blurted, moistening his lips.

The words fell into a pool of anguished silence so complete that the ticking of the clock on the mantelpiece sounded loud in Claire's ears. "Gambling!" she gasped. "Oh, Jeremy, how could you do anything so foolish?"

"One has to do something with one's free time," he replied, a defensive note in his voice. "I went to this place, this club, with some of the fellows from the bank. Besides, at first I won quite consistently. It really seemed that I had a knack for it."

"How much money did you lose?" Claire cut to the heart of the matter, not bothering to inform her young brother that letting greenhorns win at first was the standard procedure in a certain class of gaming establishment.

There was another uncomfortable silence. Claire's eyes never left her brother's frightened face. "Nearly four hundred pounds," he admitted reluctantly.

"But how could you? You didn't have that kind of money to lose. I don't understand, Jeremy. Did you sign some kind of paper guaranteeing payment? Is that possible? Punting on tick, as the gamblers say?"

"It doesn't work like that — at least, perhaps in the big clubs, where the members are all known to one another..." His voice trailed off.

Claire asked quietly, "How could you lose money you didn't have, Jeremy?"

He swallowed convulsively and looked away from his sister's face. She waited, not helping him, and at last he said, "I took it from various accounts in the bank." At her indrawn breath of dismay, he rushed on, "I need not tell you I meant only to borrow it for a few hours. I was doing so well, you see, but it was just piffling amounts, my own money, and I thought if I could win a few substantial bets I could improve my situation materially, perhaps move out of that ramshackle rooming house." Again his voice trailed off under his sister's appalled stare.

"You took money that didn't belong to you to *gamble* with?"

"You needn't make it sound as if I had stolen the money. I told you I intended to return it right away."

"Let us be quite clear on this point, Jeremy," Claire said bluntly. "What you intended is of less than no importance, and 'borrowing' involves requesting permission to use something that belongs to someone else. What you did was to take money that did not belong to you without permission, and that is stealing."

"I didn't look on it as stealing," he persisted miserably.

"Well, that is the way the bank will look upon it."

"That's why it is so vital to put the money back before the loss is discovered."

"And you thought I might have four hundred pounds to give you? If I had that kind of money, you would not have to live in cheap lodgings and I would not live here, a charge on Sadie and Samuel."

"I … I thought you might be able to borrow the money. Would the Mullinses —?"

Claire shook her head. "They don't have that kind of money either. This house didn't cost that much to build."

Jeremy rose quickly from the chair, avoiding his sister's eyes, and walked over to the window with his back to her. "What about that rich lord who has been dangling after you lately — what is his name — Mostyn?"

"How do you know about Lord Mostyn?"

"Oh, the fellows at the bank follow the doings of the current rages of the theatre world, and Clairisse Deschamps is very much in the forefront, along with Miss Euston of Covent Garden. Don't worry, no one knows you're my sister," he reassured her, having glanced over his shoulder at her sharp tone. Now he turned back to the window again and continued, "This Lord Mostyn would give you the money in the wink of an eye, would he not?"

This time the silence stretched until Jeremy's nerve gave out and he pivoted with the greatest reluctance to confront his sister.

Claire sat motionless, her face devoid of expression while her eyes searched his, shifting and shamed. "Do you know what Mostyn will expect from me in return, Jeremy?"

"Why shouldn't he make you a loan without expecting anything in return, just as a matter of business in accommodating a friend?"

"Perhaps he might if I could tell him when he could expect to be repaid, just as a matter of honour between acquaintances. How long do you estimate it will take us to repay four hundred pounds?"

The youth was as colourless as his sister by now and desperation rang in his voice. "Claire, do you not realize I could be prosecuted if the money is not put back?"

"Yes, of course I do. Is that what it comes down to, then, my virtue in exchange for your immunity from prosecution?"

Perspiration stood out on Jeremy's upper lip and he swallowed dryly. "No, no, forgive me, I scarcely know what I am saying, but I swear I'd never ask anything of you again, Claire. I've learned my lesson, I promise you."

"I'll try to think of something, but go now, please," Claire said dully. Now it was she who averted her gaze, and after a second or two of indecision, Jeremy grabbed his hat from the table and almost ran out the door. For another second Claire remained stiffly erect, and then a shudder shook her frame and she buried her face in her hands, rocking back and forth in mute despair.

When Mrs. Mullins appeared in the doorway to the parlour a few minutes later, she thought at first that the room was deserted until her roving eye located Claire standing silently by the lace-curtained window, staring out.

"What is ailing Master Jeremy?"

"He has a head cold," the figure at the window replied without turning around.

"There's more than a cold bothering that lad. He looked well-nigh distracted and he wouldn't meet my eyes. That's a sure sign that he's done something he's ashamed of. Is the lad in trouble, Miss Claire?"

Claire heaved a sigh and nodded. "Yes, but I can't tell even you just yet, Sadie. I must think what is to be done for the best."

"Best for Jeremy or best for you? He's nearly twenty and a man grown. It's high time he stood on his own two feet and stopped running to you to pull his irons out of the fire."

"Twenty is rather young to be completely on one's own, Sadie," Claire said soberly.

"And how old were you when you were left high and dry by poor Mr. Yelland, God rest his soul, without any golden apprenticeship to lead to a respectable career?"

"I was not quite high and dry, Sadie, I had you," Claire said, looking at her champion with affection, "and Papa truly believed my future was settled with Mr. Heaton."

"Well, Miss Claire, my advice is to let Master Jeremy get himself out of whatever trouble he's gotten himself into; he'll be a better man for it."

"Will he?" Claire's lashes veiled her eyes, but there was a forlorn droop to the soft mouth that caused Mrs. Mullins to cease her arguments.

"Why don't you rest on your bed this afternoon, my love, or you'll be in no case to give a performance tonight, not after the scenes you've endured last night and now with Master Jeremy."

Claire's fingers had slipped into the hair above her temples and she was kneading the area unconsciously. "I am rather fatigued this afternoon. I believe I will lie down for an hour or so." She summoned up a weak smile as she brushed by the woman near the doorway, patting her shoulder in gratitude.

Claire achieved privacy but little relaxation that afternoon, though she dutifully lay on her bed for nearly two hours. Jeremy's predicament had driven her own problem out of her head until he had suggested Lord Mostyn as the source of the money he needed to prevent the discovery of his theft. After last night Mostyn was out as a potential banker, of course, but she had been too crushed by the discovery that her brother would not scruple to barter her virtue for his immunity from the natural repercussions of his criminal action to take in the hopelessness of the situation at the time. She had something over one hundred and twenty pounds in the bank, which represented all the security she possessed in the world, not that it really signified. It was no less impossible to ask for a loan of three hundred pounds than for four hundred.

Considering the problem solely from Jeremy's point of view, discovery would indeed ruin his life. His career would be over before it began, and imprisonment would be a living death for one raised to ride over his own acres. It was not his fault that he had not been bred to habits of economy. Perhaps she should have anticipated that he would be easily led from his path of respectable poverty, which must seem endless to a youth of ardent spirits. He was all the family she had, and she loved him, faults and all.

Claire stared up at the ceiling, trying to analyse the situation dispassionately. Lord Mostyn was not the only man to wish to make her his mistress since her debut on the stage, but he was the only one who had threatened her sense of personal security. She'd have fought to the death to prevent him from having his way with her, but this was a case of an instinctive and deeply felt aversion to the man personally. Among her other would-be protectors, surely there must be one who was not personally repugnant to her. Never having felt the least *tendre* for a gentleman, the whole concept of submitting to a man's desire to possess her bodily was inconceivable, but this was no less true in the case of an honourable offer of marriage. She had certainly never been tempted to relinquish her respectability in exchange for worldly advantages. The question was: could she make a sacrifice of herself for Jeremy?

By the time Claire reported to the theatre that evening as Clairisse Deschamps, she had come a long way toward convincing herself that she could do what was necessary to save her brother, though she could not take the sacrifice one step further and convince herself that she could accept the loss of her reputation with anything approaching equanimity. This would eliminate any chance for her to assume what Sadie would call her rightful place in the scheme of things eventually. She would never be able to go back to the life she had known, never be able to establish herself respectably or raise a family. She feared she was no more able to put a good face on her dutiful action than her aunt had been able to do when she had submitted to the distasteful — to her — task of introducing an unwanted niece into society.

This thought gave her pause. Would Jeremy come to resent her for her unwilling sacrifice the way she had resented her aunt? It seemed very likely, and it would never do, because then she would lose him as surely as if he were transported to a penal colony in the Antipodes.

There was one other very real concern if she decided to rescue Jeremy, and that was Sadie. Her nurse would fight tooth and nail to prevent such a sacrifice on her part, out of pure love for the motherless little girl she had taken to her heart almost twenty years ago. Watching without appearing to do so as Sadie bustled about the dressing room making her ready for the performance and assisting the other ladies as needed, Claire felt herself sinking under an increasing weight of oppression. She longed to go back a month or so to a time when life had seemed relatively uncomplicated and the prospects for the future vaguely optimistic.

Claire's performance that night was not one of her finest. She was unable to raise her acting above the level of mechanical reaction and was relieved when the final curtain fell. As previously decided, she kept away from the green room and slipped away to meet Samuel, who escorted her home. At the last moment before she left, the stage manager handed her an envelope which had been delivered to the theatre that afternoon. It was not unusual to receive messages and invitations from admiring gentlemen. She tucked it into her reticule and hastened away to meet Samuel. Weary from the emotional stresses of the day following a disturbed night, Claire never gave the note another thought as she made quick work of the nightly routine and tumbled into bed.

CHAPTER 5

Claire arose rather heavy-eyed the next morning, and no closer to a solution to the pressing situation than before she had retired. As her uninterested glance fell on the reticule she had dropped near the wig stand on the dresser, she recalled the note she had received and took it out of the bag. The handwriting was unfamiliar, bold and fairly slanting, with well-formed letters. The communication was brief:

Dear Miss Deschamps,

It is my earnest desire to speak with you at your earliest convenience on a matter of some urgency. Will you drive with me tomorrow afternoon at two? If you agree, I will meet you at the corner of Bridges and Russell streets at that hour.

Your obedient servant,

Egon Hollister

For several minutes, Claire studied the unrevealing few lines for some hidden message, aware of an initial tingle of excitement that she soon subdued. Doubtless Sir Egon desired to make it clear that he would prefer her to discourage his young cousin's attentions. Surely by now she had gotten past the stage of being hurt by examples of what was the general opinion of women who embraced a thespian career. She told herself the only reason she was inclined to accept the invitation and put herself in a position to be insulted was a sense of guilt at having dashed away without thanking Sir Egon for his timely rescue the other evening. This was what she told Sadie when that suspicious lady expressed her disapproval at the proposed outing.

"Like as not, this sir got the wrong impression t'other evening and is planning to try his hand where Mostyn failed," Sadie said flatly.

"Somehow I do not believe Sir Egon has any personal interest in me, Sadie, but be that as it may, I feel obligated out of common civility to repair the omission of that night. I never said a word of thanks to the man."

Mrs. Mullins grumbled as a matter of form, but subsided more quickly than was her wont. She was more interested in reopening a discussion of Jeremy's visit, which her intimate knowledge of Claire told her was of crucial importance to the girl, but Claire fobbed her off again.

"I haven't quite worked through my plan, Sadie, so please bear with me a little longer."

Miss Yelland found it unexpectedly difficult to decide on an outfit in which to drive out with Sir Egon. After checking on the weather every hour and rejecting several of Sadie's suggestions, she finally settled on a black velvet spencer worn over a walking dress of narrowly striped black-and-white cotton, which she fancied made her look tall and dignified. There was nothing dignified about the black velvet bonnet whose wide poke was lined in pleated white satin, however. With its high crown trimmed with a band of the satin, it was frankly dashing. Black kid half-boots and white kid gloves completed the costume, and Samuel, who was going back to the shop after a late lunch, ventured the opinion that she looked "right smart." Coming from the kind but nearly inarticulate Mr. Mullins, this was high praise indeed. Sadie, made as uneasy by an occasional flash of eagerness today as she already was at the general air of anxiety that had hung over Claire since her brother's visit, lavished no compliments on her darling that day. She watched Claire set out with Samuel for as far as their paths agreed with misgivings that she did not attempt to conceal.

Claire was still a hundred or so feet from the designated meeting place when Sir Egon pulled up ahead of her in the phaeton she had nearly crashed into — was it only two days ago? He did not have his groom along this afternoon, an indication that he desired privacy for his purpose. Either she or Sadie must be correct in guessing this purpose.

Claire projected an attitude of neutrality as she greeted Sir Egon politely and accepted his extended hand to climb up into the phaeton in one swift graceful movement. Having become accustomed over the past six months to being looked over like a farm animal at Smithfield Market, she was easily able to maintain her composure under the measuring look he bent on her during this operation, though his eyes held none of the admiration that she was used to seeing in similar circumstances.

"Ready?" he asked briefly, preparing to give his horses the office to start.

"Quite," she replied, equally brief. She directed her gaze toward the side of the road until he had the bays moving smoothly together, at which time she swivelled slightly toward him, presenting him with a bit more than a profile should he wish to speak to her.

He did not immediately avail himself of the tacit invitation, keeping his eyes forward, so Claire was able to study his profile freely in her turn. She had thought his eyes uncommonly fine at their first meeting. Now that this dominating feature was reduced to an enviable length of dark lash, she decided his face was arresting rather than handsome. There was no fault to be found with the slightly aquiline curve to his nose and the strongly carved jaw, but those faint vertical lines in his thin cheeks aged him and gave a rather grim cast to his countenance. A smile might considerably improve his appearance, but she had not been privileged to see Sir Egon smile in their previous brief encounters.

Claire approved his taste in clothes. No true aspirant to fashion distinction would have settled on a coat with such a modestly styled collar and lapels, but to her knowledgeable eye the claret-coloured superfine fabric was of excellent quality, and she could tell that the cut and fit were superb by the ease with which the sleeve construction accommodated his muscular motions in driving. His linen was also of the finest quality, though his shirt points were not nearly so high as his cousin's and would not restrict his head movements, since his cravat was neatly but not extravagantly tied. His inexpressibles were dove-coloured and closely moulded to strongly muscled thighs, disappearing beneath black Hessian boots of mirror-polished leather.

Sir Egon turned and caught her staring, but since he must have been aware that she was studying him — indeed, by his continued silence, he had made it difficult for her to do anything else — she was easily able to prevent a blush from rising into her cheeks. She gave him a cool look of inquiry and waited for him to speak.

"You must be wondering why I requested this meeting, Miss Deschamps?"

"Whatever the reason, sir," she said in her beautiful warm voice, "it has afforded me an opportunity to thank you for the singular service you rendered me the other night. My only excuse for being remiss at the time is that I was in great distress and, knowing nothing about you, I simply obeyed my instinct to fly to safety. I do thank you now, most sincerely."

Claire met his searching look unwaveringly. He did not speak for a second or two, and when he did, she received the impression that he had altered what he had intended to say.

"Why did you accept Mostyn's invitation? Surely his reputation was not entirely unknown to you?"

"I am not so well-established in the theatre world that I can afford to antagonize well-connected persons like Lord Mostyn." She shrugged her shoulders and continued with a slightly bitter intonation, "It was never my intention to embarrass him; in fact, it was my hope that I had made my sentiments sufficiently plain that a gentleman would have no choice but to accept my decision. Obviously my judgment was faulty in believing Lord Mostyn to be *au fond* a gentleman."

"Whatever your intentions, I would say that you have certainly succeeded in antagonizing Mostyn."

There was a conspicuous lack of sympathy in Sir Egon's voice or manner. Claire gripped the inside of her cheek between her molars but returned no answer, determined to betray no emotion in the presence of this cold-hearted man. She kept her gaze on the shops they were passing. Let him look at her profile for a time.

"Do you enjoy the life of an actress, Miss Deschamps?"

"I enjoy performing on the stage with a talented group of people, helping to make the words of other talented people come alive to an audience."

"And do you like being the object of improper advances from Mostyn and his ilk?"

"If your purpose in inviting me to drive with you was to insult me, sir, you have now accomplished your goal. If you will please set me down over there, I will have no trouble finding a hackney carriage at this hour."

"My purpose, Miss Deschamps, is not to insult you but to learn something about you."

"I cannot conceive of what has prompted this interest in one so far beneath you, sir. If you wish for my assurance that I shall not entertain any improper advances from your young cousin, you have it. Now, I must request you to set me down at once."

"Hoity-toity," he said softly, watching angry lights flare into soft amber eyes. "My young cousin will not trouble you with any improper suggestions; he thinks you pure as the driven snow."

"While you know otherwise?" she snapped. Too late she regretted allowing him to badger her into unbecoming retaliation.

"Let us just say that I am no longer young and credulous. But please believe, Miss Deschamps, that I have no wish to insult you or quarrel with you. I brought you here to put before you a proposition, which I hope you will give serious consideration."

Claire's white-gloved hands gripped each other tightly in her lap. So Sadie had been right. He was going to offer her a *carte blanche*, though she would swear he felt no attraction to her. She kept her eyes on the side of the road, intent on retaining both her temper and her dignity under trying circumstances.

"I am not proposing to make you my mistress, Miss Deschamps, but my wife," he said coolly, "so do not poker up, there's a good girl."

That brought her head around in a flash. "Your wife?" she echoed in patent disbelief, her eyes widening.

"Yes, as in marriage. A temporary marriage," he added.

Claire's good intentions disintegrated under this new provocation. "Sir, I do not know whether your senses are deranged or you merely possess a reprehensible sense of humour, nor do I care particularly, but I have endured enough. If you do not stop this carriage immediately, I shall create a scene worthy of the stage, which, if it cannot cover you with embarrassment, will at least bring you a good deal of hostile attention."

"I believe you would, but I assure you such desperate measures are unnecessary. If after you have heard my proposition you still wish to leave the carriage, I promise you shall do so, on my word as a gentleman."

"Another fine gentleman," she said, curling her lip.

"Madam, you will find that you may trust the word of a Hollister," he retorted, nettled at last. "I am proposing a straight business proposition. I wish to employ your services as an actress for a short period of time, and naturally I expect to pay you well for these services."

"You mean," she said slowly, "you want me to pretend to be your wife?"

"Not pretend. I fear it will be necessary to go through with a legal ceremony, which we shall ultimately dissolve through another legal process called divorce."

"Thank you, I am familiar with the term."

"And for your services," he went on in the same patient manner of teacher to dull student, "I am prepared to pay you five hundred pounds."

Claire stared into those deep brown eyes, trying to discover the truth of this extraordinary proposal. "Why?" she asked at last.

"Because in accommodating me thus you will have earned the money by the time the charade is over."

She waved a dismissing hand. "I meant why do you require a temporary wife?"

"That I do not propose to tell you. I have my reasons."

"I see. Well, I have heard you out and I would like to get down now, please."

"You have scarcely given the proposition fair consideration," he protested.

"I gave it all the consideration it deserves. It sounds like a havey-cavey scheme to me. For all I know, you might be involving me in something criminal."

"There is no question of illegality or criminality."

"I'm sorry, but I don't know that."

"Very well," he said after an antagonistic pause that she did not attempt to end. "I need to be married in order to be considered as my grandmother's prospective heir."

"I ... see. Then my performance would be for your grandmother's benefit?"

"Hers and any other relatives who may be present at Belhaven."

"Where is Belhaven?"

"Near Rye and Winchelsea in East Sussex."

"We would have to go there?"

"That's correct, within the next few days."

Sir Egon returned his full attention to the horses, leaving Claire to make her decision in peace, if such a term could be applied to the turmoil in her mind at that moment. She mistrusted the whole scheme and had decided that Sir Egon was a very disagreeable personality, but the offer of five hundred pounds had come as an answer to prayer. If she could have contemplated an irregular connection with the repulsive Lord Mostyn or another of his ilk, how could she hesitate at an impersonation which would not leave her dishonoured? A divorced woman might be beyond the pale in society, but in the case of a simple nonconsummation, surely an annulment would be possible. Nobody's fool, Claire was conscious that she was getting into deep waters, but this mad scheme seemed the lesser of the two evils. She firmed her resolution and said, "I will do it on two conditions."

"Name them."

"There is to be no question of any conjugal privileges during this temporary marriage, and —"

"You flatter yourself, Miss Deschamps. Quite frankly, your attractions are not such that I shall be tempted to press any claims the law allows me."

"I would prefer your word as a gentleman, that famous word of honour of which you boasted a few moments ago," she said dryly, hiding her annoyance at the gratuitous insult to her charms.

"You have it. What is your second condition?"

"I would like three hundred pounds before we leave London."

"What guarantee have I that you will not leave London with my three hundred pounds?"

"The word of a Yelland, which is as good as that of a Hollister."

"Yelland? What is this?" He turned a frowning glance on her calm face.

"My real name, which I assume you will require for the special licence. Clairisse Deschamps is only a stage name."

"What is your given name?"

"Claire."

"Claire." He produced the word slowly, as though tasting it. "At least that sounds real," he said unexpectedly. "Very well, Miss Claire Yelland, you may consider yourself betrothed. There will be numerous arrangements to make over the next few days. We can discuss them on the way to your home."

"No," she replied swiftly. "I have no intention of allowing you or anyone to know where I live. I will meet you wherever you say for whatever it is necessary to do, but I will go home alone."

Sir Egon argued against this arbitrary decision, but in the end he was forced to give way as Claire remained adamant on this point. He agreed to meet her at the same time on the following day to give her the pertinent information regarding the actual ceremony. He then bade her an unsmiling goodbye and touched his hat briefly after depositing her at the corner of Bow Street at her request.

Claire stared after the departing phaeton until it disappeared around the corner, her thoughts in a whirl behind the calm facade she had developed as a necessary weapon of survival in her strange new life. She could not quite believe she had just committed herself to a deception beyond anything she had ever achieved on the stage, and moreover, a deception that could have far-reaching consequences for the rest of her life. She headed with slow steps back to the Mullins residence. Her self-appointed guardian was going to oppose this undertaking with all the strength of her being, but there was literally no other recourse if Jeremy was to be spared the gruesome consequences of his rash behaviour. Sadie was a firm believer in assuming the responsibility for one's own actions, and so was she in theory, but how could she let her brother's life be ruined before he was even fully adult? Besides, she believed him when he said he'd learned his lesson.

It seemed that Mrs. Mullins did not share Claire's confidence on this vital point. Even when the situation had been explained to her in painstaking detail, with emphasis on Sir Egon's total lack of interest in her person, Sadie could not regard the scheme with anything but abhorrence.

"How can you sit there and say without a blink that you'll be able to take up your life again when this episode is over? What kind of life does a divorced woman have?" She held up a hand as Claire's lips parted. "No, do not explain to me again the difference between divorce and annulment, because it won't make a particle of difference to how you are regarded. What respectable man would marry you after this escapade, tell me that if you can?"

"How many respectable men have been seeking my hand in marriage these past six months?" Claire's words were accompanied by a twisted little smile that struck at Sadie's heart.

"You could bring Mr. Blyden around your thumb in a fortnight if only you would exert yourself," she predicted confidently.

"I thought we were talking about men, Sadie. Geoffrey Blyden is a boy yet, and what he feels for me is infatuation or calf love at the most. He doesn't even know me. All he sees is the exciting actress Miss Clairisse Deschamps."

"Because that is all you've allowed him to see!"

"Would you have me take advantage of his youthful adoration to trick him into offering for me? What kind of a person would that make me?"

"A married woman!" Sadie retorted. "What makes you think he is so helpless? He's older than you are and would be fortunate to have you for a wife."

"Only if I thought myself equally fortunate to have him for a husband, which I do not. I am persuaded I was meant to remain a spinster and keep house for Jeremy eventually."

"Not if I have anything to say in the matter," Mrs. Mullins declared in a perfectly audible undertone that Claire elected not to hear.

"Sadie dear, we are wandering from the point, which is my imminent sham marriage to Sir Egon Hollister. Nothing you have said or will say could make this solution to the immediate problem anything less than a godsend from my point of view. I gather time is a pressing consideration for Sir Egon, which means we must put our heads together to adapt my rather eccentric wardrobe to make it unexceptionable for a newly married lady on a visit of ceremony to her husband's grandmother, who, my instincts tell me, is something of a dragon."

"I don't like the idea of his dragging you off to the country, where you won't have anyone to support you in case all is not as it should be," Sadie complained, but she could not resist a challenge to her fashion awareness. Though she continued to espouse new arguments against the plan in the next two days, her busy fingers were engaged in removing trims from some articles of clothing and refurbishing others to nullify the black-and-white theme that had set the "Iceberg" apart from the rest. At the showroom of a dressmaker friend of Sadie's, they were fortunate enough to find a pelisse and two evening gowns in an advanced stage of construction that had been put aside because the woman who ordered them had had to go into mourning unexpectedly. All were perfect for Claire's colouring, and what was more to the point, dagger cheap under the circumstances. Even with the advance of three hundred pounds, Claire's savings would be almost entirely depleted to make up the sum Jeremy required.

Although with each passing hour she was coming closer to becoming the wife of Sir Egon Hollister, Claire came no closer to a personal rapprochement with the stern-faced baronet in the last brief meeting between the parties to the arrangement before the actual ceremony that was to unite them in the eyes of the church and the law. He did not even bother with a greeting, plunging instead into a renewed argument to find out where she lived when he picked her up the next day in his carriage.

"You don't seem to understand, sir, that when this mock marriage has served your purpose, I shall have to resume my life as it was before we met. How much better for both of us, do you not agree, if we make it a total separation, with no contact except through your attorney?"

"That sounds logical enough, but I have a strong conviction that you are concealing something vital from me. How do I know you do not already have a husband whose existence will invalidate our arrangement and cause me to lose my inheritance?"

"I am not now nor have I ever been married. I live with my old nurse and her family, who should not have to be disturbed by Clairisse Deschamps's admirers in their home. There is no mystery about it, but I shall continue to maintain the secrecy for their protection," she declared, elevating her pointed chin and giving her intended husband a level look that confirmed his earlier impression that in Miss Yelland he was not dealing with a meek, compliant female despite her pleasant manner. He was forced to accept the situation, though his mistrust of her was far from mitigated.

She listened without interruption to his arrangements for the ceremony to be performed at St. Martin-in-the-Fields in two days' time by special licence, which he was in the process of procuring.

"Is there anyone you would wish to have present as a witness?" he asked as an afterthought when he had given her the pertinent details.

"Well —" she blinked and hesitated, summoning her acting skills to the fore — "I had not really thought about it before, but one of the dressers at the theatre has been very kind to me. Perhaps she would like to come." Sir Egon being amenable to this suggestion, it was agreed on between them.

The truth was that Sadie had flatly refused to permit her chick to marry without her support on that momentous occasion, and incidentally to check that all was legal and above-board. Also she was burning to see for herself the man who had presumed on one day's acquaintance to embroil her darling in this act of mockery. Afraid at first to jeopardize her cherished anonymity, Claire had relented only after extracting a solemn promise that Sadie would act the part of a casual acquaintance in the presence of Sir Egon.

It was more of a wrench to give notice that she was leaving the theatre company than Claire could have anticipated when she had taken to the stage in desperation seven months earlier. Whatever her difficulties adapting to the life of an actress offstage, the thespian craft itself had become important to her and she had been proud of her progress in acquiring and perfecting the necessary skills for the performance of it. She ran into no practical hitches in severing the ties, perhaps because it was anticipated that Lord Mostyn would act against her. She did nothing to discourage the popular assumption that she was cutting her losses by leaving voluntarily, but she walked away from the theatre for the last time with an accretion to the mound of sadness that had accumulated with all the significant losses in her life to date. Whether it was another closed chapter or merely a pause to turn the page, she couldn't presume to guess at the moment, but it was a sombre moment.

What to tell her brother was another question that troubled Claire in the short period before her marriage. She would have preferred to keep from him the knowledge of the arrangement by which she was able to redeem his debt, but she could not simply vanish from London for a time without telling him some story to account for her absence. Sadie opposed any solution that would keep Jeremy in the dark about the extent of his sister's sacrifice for him, and vowed she would tell him the truth no matter what Claire decided. Faced with this ultimatum, Claire had no choice but to lay the whole matter before him. She was somewhat taken aback by his disapproval of the plan, despite his relief at evading the spectre of prosecution that had tormented him.

"A divorce? But that is scandalous! You'll be ruined!"

"A divorce cannot do my reputation any more harm than becoming someone's mistress would," Claire protested.

"But that would be Clairisse Deschamps. No one would ever have to know that Clairisse Deschamps is really Claire Yelland when it is over … in later years, I mean," Jeremy stammered.

Claire's eyes narrowed. "I am telling you plainly that I do not intend to enter into an immoral liaison when this alternative is available to me. If I cannot get this money to save you from being prosecuted, it will be you who sullies the Yelland name. Either way, the fair name of Yelland must suffer, it would seem. Which is to be, Jeremy, a prison cell for you or a divorce for me? It is your choice."

"I do not think I should survive a prison term," the young man said miserably, looking at his sister with shamed but desperate eyes.

"That's settled, then. Sadie will give you the money after the ceremony tomorrow. I shall be leaving immediately with Sir Egon for his grandmother's estate."

"Does this man Sir Egon know what I've done?"

"He doesn't know you exist."

Jeremy looked even more miserable if possible, and this time Claire received the impression that it was partially on her behalf. "Why does he think you are going along with this charade, then?"

"I don't believe Sir Egon Hollister has asked himself that question," Claire said lightly. "An actress is not important enough in Sir Egon's scheme of things for her feelings or motivations to be of any interest to him."

Jeremy bit his lip but said no more. When brother and sister parted, however, he embraced her with unusual warmth. Knowing this to be his attempt at apologizing, Claire felt an infinitesimal lightening of the cold weight of apprehension lying in the pit of her stomach.

CHAPTER 6

Sir Egon Hollister paced up and down the pavement outside St. Martin-in-the-Fields as the appointed hour for his wedding struck. He was not altogether certain that the mysterious Miss Yelland would actually put in an appearance and, if the truth were told, was of two minds whether a failure to appear would be for good or ill. At this moment his thought processes defied description, though they were anything but calm and rational. Five years ago, he never could have envisioned that his marriage would be a hole-in-corner affair undertaken in a spirit of bitterness and spite with a woman — a stranger — for whom he entertained none of the recommended feelings for persons contemplating wedlock. In fact, he had selected his bride-to-be precisely because she was everything his grandmother would most abhor. He had been in a mood to strike out at the woman who had been able to sever the closest ties of affection apparently without regret rather than accept that she could not enforce her will on him in the area of his marriage.

Now that he had had several days in which to cool down his blood, he could only wonder what he had accomplished by his rash decision beyond an unnecessary statement of his independence. Unless his grandmother had grown dotingly fond of Melissa in the past few years, she would hate making Jack Blyden her principal heir, but this *mésalliance* he was about to contract could easily drive her to that point. No amount of rage or denial could alter the fact that he loved Belhaven. He had been raised to expect that it would be his one day, and it would hurt like blazes to see Jack and Melissa inherit the estate.

On the other hand, he would never allow his grandmother to foist the inoffensive nonentity that was Miss Winward onto him as the price of his inheritance.

He didn't want a wife at all, but at least in Miss Yelland he need not worry about emotional tethers. The actress possessed more than her share of good looks, but that obvious sensual appeal she exuded held no allure for him. He had always been attracted to the elegant blond beauty typified by Melissa, and five years' exposure to the charms of Latin ladies had not altered this preference. Her lovely voice was the only quality he wholeheartedly admired in Miss Yelland, though he conceded a grudging respect for the mental coolness she displayed under pressure.

At this point in his pacing, Sir Egon was brought up short by the sudden proximity of two ladies, one in her early twenties and the other some dozen years older. He had not noticed their approach and had to sidestep quickly to avoid bumping into the younger of the two.

"I beg your pardon, ma'am. I fear I was lost in thought and unmindful of my movements."

"Well, marriage is a very serious step and certainly warrants a good deal of thought," the young lady said with a slight smile.

Egon started and stared. "How did you know…?" His voice vanished and his stare intensified as he assimilated the cool amusement in a pair of large amber-toned eyes set at a tilted angle in a heart-shaped face. His glance roamed over a broad creamy brow and lingered on a widow's peak of smooth tawny hair that disappeared beneath a sage-green bonnet. The well-defined cheekbones and narrow nose struck a chord, as did the pointed chin beneath invitingly curved lips that were no longer artificially reddened. Startled recognition in his dark eyes produced a widening of the lady's lips, which parted to reveal perfect teeth.

The smile was not destined to be long-lasting.

"What have you done to yourself?" Egon demanded harshly.

"I merely discarded Clairisse Deschamps's wig and washed off the cosmetics." She blinked fabulous lashes which remained jet black, though he noted that her eyebrows were now just a couple of shades darker than her hair.

"Do you have any additional surprises up your sleeve, Miss Yelland?" he inquired in a soft voice shaded by a hint of menace that brought her chin up to a defensive angle.

"I do not feel I know you well enough to speculate about what you would find surprising in a woman," she returned evenly. "Sir Egon, may I present Mrs. Mullins, who has kindly agreed to serve as a witness at our ... at the ceremony."

Egon had his temper well in hand when he bowed to the sturdy figure regarding him critically from a pair of well-opened hazel eyes in an unsmiling though comely countenance.

The woman was dressed with great neatness in a dark blue pelisse of very good cut but without any of the adornments currently adopted by ladies of fashion. Her black hat was of similar quality, its sole concession to style being a pleated blue satin ribbon around the modest crown. A solid citizen with no hint of the deferential in her manner despite the small curtsy she dropped him. He took the trouble to make his greeting pleasant.

"How do you do, Mrs. Mullins? It is extremely kind of you to accompany Miss Yelland on this important occasion, and I would like to add my thanks to hers. Now, if you will come with me, ladies."

Sir Egon offered an arm to each, but Miss Yelland held back. "I believe there is one formality remaining, sir. Would you excuse us for a moment, Mrs. Mullins?"

As the older woman moved a few steps away, Sir Egon's eyebrows arched in question. "A formality?"

"A little matter of three hundred pounds," Miss Yelland replied.

His look of distaste did not cause her cool gaze to alter. He inclined his head but couldn't forbear to lodge one protest. "Would it not have been more ... seemly to wait until after the ceremony, Miss Yelland?"

"More seemly perhaps, but less practical, for what recourse would I then have should you not prove to be a man of honour? We would already be married."

"I take your point, Miss Yelland," Sir Egon replied, reaching into an inner pocket of his coat and extracting an envelope from which he took a number of notes. "You would seem to have been unlucky in your prior acquaintance with honourable men," he added politely as he handed them to her.

"But it seems my luck has now changed, sir," she returned with equal politeness. "Thank you. Excuse me, please, while I fetch back Mrs. Mullins."

He feigned surprise. "Are you not going to count the bills?"

She looked back over her shoulder. "Of course. Thank you for reminding me."

Miss Yelland seemed to have won that round, Egon conceded, his jaw set and his brooding eyes following the graceful back view she offered as she approached the older woman. After a brief exchange of words he could not distinguish, they turned back toward him.

How distasteful this whole affair was! Well, he had asked for it, and the time for turning back had come and gone. Without a word, he escorted the women into the church.

Oddly enough, Egon's senses were sharpened by the ineffable disgust he was feeling as the travesty of a marriage ceremony proceeded to its close, with a church sexton acting as the other witness. The officiating minister droned out the beautiful words of the marriage service in a musty office overflowing with books cluttering every surface, including piles on the floor. It boasted a single window whose unwashed panes permitted a weak diffused sun to filter in and accent the dust motes in the air. An aroma of old candles and dust permeated the area and provoked a fastidious sniff of disdain from Mrs. Mullins, who lifted her skirts as she brushed past one of the haphazard piles of books to take her place beside the ancient sexton, whose rheumy eyes and hacking cough caused him to resort to a none-too-clean handkerchief at frequent intervals. Egon noted that Mrs. Mullins edged as far away from her fellow witness as space permitted, her lips tightly pursed.

The only person apart from the cherubic grey-haired cleric who appeared not to be affected by the drab setting was Miss Yelland, who stood absolutely still, her face quiet and her eyes never leaving the minister's rosy-cheeked face. Egon was thus afforded an opportunity to acquaint himself with this new version of the woman who was, unbelievably, about to become his wife. Gone was the dramatic black-and-white image of the shrewd sensualist that was Clairisse Deschamps, acclaimed actress of Drury Lane. In her place stood Claire Yelland, about to become Hollister, a serenely lovely young woman simply and becomingly dressed in a sage-green sheer wool pelisse with a matching bonnet, and every inch a lady to the casual eye.

Perversely, he was more outraged at what he could only regard as her deception than gratified by the transformation. Egon hated relinquishing control of any aspect of his life, and he could not quite dismiss a feeling that the mysterious Miss Yelland had wrested control of the present situation from him, momentarily at least, by this radical switch in personalities.

"Ahem ... Sir Egon?"

Egon's gaze left Miss Yelland's clear-cut profile and went to the minister's expectant face.

"You have the ring, sir?"

The ring! He'd never given a thought to buying a wedding ring during the hectic days of preparation for his coup. His fingers began searching motions in his pockets under the unflurried eye of his waiting bride.

"I'm so sorry, Reverend; in my haste this morning I'm afraid I left the ring at home."

"No matter. You may use your signet ring for the ceremony," the kindly cleric said soothingly.

"Oh, yes, of course." Egon hastily removed the stamped gold ring from his little finger while Miss Yelland proceeded to take off her glove, as little discomposed by this hitch in the proceedings as the minister. Did nothing ever dent that iron composure of hers? he wondered savagely as he took her hand and repeated the minister's words, slipping the heavy ring onto her slender finger. Out of the corner of his eye, he caught a glimpse of Mrs. Mullins wiping a surreptitious tear from her eye with a snowy handkerchief as he released Claire's hand. Women were indeed mawkish creatures if they could derive some pleasurable sentiment from this uninspiring scene.

"I now pronounce you man and wife. You may kiss your bride, Sir Egon."

Egon started and glanced at his bride, watching him … dispassionately? Challengingly? Disappointment, regret, and distaste for the situation he had created churned within him. It was time she found out that she issued challenges to him at her peril. Deliberately he gathered the slim young woman into his arms, sensing her initial resistance and subsequent relaxation within his embrace. There was no surrender in those amber eyes, which glowed defiantly up at him as his mouth took possession of hers with unnecessary roughness. Her lips were warm, sweet, and totally unresponsive. He released her abruptly when it dawned on him that he was actually trying to coerce a response from her. He looked an apology, but she did not meet his eyes, being occupied with receiving the felicitations of the beaming cleric.

Mrs. Mullins had moved forward, and the minor rite of signing the parish register now took place, after which the wheezing sexton removed himself and his symptoms from the office with a nod of acknowledgment for the gratuity pressed on him by the groom. The small party now took leave of the minister in a silence that lasted until they were again outside the church. Mrs. Mullins walked close beside the bride, seeming almost to hover protectively, and when they reached the pavement she turned to the baronet, fixing him with a probing look.

"You are to be congratulated, Sir Egon, on having persuaded the sweetest and loveliest girl in the world to be your wife. I hope you realize your good fortune."

The girl at her side stirred uneasily. "Please, Sa… Mrs. Mullins, do not embarrass Sir Egon with a catalogue of my supposed virtues," she said softly.

Egon intervened smoothly. "Thank you, Mrs. Mullins, for your good wishes. I trust the future will reveal the full extent of my good fortune. I certainly concur that no man could have a lovelier bride than Claire, and I can see that she has a good friend in you."

"And I hope she will have a good husband in you, sir."

"Mrs. Mullins!"

Egon noted the minatory look his scarlet-cheeked bride sent her friend, but he laughed and held out his hand to the older woman, saying easily, "I trust Claire and I will study the art of pleasing each other as husband and wife. I have left my carriage at an inn around the corner, so we shall be saying goodbye to you here. Thank you again for your service to my wife this morning. I'll leave you two to say a private farewell."

Egon bowed and walked off a few paces, his face thoughtful. One way and another it had been a memorable morning. He had not been prepared for the emotional toll that would be exacted by the carry-out of this wild marriage scheme, and he had a horrid premonition that this was only the beginning. Suddenly he had no stomach for the deception, but it was too late to pull back now. There was Claire to consider, for one thing; she was now his legal wife. He repeated the words to himself, but they still had no reality for him. Anyway, his *wife* could live quite well on five hundred pounds for the next year or two, so he need not succumb to a misplaced attack of conscience on the actress's account.

Egon's expression was sterner than ever, did he but know it, as Claire walked slowly toward him, a little misty-eyed after having embraced her friend and bidden her a quick farewell. Lord, the girl was really lovely! This was a complication he had not envisioned. Egon's teeth went together tightly and the grip he took on his bride's elbow made her wince a little.

He muttered an apology and relaxed his fingers. "We go this way," he said, summoning up a businesslike air. "Did you send your baggage to the stables for my groom to bring down to Belhaven with my own?"

"Yes, last night."

Except for an automatic inquiry about her comfort, this was the extent of their conversation until Egon had the phaeton back on the city streets. Bride and groom were lost in their own private ruminations, and it was not until the vehicle came to a halt that Claire emerged from her reverie and looked around her in some confusion.

"Why are we stopping here, sir, on Ludgate Hill?"

"You'd be advised to practise calling me by my name, or we'll queer our pitch before we've been an hour at Belhaven," he said tartly. "I have an errand in there. Do you think you can hold the horses for a few moments?"

Claire nodded and accepted the reins. She watched his broad shoulders disappear into a shop and her eyes found the sign: Rundell and Bridge, one of the premier jewellers in the capital. So he had lied about leaving the wedding ring at home this morning. Well, she had thought as much at the time, despite his quick-witted pantomime of searching his pockets. She composed her features into a pleasant mask and greeted him serenely on his return some ten minutes later.

Egon accepted the ribbons back and put a small package into her hands. "Here, you'd better have this."

Claire handled the package gingerly, turning it slowly in her fingers.

"It won't bite; open it," he commanded.

Thus admonished, she obeyed, removing the wrappings with delicate precision. She opened the little box and gasped audibly at the contents, blinking her cat's eyes at Egon. "I'll wear the wedding ring, of course, but surely the engage… the other is an unnecessary extravagance?"

"The emerald? If we are to convince my grandmother that I'm so wildly gone in love that I'd marry within a month of returning to England after a five-year absence, it will take more than that bauble to do the trick. I have some jewellery that was my mother's. I'll have my man bring it down to Belhaven in a day or two — if we last that long," he added.

Claire did not question this cryptic remark, and after a moment he glanced over to see her still holding the box in her gloved hands, her eyes fixed on the contents. "If you are waiting for me to do the honours," he said dryly, "I must tell you that a city street full of noonday traffic is scarcely the setting for a romantic gesture, even if I could perform it without jeopardizing our bodily safety."

Hastily Claire transferred the box to her right hand while she struggled to remove the tan glove from her left at the same time. Eventually she accomplished the chore and removed the signet ring, which she held out to him hesitantly.

"Drop it in my pocket," he ordered, and she did so, making sure it was safely inside before slipping first the wide gold band and then the large oval-shaped emerald in its diamond setting onto her finger. Womanlike, she could not resist holding up her hand to admire the effect.

Catching his eye fixed on the rings, she spoke quickly to cover her confusion. "They fit perfectly. Thank you, sir … I mean, Egon. It is a magnificent ring."

"It was a matter of pure luck that the emerald was made up in a small size, which I guessed would be right from the way the signet had fitted you. That's why I chose that particular ring over a diamond."

"I see. Well, it is perfectly beautiful and I shall enjoy wearing it. I'll return it, of course, when we … that is, after this is over."

"It's yours. Keep it. What should I want with the damned thing?"

With this blunt statement all conversation between the bridal pair ended for more than an hour.

They were well into the Kentish countryside when Egon pulled up to a respectable coaching inn. "If you will like to go in and order luncheon for us — the ordinary here is quite acceptable — while I see to the horses, I will join you presently. They should run to a private parlour at this time of year."

Claire murmured acquiescence and climbed down with the assistance of an obliging ostler. When Sir Egon entered the private dining parlour ten minutes later, he found his bride comfortably established in a Windsor armchair in front of the fireplace, where a small coal fire burned. She was holding out her hands toward the heat while a waiter set up a table with crockery for them.

"Have you been cold?" he demanded. "I decided to take the phaeton at the last minute because the weather was so fine this morning, but we can finish the journey by post chaise, if you are uncomfortable."

"No, no, I like an open carriage, and I am enjoying the scenery. I have never been south of London before. I am persuaded it will not be too cold. My pelisse is made of wool and I am wearing kid half-boots."

She had removed the pelisse, revealing a most becoming walking dress in a lighter shade of green that featured a triple flounce at the hem. Now she rose and seated herself at the table at the waiter's invitation. Egon removed his grey beaver and tossed his gloves inside it before allowing the waiter to assist him off with his drab driving coat with its half-dozen shoulder capes. He joined her at the table after giving the waiter a low-voiced order, and began lifting the covers off the various dishes, exclaiming with satisfaction as he did so. "Ah, cold roast beef. Good! Driving is hungry work. And here, if I am not mistaken, we have a raised game pie that smells inviting. May I give you some?"

Claire accepted a small portion of the game pie and helped herself to a spoonful of buttered carrots, refusing all the other offerings. Egon set about replenishing his strength with a will, but he was aware that his bride actually ate little of what was on her plate, though she pretended to do so when he looked her way. Though he recognized the irrationality of the emotion, his irritation with her increased as she sat there like a polite schoolgirl, speaking when spoken to. He welcomed the reappearance of the waiter carrying a bottle of champagne, which he opened with a satisfactory pop that made Claire jump.

"Thank you, we'll serve ourselves now," Egon said, holding out his hand for the bottle and dismissing the man. He poured out two glasses of the sparkling liquid and handed one to his reluctant companion across the table. "I believe a toast is appropriate, don't you, on this auspicious occasion? To a successful alliance," he proposed, trying to clear his voice of undertones as he raised his glass and drank deeply.

The polite stranger opposite him lifted her glass and sipped once, her cool cat's eyes never leaving his face. "May I ask you something, sir ... I mean, Egon?"

"Of course."

"Why were you so annoyed earlier to see how I really look?"

"If I was annoyed at anything, it was at the discovery that you had deceived me. You were not what I thought you."

She appeared to consider his words, then rejected them with a shake of her head. "I feel it was more than that. If I understand the purpose for this charade, you should have been pleased at the change. Am I correct in assuming that you married to comply with your grandmother's insistence that her heir be a married man?"

"My grandmother will not consider me as her heir unless I am married."

"I apprehend that as you have recently returned to England, you might not yet be in a position to select a wife on the basis of personal preference. I can even understand that a misogynist might prefer to select a wife in name only on a purely business basis, as you have done," she continued, staring at his unrevealing face for a clue as she tried to fathom his reasoning. "You are no green youth. Your cousin might possibly believe that Clairisse Deschamps would be acceptable to Lady Hollister, but you must know that I am much more likely to win her approval."

"Must I?"

Claire tilted her head, her amber eyes boring into his; then she shrugged defeat. "If you really wish to gain her approval of your choice. I see that you do not intend that I should know your real thoughts on the subject. I must assume that you thereby accept the possibility that in my ignorance I might blunder in my portrayal. I intend to carry out my end of the bargain to the best of my ability, but I shall have to rely on you to direct my performance."

Having had her say, Claire returned her attention to her plate, but she did not touch the champagne glass again.

"Who are you?" Egon demanded after a long moment of silence in which he refilled his own glass and drank it down again.

"I have told you."

"You've told me nothing beyond your name, and I have no way of proving even that is true. How old are you?"

"Two-and-twenty."

"Who are your parents?"

"My parents are dead."

"Who were they? Not French *émigrés*?"

"No." She did not elaborate.

"Your manners are polished, your accent is impeccable, your demeanour poised and assured, all qualities that might have been acquired through stage training. Were they?"

She hesitated, then said, "No."

"So you are from a class of society that does not ordinarily send its daughters onto the public stage?"

"Does it really matter for your purpose?"

He ignored this and pursued his own line. "What made you become an actress?"

"The necessity to earn my bread and butter."

"Surely there were more respectable alternatives?"

"There were not. None that paid as well."

"I see. Money is very important to you, I take it, Miss Yelland?"

She did not correct his use of her maiden name. "Money is generally important to those who have none, Sir Egon."

"More important than your self-respect?"

Her eyes narrowed but her voice remained even. "You know nothing of my self-respect."

"I think you bartered it and your virtue for money long before I came along."

He thought she lost a little colour at this calculated insult, but her eyes did not waver as she said stonily, "You are mistaken."

"I think not, but wrangling will serve no purpose, especially since we shall be obliged to put on an act of newly wedded bliss in about three hours from now. If you have finished, we should be on our way."

Without a word, his bride rose to her feet and began donning her pelisse.

There were no words wasted between them during the rest of the journey. Beyond occasional brief inquiries into her comfort, Egon addressed no remarks to his new bride. Her answers, always denying discomfort, were even briefer and, together with rare exclamations at the serene beauty of the passing scene, comprised her total verbal contribution. She sat quietly, neither restless nor fidgety, but Egon was aware of her as he had never been aware of a woman before. Not even at the height of his love for Melissa had he sensed her slightest movement, listened for her breathing, and speculated endlessly about her thoughts, which must go to prove that dislike could be more all-engrossing mentally than love.

And the worst of it all was that he desired to remain mentally aloof from her, which was why he was so annoyed that she had come so close to a shrewd understanding of his reasons for this scheme. She had guessed that he had not been pleased to see her refined appearance and had come close to discovering that he had selected Clairisse Deschamps to parade as his wife in the full knowledge that she would be unacceptable to his grandmother. Small wonder she could make little sense of the situation without his cooperation.

She could not know that she had succeeded in holding up his behaviour to his own clearheaded judgment, a judgment that had obviously been in abeyance since he'd first read his grandmother's letter. Granted, he'd have had his moment of cheap revenge when he paraded a rouged and bedizened Clairisse Deschamps before his family, but what then? He'd have driven Gran into making Jack or Michael her heir, thereby succeeding in performing the idiotish feat of cutting off his nose to spite his face.

Perhaps he had given up too soon. Once he'd decided that he would not marry at his grandmother's command, even for Belhaven, he'd fatalistically conceded the loss of his patrimony and contented himself with planning this flamboyant gesture of defiance. Now, thanks to Claire Yelland's obvious quality, despite her lack of morals, there was a slim chance that he might be able to satisfy his grandmother's requirements on the surface at least. Even with Claire's enthusiastic cooperation, they were about to walk across a minefield without a map. No matter how skilled an actress she was, their charade of wedded bliss was not going to hold up under minute and continued scrutiny. Suppose Gran actually took a liking to his sham wife and demanded that the couple make their home at Belhaven? Then the fat would really be in the fire. He and Claire had not discussed a term to her employment, but the clear understanding had been that it would be temporary. If he'd thought beyond the brief visit to Belhaven at all, which he had not, he'd have expected that Claire would simply go back to her own life and await his petition for divorce.

As the new pair of horses ate up the distance to Belhaven at a steady rate, Egon confronted the complexities of the situation he had blindly created, and was appalled. Why had he not anticipated that to sue for divorce during his grandmother's lifetime would be to undo all his efforts? And had he so little compunction for one who had done him no harm as to expose Claire to the scandal of being labelled an adulteress? Of course, he could allow her to bring the actual petition; that would be the more honourable course. Good God, what a coil! His brow furrowed and the grooves in his cheeks deepened as his lips set grimly. The only explanation that made any sense was that he had been suffering from a spell of dementia these past several days.

He could still retreat, return Claire to the tawdry little life she had chosen for herself, turn his back on Belhaven forever. All he had to do was turn the horses around and pretend these few days had never happened. If he and Claire parted immediately, an annulment might be possible to wipe out the mistake, with no one the wiser. His hands actually tightened on the ribbons, and the horses slackened their pace accordingly.

"Are we nearly arrived, sir?"

He stared down into that cool, controlled face and experienced the now-familiar stab of irritation. Why should he be suffering qualms of conscience on this woman's account? He had not coerced her to accept the offer; she had elected to take on the role because she was hungry for riches. If he called off the impersonation at this point, she would have gotten three hundred pounds out of him, a not inconsiderable reward for one day's minor inconvenience to herself.

He dropped his hands and the horses spurted forward again. "No, it will be at least another half-hour before we arrive, which is all the time you have to learn to use my name, Claire, my pet, before the curtain rises on your most important performance to date."

He spotted the dislike in her eyes before they were veiled by that forest of black lashes, and perversely was pleased to uncover a chink in her armour of self-possession, even though said chink might be supposed to bode ill for her successful portrayal of an adoring new bride.

CHAPTER 7

"Once we go through those gates up ahead, we shall be on Belhaven land."

Claire made no comment on her husband's terse announcement. For one thing, a sudden attack of preperformance nerves had her in its uncomfortable grip, tightening her stomach and throat muscles and drying out her lips so that speech seemed a physical impossibility just then. Even without this impediment, it was unlikely that she would have tried to improve the moment with her own contribution. It seemed every time she opened her mouth, she merely afforded Egon another opportunity to snipe at her. She was still smarting from his low opinion of her morals pronounced during their luncheon at the inn. The fact that he had not delivered this harsh judgment in the heat of an emotional quarrel, but with a cool deliberation, made it all the more wounding. She had been engaged since then in the necessary but essentially unrewarding exercise of trying to bring to the forefront the Christian precepts she had learned in the nursery, in order to keep from offering unwise retaliation. Turning the other cheek, while beautiful in its theological conception, had little to recommend it as a smoother of ruffled feelings. Stern self-discipline and a very unchristian desire to deprive the beast she had married of the satisfaction of rattling her composure or discovering the extent of his ability to hurt her provided a more workable basis for exerting control over her own conduct in her dealings with him. Being thin-skinned would be a decided disadvantage while she was playing her part in their deception.

Accustomed to painstaking analysis and study of a character before she attempted a role on the stage, Claire felt she was being thrust into the upcoming performance with no preparation or plan of any sort. Worst of all, Egon, who should have been coaching her and guiding her actions, was being unhelpful to the point of obstruction — and deliberately so, she felt sure, though *why* was a question still shrouded in mystery. She tried to comfort herself with the thought that all would doubtless be revealed in the fullness of time, and the knowledge that Egon would have no one to blame but himself if his own plan went awry through lack of knowledge on her part.

Claire dimly recognized that the road was winding through some very pretty parkland, but she was too nervous to assimilate any of the details as she kept her cold hands tightly clasped and her eyes fixed in front of her. When the house came into view suddenly, she was moved out of her self-absorption by admiration of the graceful brick structure. "Oh, it's lovely," she murmured, her eyes taking in the large sash windows symmetrically placed and the handsomely proportioned entrance facade.

"It isn't a grand house, but it is nice, isn't it?" Egon said with the first approving look he had ever cast in her direction.

As they pulled to a stop before the central bay, she was mentally registering the note of eagerness that had sounded in his ordinarily clipped tones. She had thought him totally emotionless; it was encouraging to learn that something could arouse him to enthusiasm, even if it was only a building.

"Wait here," he commanded, tossing her the ribbons. He jumped down, ran lightly up the short flight of steps to the black-painted entrance door, and banged on the knocker.

Claire watched the impatient tapping of her husband's foot still as the large door opened. After a short, unintelligible conversation with the footman who appeared, both men returned to the phaeton, the footman to take Claire's place as Egon lifted her down with more care than she would have expected. He was assisting her up the steps when a tall, stately individual in a dark coat came through the door to stop short at sight of the guests. His face convulsed into a smile that must surely jeopardize his standing as a proper butler; then he rushed forward again.

"Master Egon, what a wonderful surprise! Come in, come in."

"Hello, Boynton. You don't look a day older than when I left." Egon fairly leapt ahead of Claire to grasp the butler's hand. As he wrung it heartily, he was patting the man's shoulder in a way that stopped just short of being an embrace. "It's good to see you in prime twig, Boynton. I swear you haven't added a single grey hair in five years," he declared, smiling broadly.

"You are the one who put them all there, Master Egon," Boynton replied with a slight twitch of his lips and a return to his normal dignity. "Why did you not advise us of your arrival?"

Claire gasped, her eyes huge as she squeaked, "Isn't your grandmother expecting us?"

Her husband's face assumed a bland expression as they moved inside. "It all happened so quickly, there wasn't much point in sending off a letter when we would most likely arrive ahead of it," he said with careless good humour. "Boynton, this beautiful but scandalized lady is my wife. Claire, may I present my grandmother's butler, the rock upon which this household depends?"

Claire's smile held no reservations. "How do you do, Boynton?"

"Very well, my lady. May I be the first to welcome you to Belhaven?"

Though the butler's manner had reverted to a professional mien, Claire had the comforting feeling that at least he was not concealing disapproval of her person.

"By the way, Boynton, my groom should arrive with our baggage within the hour," Egon warned.

At that moment, a door toward the back of the gracious entrance hall opened and a tiny, birdlike lady of indeterminate age fluttered out, intent on heading for another door across the hall.

"*Mamzell!*"

Her husband's voice, almost boyish in its elation, riveted Claire to the spot and she watched in fascination as the tall man left her abruptly to stride over to the little lady, who had thrown up her hands in a broad gesture of surprise. He seized her in his arms and whirled her off her feet in an exuberant circle, heedless of her squeals of protest.

"Let me down! Fie on you, *mon mauvais!* I can see you are as wicked as ever," she scolded incessantly as he kissed both cheeks before gently setting her on her feet again. He kept his arm about her shoulder and walked with her toward the others.

"I fear there has been no conversion to sainthood yet, Mamzell, but don't cease your prayers to *Le Bon Dieu* to save me from eternal damnation. I am convinced those prayers saw me through many a battle. And I want to thank you for your letter on my birthday each year, though it went much against the grain with me to obey your instructions not to reply."

"It was better that you did not, *mon p'tit*, all the post is delivered to Lady 'Ollister's office." She shrugged expressively. "It was to keep the peace, *tu comprends?*"

The tall elegant man and the tiny, slightly untidy woman with crimped salt-and-pepper locks escaping from the cap that Egon's embrace had set askew were an oddly assorted pair, Claire could not help thinking, but the affection between them was heart-warming to witness. She subdued a foolish twinge of wistfulness at being on the outside of the charmed circle and stood quietly as the engrossed pair approached. She had experienced two shocks in as many minutes since their arrival at Belhaven and needed a respite in which to catch her breath. The first had been the welcome realization that the severe individual toward whom she was supposed to demonstrate the mindless devotion of a new bride was not quite the unfeeling creature she had been given to suppose by his demeanour toward herself. The second shock, the discovery that their arrival was unexpected, was much less welcome and might presage a difficult scene to come, when Egon met his grandmother, if, as she was coming to suspect, there already existed an estrangement between the two.

The voluble little Frenchwoman in Egon's fond clasp glanced her way for the first time, and Claire rallied her scattered forces for the performance that was about to begin. She asked herself how she would be feeling at this moment if she really were his adored bride, and the answer came bouncing back: anxious — anxious about her reception by her husband's loved ones and, above all, anxious to make a good first impression for his sake. She sent an imploring glance to Egon, then shifted her gaze to the woman he called "Mamzell," straightening her shoulders and moistening her lips with a quick nervous gesture, not quite daring to smile.

Somewhat to her surprise, Egon responded with a gallantry that struck her as wholly natural. He removed his arm from the Frenchwoman's shoulders to take her hand while extending his other arm to gather Claire close to his side under the benevolent eye of the butler and the alert, curious gaze of "Mamzell."

"Forgive my temporary abandonment, darling," he said, smiling down at Claire before turning once again to the Frenchwoman. "Mamzell, I'd like you to meet my wife, Claire. Darling, this is Mademoiselle Clothilde Ducroix, who has been my grandmother's companion and my good friend for many years."

As Claire dropped a smiling curtsy to the older woman, the latter clasped her hands in front of her meagre breasts in a gesture of Gallic delight, casting her eyes upward at the same time. "*Mais ça c'est magnifique! Je rémercie mille fois au Bon Dieu. Bienvenue,* welcome, Claire. *Vous êtes aussi belle que vôtre nom, qui est français.* I can see already that you are just what *ce coquin* has needed." Mademoiselle Ducroix took both of Claire's hands in her fragile little claws, squeezing them with unexpected strength.

"*Je suis heureuse de faire vôtre connaissance,* Mademoiselle Ducroix. *Vous êtes très gentile.* Thank you for your kind welcome."

"How you are fortunate, *mon mauvais.*" Mamzell's snapping black eyes returned to Egon, who had managed to look like a proud new husband during the exchange.

"I am well aware of my good fortune, Mamzell," he said with a little smile that Claire didn't quite like, though his words were harmless enough. "Is Grandmother having tea in the drawing room at this hour? Shall we go right in?"

"Yes, they are there, *mon cher*, but I think I had best see about your apartment, *n'est-ce pas?* You take your wife in to meet Lady 'Ollister. *Au revoir* for now, *ma petite*," she said to the bemused Claire, who stood five feet, six inches in her stockings, more than half a foot taller than herself.

"I'll announce you, Master Egon," Boynton offered as the Frenchwoman fluttered away to find the housekeeper. "If you will come this way, Lady Hollister."

Claire had time to wonder if the butler intended to introduce her husband as "Master Egon" as she allowed herself to be led through a door at the back of the hall that opened on a corridor running parallel with the front of the house. She had not thought of herself as Lady Hollister, and it gave her a queer little pang to hear the title fall so naturally from Boynton's lips.

The drawing room was a large apartment at the back of the house on the ground floor. That much Claire took in before Boynton announced, "Sir Egon Hollister and Lady Hollister, my lady."

Claire had been aware of a murmur of conversation as they entered, and now was conscious of sudden complete silence as what seemed to be dozens of eyes turned to stare at them. Her hand crept into Egon's unplanned, and he held it firmly, giving her a little nudge to get her moving again. Her eyes instantly lighted on the regal white-haired woman behind the teapot set on a table in front of a long sofa. She must have imagined that the woman's dark eyes had come to blazing life at the mention of her grandson's name, because when she had put her cup down carefully and looked up again, those eyes that Egon had inherited were as indifferent as his habitually seemed.

"Hello, Gran, how are you?"

Was this quiet, controlled man the same boyish individual who had indulged in boisterous greetings with the butler and

104

Mamzell just minutes ago? Claire could feel Egon's tension as he waited for his grandmother's reply.

"I am tolerably well for someone of my advanced years, thank you, Egon," Lady Hollister replied in precise measured tones. "May I inquire why you did not see fit to inform me of your marriage if I am to assume from Boynton's announcement that this young woman is your wife?"

"There was really no time, Gran. I found your letter waiting when Claire and I returned yesterday evening from a brief wedding trip. We simply turned around and headed down here. I couldn't miss your birthday celebration, could I?"

Claire's discomfort escalated in the pause that followed this blatant lie, and it was not all attributable to the painful pressure being applied to her hand by her loving husband. She was grateful that she was still wearing her gloves. She concentrated on maintaining what she hoped was a pleasantly unconscious expression in the face of the undercurrents she sensed. Her poise was challenged immediately as that beautifully coiffed white head in the exquisite lace cap turned in her direction. A lorgnette on a chain appeared from among the folds of Lady Hollister's mauve taffeta gown and was deliberately raised to her eyes.

It is not an easy thing to withstand a rude scrutiny through one of these instruments, but by now anger had come to Claire's rescue. This and her stage training stood her in good stead as she remained perfectly still, never taking her eyes off the figure behind the tea table until the lorgnette was lowered once again.

"At least she doesn't look like someone you found on a stage somewhere," Lady Hollister said with a caustic inflection.

"Claire looks what she is, Gran, a lady," Egon put in with that quiet note of menace in his voice.

Claire knew she had lost colour at Lady Hollister's uncanny shot in the dark; in fact, if Egon's grip on her hand had not been so uncomfortably tight that she was concentrating on not crying out in pain, her knees might have buckled at that point.

"Come, come, child, what is your name — Claire? I assume you do speak when this hot-tempered grandson of mine permits it ... or orders it?"

"How do you do, Lady Hollister? I am happy to be here in your lovely home."

"You have a beautiful voice, Claire. I hope you sing. I have a great fondness for vocal music."

"I fear my voice has not really been trained, ma'am," Claire replied, trying to keep up with the rapid conversational shifts.

"At this point it seems a trifle redundant to insist upon making proper introductions," Egon chimed in with a whimsical smile.

"Claire and I will become properly acquainted in good time, never fear," Lady Hollister assured her grandson, and Claire wondered if there was a threat lurking behind the words. "Meanwhile, there are certain necessary introductions to be made. Egon, I believe you remember Miss Winward from Fourways, and Melissa you know, of course, but I think you cannot have met Michael Dunston's wife. Jessica, my dear child, this is my eldest grandson, Egon Hollister, and his wife, Claire, who is apparently a newer bride even than you."

A sweet-faced young girl rose from one of a pair of armchairs at right angles to the sofa on either side of the tea table and came toward the newcomers. Egon bowed smilingly over her hand.

"Michael is to be congratulated, Cousin Jessica."

The girl blushed and stammered a greeting. Claire and she exchanged quick smiles and handshakes before Egon took over, turning to a plain, intelligent-looking young woman who had sat composedly on the sofa next to Lady Hollister through all the drama.

"Miss Winward, how do you do? It has been a very long time since I have had the pleasure of meeting you. May I present my wife?"

As the two women murmured appropriately, Claire was conscious that the remaining person in the room had laughed, a low and inviting sound.

"Is it finally my turn, Egon?"

The speaker, sitting at her ease across the tea table from Jessica Dunston, was the most beautiful female Claire had ever seen, incorporating perfectly modelled features in an oval face of the fairest colouring. Her hair, worn in the latest fashion, was a pale golden blond, her eyes were large and deep blue, and her smile enchanting. All this enchantment was directed at Egon, who seemed to be making a deliberate attempt to resist its power. He did not return the smile, saying gravely as he bent over her extended hand, "You are looking wonderfully well, Melissa. May I present my wife, Claire? Darling, Melissa is my cousin Jack Blyden's wife."

"And a good friend of your husband's, Lady Hollister. How do you do?"

"I am delighted to meet you, Mrs. Blyden," said Claire, who was no such thing. To a person used to analysing speech patterns, Mrs. Blyden's light languid voice had held a significance meant for Egon, not herself, a significance that had not escaped him, though he chose to ignore it.

"If I know Boynton, he will have ordered fresh tea," Lady Hollister said, taking the reins back into her own hands. "You may come sit beside me, Claire, and tell me how you met and

107

enslaved my grandson in the short time he has been back in the country."

Egon produced a quite creditable laugh as he helped his wife off with her pelisse. "Let my poor girl get some hot tea into her first, Gran, before you begin the inquisition. We drove down in an open carriage, and I am persuaded the poor darling is half-frozen, though she never uttered a word of complaint. Let me do the talking," he hissed in an aside to Claire as he laid her green pelisse over the back of a chair with his driving coat before escorting her past Mrs. Blyden's chair to the sofa. He dragged up another chair and placed it between Mrs. Blyden's and the sofa for himself.

"You must not allow Egon to treat you like one of his troopers, Lady Hollister, and you still a new bride," Mrs. Blyden said with another soft laugh.

"I wanted to come in the phaeton," Claire explained in her warm voice. "I had never been in the country south of London before, and one can see so much more from an open carriage. It was a lovely drive."

"Where are you from, Claire?" This from Lady Hollister.

"Originally from Northumberland, Lady Hollister, but I have been living in London."

"So you and my grandson met in London?"

"Here comes Boynton with more tea, Gran. Let Claire have hers in peace while I tell you the romantic story of our courtship."

"How exciting. I can scarcely wait," said the beautiful Mrs. Blyden in bored accents.

"You may be sure that I at least am all attention," Lady Hollister said in her precise manner as she poured out a cup of tea for Claire and looked on with something less than indulgence as Egon helped himself from the sherry decanter Boynton had taken it upon himself to add to the tray.

Claire accepted her tea, profoundly grateful to have Lady Hollister's attention shifted to her husband. She had discovered it was more difficult to perform for one lynx-eyed old woman than for a couple of thousand strangers when one was unsure of one's lines.

"Actually, Gran, if I led you to believe there is an exciting story behind our marriage, I must apologize, for it is no such thing. Claire has been living with an aunt since her parents died. We met and knew almost immediately that we wished to spend our lives together, but we would not have married in such haste except that Claire's aunt was about to move back to Northumberland. I had no intention of conducting a long-distance courtship, so here we are."

Mrs. Blyden sighed gustily. "And I was all prepared for a romantic saga of cruel guardians and flights to Gretna Green."

"Do not talk nonsense, Melissa," Lady Hollister said. "I should hope Egon is well past the age of such foolish traipsings."

"I don't know whether to thank you or not for that defence, Gran." Egon turned his dark eyes on the young woman quietly sipping her tea. "Had it been necessary, I think I might have challenged all manner of wicked guardians to win Claire." His voice had a ring of quiet sincerity that startled Claire, whose glance sank back to the contents of her cup.

"You have made your bride blush, Egon. How ungallant of you," Mrs. Blyden observed at his other side.

Claire welcomed a diversion just then in the person of Mademoiselle Ducroix, who flitted into the room trailing her shawl that had slipped off her thin shoulders.

"Clothilde, look who is here! Your pet lamb is back and he has brought a wife with him," Lady Hollister announced in soft but commanding tones.

"*Mais oui*, my lady. I was in the hall when Egon and Claire arrived. It is a great happiness, is it not? I have ordered the green suite prepared for them, if that is agreeable?"

"Yes, that's fine. Don't stand there dithering, Clothilde, come in and have your tea." Lady Hollister was already pouring out another cup for her companion, who accepted it and took the chair that Egon placed near Mrs. Dunston. She took an appreciative sip of her tea and then leaned forward, addressing Egon.

"Your baggage has arrived, *mon cher*, but with only a groom. Where are your man and Claire's abigail?"

Claire buried her nose in her teacup again, content to let her husband handle this new complication. He had had a story ready to account for their hasty marriage, one of such simplicity it could not be questioned. She could only trust that his invention would not fail now.

"My man will be here in a day or two, but I fear Claire's maid went north with her aunt's household, and we have had no time as yet to engage another. I have been acting as a very unskilled abigail since our marriage."

Claire knew her cheeks were flaming, but she kept her eyes on her cup. Drat the man! Had he no sensibility at all?

"But your beautiful hair, *chérie*; it must be very long, *non*?" Mamzell was astonished, and Claire felt it was time to intervene.

"I generally wear my hair in this simple chignon, Mademoiselle Ducroix; it is really no trouble."

"Well, tonight you shall have Estelle to do the hair. She has a flair," Mamzell declared.

Claire glanced fleetingly at Lady Hollister, who nodded agreement. "Yes, Clothilde is correct. The girl is an impertinent piece, but she is very good at dressing heads. You'd better have her as your maid while you are here, Claire."

Claire thanked her hostess quietly and subsided into the background as Egon asked his cousin's beautiful wife where the men were at that hour.

This first meeting with her husband's family had not been as difficult as it might have been; at least no one had been overtly hostile. She had not expected to find so many people in residence, but perhaps there was safety in numbers. Lady Hollister's large dark eyes were remarkably like her grandson's, and even more penetrating. At least Egon had never levelled a quizzing glass at her! The tea, far from reviving her, seemed to be having a lowering effect. Being an essentially honest person, Claire was rendered acutely uncomfortable by the deception she and Egon were practicing on his family. Her situation in London had been so desperate that she had jumped at this employment when it was offered. She had given no thought to the victims of their pretence until they had actually arrived at Belhaven, but now she could think of little else. How Lady Hollister would despise her if she knew the truth! And though she couldn't account for the swiftness of the feeling, Claire was unhappily aware that she rather strongly wished for Lady Hollister's approval. She sat beside the straight-backed matriarch, still lovely at four score years, and felt like the lowliest creature on the face of the earth.

A maid entered the room and spoke to Mademoiselle Ducroix, who looked across at Claire. "Your apartment is ready now, *chérie*, and I think just in time, no? That long drive has fatigued you, but you will be refreshed by a rest before dinner."

"Yes, Claire, do go upstairs with Clothilde. Not yet, Egon," Lady Hollister added as her grandson made to rise. "I should like to have a little talk with you. We meet in here at seven, Claire."

Thus dismissed, Claire excused herself to the company and followed Mamzell out of the drawing room. She was aware of many eyes on her back and thankful for the stage experience that enabled her to maintain an unhurried, confident pace during her exit.

Mamzell kept up a stream of inconsequential chatter as they regained the entrance hall and ascended the marvellous main staircase with its lovely pattern of gold-painted wrought-iron leaves and vines that took the place of conventional balusters. Claire tried to look interested in her companion's rambling discourse while still keeping track of the turns they were taking along auxiliary corridors. She concluded that there must be wings to the house that had not been visible on their approach.

At last Mamzell paused in front of a door and threw it open.

"So, *chérie*, here we are at last, the green suite. *C'est très charmant, non?*"

Charming it was, and Claire's praise for the cosy sitting room with its choice green brocaded upholstered chairs and draperies was quite sincere. The adjoining bedchamber was equally attractive, but it took a much greater effort on the new bride's part to express her admiration, for her eyes had winged to the scattering of baggage in front of the massive tester bed with its green-and-white-print curtains.

Following her glance, Mamzell gave an exclamation of satisfaction. "Ah, *bien, vos bagages sont ici*. I shall send Estelle up to unpack for you at once, Claire."

Claire nodded and smiled, but the instant that Mamzell, still chattering, closed the sitting-room door behind her, the fixed smile crumbled. Her eyes went back to the four pieces of baggage. Only the two smaller portmanteaux belonged to her. She glanced again at the big bed and then her eyes did a swift circuit of the room. There were only two doors, the one that led to the sitting room and another which she immediately approached. It opened into a very small room containing an armoire, a washstand, a mirrored dressing table, and a daybed of sorts. There was one other door, and she hurried over to it, her heart pounding and her lips forming the words, "Please let it be another bedchamber."

Claire flung open the door and found herself staring at a similar door across the corridor. She stood there transfixed for a long moment until the sound of voices somewhere further along the corridor made her close the door soundlessly.

CHAPTER 8

It was half-after six o'clock when Egon entered the sitting room of the green suite to see his freshly coiffed and gowned bride sitting in one of the brocaded armchairs with an open periodical in her lap. She cast this aside at his entrance and sprang out of the chair.

"Egon, you must —"

"Allow me to compliment you, my dear Claire, on your charming appearance. That champagne silk with the coffee-coloured ribbons and lace inserts is vastly becoming, and if the pert Estelle is responsible for your coiffure, then she does indeed have a flair," he said admiringly, but his agitated wife brushed aside these compliments.

"Never mind that! Egon, you've got to do something. This suite won't do at all!"

"Now, I would have thought, as a poor refugee from the stage, you would relish the luxury of this handsome apartment. What is there about it that offends your aesthetic sensibilities?"

Her husband's suave provocation had the effect of a dash of water in Claire's face. She might have known he would be deliberately obtuse. She took a calming breath and said in more moderate tones, "I did not mean any criticism of the decor, as I am persuaded you know. My quarrel is with the … arrangements. There is only one bedchamber."

"Why should you find this surprising? We have, after all, advertised ourselves as a newly married couple. The suite does contain a dressing room, if I remember correctly."

"Yes, but it is a poky little place with only a small rickety daybed."

"I am deeply touched by your wifely concern for my comfort, but I shall manage very well, unless you are volunteering to trade sleeping quarters with me?"

"I am not," she said shortly, turning her shoulder on him to return to her chair.

Egon brushed his fingers across his chin and cheeks. "Have they sent up any hot water? I have to shave before I change for dinner." He was undoing his cravat as he spoke, and Claire swallowed nervously as her eyes followed the movements of his fingers. She had not bargained for such domestic intimacy.

"Yes, a servant brought up a can of hot water about ten minutes ago. It is in the dressing room."

"Good. I'll need to hurry to be downstairs again by seven."

He would have vanished into the bedchamber, but Claire couldn't prevent herself from asking, "What kept you so long? What did your grandmother say about our ... about your marriage?"

"Convincing though we were — though I must tell you I don't feel that your performance was quite as inspired as my own — my grandmother is a downy one and she has not been completely taken in by our parade of connubial devotion. The fortuitous timing sticks in her craw, but she cannot disprove it. The only person who could do that is not here, thank heavens."

She stared at him, her mind working rapidly. "Do you mean your cousin Geoffrey?"

"Exactly, my love. How quick you are. I chose an able confederate."

"Egon," she began hesitantly, "does it not bother you, the deception, I mean?"

His eyes narrowed. "Scruples, Miss Yelland? You surprise me. No doubt we could have a fascinating philosophical discussion on the subject, but owing to my reluctance to invade your privacy earlier, which I trust you will chalk up to my credit eventually, I have left myself little enough time to change for dinner. I should warn you that my grandmother is a stickler for punctuality."

This time Egon did disappear through the door into the bedchamber, leaving Claire feeling rebuffed and out of sorts.

The man had a positive genius for putting her in the wrong!

She picked up the discarded copy of *La Belle Assemblée* and opened it at random, knowing it for a vain endeavour. Her mind was too unquiet to concentrate on the printed word, nor was she moved to a pleasurable acquisitiveness or envy by the depiction of a tall svelte female in an elaborate ballgown staring out from the pages. For a short time after their arrival at Belhaven, it had seemed to her that she and Egon had presented a united front, anticipating each other's actions as if they could communicate without words. Coming on top of his manifesting a much more appealing side to his nature than he had ever let her glimpse, it had filled her with a strange sort of excitement. She had actually enjoyed their playacting despite her basic aversion to the deception.

His appearance just now had put a quick end to any foolish sprouting hopes that they might deal more comfortably together in future. He could not have made it any clearer that he despised her personally — not that this should trouble her in the least, because she disliked him intensely — but the constant awareness of his thinly veiled animosity was going to increase her difficulty in sustaining her role in front of his family. It would be so much simpler if their attitudes toward each other were neutral. It meant she was not going to be able to relax her vigilance for an instant lest she betray the real state of affairs between them.

The magazine was open to the same page when Egon reappeared a few minutes later carrying his black evening coat, impatience in the set of his features.

"Claire, will you put the studs in my right sleeve cuff? I have just spent an annoying few moments fumbling with them. I don't want to be late."

"Of course." Conscious of his dark gaze on her as she moved into position to perform the task, Claire dropped her glance, unconsciously displaying the luxuriant curl of her extraordinary eyelashes against her soft cheek. Electricity crackled in the space between them and her fingers were none too skilled either.

"There, it's in."

"Must you be so prodigal in your use of French scent? You smell like an expensive brothel."

Twin spots of colour flamed into Claire's cheeks as she recoiled from him, and her thin nostrils flared, but her voice was soft and uninflected. "I'll remember to use less in future. Shall we go down now?"

"Claire, I beg your pardon! That was inexcusable."

She glanced briefly into his taut countenance with the vertical grooves emphasized in his thin cheeks. "Hadn't you better put on your coat? It is growing late."

Not a syllable breached the wall of silence behind which Sir Egon and the new Lady Hollister re-entered the drawing room only a minute or two after the appointed hour. By then Claire was actually relieved to go amongst a crowd of strangers whose presence would serve to divert her thoughts.

The cast of players this evening was the same as at tea, with the addition of two men who must be Egon's cousins. They were standing together talking to Miss Winward and Mrs. Blyden. The younger man must be Michael Dunston. He was ruddy-complexioned, with a mop of tight brown curls, and he had an ordinary, good-humoured face. He was slighter in build and shorter in stature than his cousins. Claire would have had no difficulty in identifying Jack Blyden in a room full of men, thanks to his strong resemblance to his brother, Geoffrey. The elder brother, equally blond and well-formed, was even more impressive of feature, but Claire searched his handsome countenance in vain for what she could only call Geoffrey's "niceness."

As Egon took her arm to steer her over to this group, Mr. Blyden turned more fully to face her, his eyes traveling from his returned cousin to roam her person with the unsubtle sort of appreciation she had grown accustomed to as Clairisse Deschamps. One hand crept up to finger his cravat in a typical gesture of male vanity.

"Claire, my love, these two under-bred specimens are my cousins Jack Blyden and Michael Dunston. You have my permission to snub them if they forget their place or get above themselves."

Claire smiled nicely at both and murmured their names, whereupon Mr. Dunston's engaging grin broadened. "Call me Mike, Cousin Claire, or I *shall* think you are snubbing me. Egon, you old reprobate, I'm glad to see you back." He pummelled his cousin's shoulders when they shook hands, giving every appearance of delight at the reunion.

"Yes, congratulations, cousin, on returning unscathed to our shores," Mr. Blyden drawled before turning to bow to Claire.

"Does the lovely lady come under the heading of spoils of victory?"

"No, under the heading of underserved good fortune," Egon said shortly.

"That goes without saying, coz. I am delighted to see your sojourn in the military hasn't dimmed your fabled eye for beauty." Mr. Blyden's drawl grew caressing as he carried Claire's hand to his lips. "Welcome to the family, Cousin Claire. You'll find me very much at your service."

To Claire's relief, Boynton appeared at her elbow at that moment with a tray of glasses, sparing her the necessity of replying to this fulsome gallantry. She accepted the sherry, conscious of a mocking light in Mrs. Blyden's beautiful blue eyes before the latter managed by means of a small but efficient movement to isolate herself and Egon from the others as she asked him a question. She kept him engaged for the next ten minutes, during which period Claire attempted to satisfy his cousin Michael's requests for her impressions of Belhaven, to parry his cousin Jack's heavy-handed gallantries, and to include the observant but reticent Miss Winward in the conversation at the same time, all the while affecting not to notice the air of intimacy enveloping her husband and the lovely Melissa. By the time Boynton announced dinner, she was exhausted from her endeavours and her jaw felt stiff from smiling.

Claire had not been so busy keeping her own balls in the air that she had failed to note that Lady Hollister had closely monitored Egon's conversation with Mrs. Blyden, though she could have heard none of it from her position on the sofa, where Mademoiselle Ducroix was holding forth on some topic, complete with expansive hand movements, for the benefit of young Mrs. Dunston. Subsequently, Claire noted that Lady

Hollister kept her eldest grandson at her right hand at table and placed Jessica Dunston on his other side, while seating Mrs. Blyden as far away from him as space permitted. Claire was placed between Egon's cousins, the only lady to be honoured with two masculine partners.

During her stage career, she had accumulated enough experience at dividing her attention among numbers of competing males to have no difficulty in keeping two conversations alive during the course of a rather sumptuous dinner. Not wishing to draw any attention to herself, she maintained a careful pretence of partaking liberally of the tempting array of dishes in both courses, but her appetite seemed to have deserted her following the pathetic farce of a wedding ceremony she had endured in that dreary, musty church office. She hadn't felt really normal inside herself since, a condition periodically exacerbated by the gratuitous insults her husband delighted in flinging at her just when she thought she had mastered her previous agitation and could proceed with the distasteful pretence in an efficient, unemotional manner. Even though he kept young Jessica well-entertained, judging from her frequent smiles, and chatted quietly with his grandmother, he still had time to rest an enigmatic but disturbing glance on his bride with enough regularity to ensure her continued loss of appetite.

All things considered, Claire was very ready to join the parade of ladies out of the dining room at Lady Hollister's signal, even if it meant she would be subjected to an inquisition into her background from the old lady before the men re-joined them. It was as inevitable as the changing of the seasons that Lady Hollister was going to try to find out everything worth knowing about her newest granddaughter-in-law sooner or later. She had determined to stick to the truth of her family circumstances in general. It would be easier on her memory if this visit lasted for more than a few days, and she was reasonably sure that Egon was not planning to pass her off as an heiress or some such unlikely thing. In fact, she still held to the unsupported but intuitive conviction that pleasing his grandmother had not been an object with Egon when he had chosen Clairisse Deschamps as his bride; quite the opposite, though such a course seemed quite illogical.

As the ladies disposed themselves about the drawing room at their ease, Claire elected to sit in one of the armchairs placed by the tea table. She would be near enough to converse with Lady Hollister without the disadvantage of being pinned to her side on the long sofa.

As it turned out, beyond a few initial inquiries into the comfort of the accommodations assigned to the newly wedded couple and a well-phrased compliment on Claire's hair that gave that young lady a chance to express her gratitude for the loan of the clever Estelle, Lady Hollister showed no inclination to question the newest addition to the family.

She beckoned Mademoiselle Ducroix to her side to discuss some household arrangements, leaving Claire alone with her slowly relaxing nerves for the moment. Jessica Dunston and Melissa Blyden were glancing through a periodical to check on some point that had arisen earlier, and Miss Winward had gone back to her room for a shawl directly from the dining room.

This young woman came into the room a moment later wearing a paisley shawl over her thin muslin gown. After a quick glance around the room, she pulled a chair nearer to Claire's and sat down with a polite smile.

Claire returned her smile. "I believe Lady Hollister introduced you as being from Fourways, Miss Winward. Is that the name of your home?"

"Yes, Fourways is my father's estate. It is located some five or six miles from Belhaven."

"I have been most impressed by the lush green countryside with its gentle hills on our drive into Sussex today. Is it sheep country?"

"There are sheep all over the downs, of course, but there are a variety of crops grown too, and orchards. We grow mostly wheat and corn at Fourways, in addition to various vegetable crops." She sighed. "I feel I have been away for a very long time, though thanks to you, I shall be able to bring my visit to Belhaven to a close now. I plan to send a message to my home tomorrow morning, and may leave in the afternoon if my father sends the carriage."

Claire blinked in surprise at the quiet-faced young woman regarding her dispassionately. "Thanks to me you can curtail your visit? I'm afraid I do not understand, Miss Winward."

Cool hazel eyes studied her for a moment. "No? Well, I suppose Sir Egon might not have told you the whole situation. Perhaps he did not know himself, though if I know Lady Hollister's style at all, she probably made it crystal clear to him that he was still expected to marry me."

"To … to marry you? Miss Winward, I … I don't know what to say! If I am responsible for injuring you, please believe it was not intentional. I … I had no idea!" Claire's eyes reflected her distress as she sat biting her lip.

"You have done me no injury, and neither has Sir Egon," Miss Winward corrected in her cool manner. "The marriage scheme has been a distant hope long cherished by my father and Lady Hollister. They are both highly opinionated and determined persons and they refused to relinquish the idea, even though Sir Egon joined the army five years ago to escape the match."

"I … I had no idea," Claire said again. "If … if you ever cherished any warm feelings for Egon, I can only say I am deeply sorry."

"Thank you, but there is no need for sympathy. I wished for the match no more than your husband did, but I let my father persuade me to agree five years ago when I was too young to stand up against him. I was not best pleased to learn that Sir Egon had returned to England still unattached, but I had given my word to my father and he had no intention of releasing me from my promise. Your marriage has achieved that. Actually, I feel no inclination toward the institution of marriage. My limited acquaintance with the male sex has not led me to hold them in either awe or reverence — or much affection either," she added in a dispassionate style that was reminiscent of Lady Hollister.

Claire's eyes twinkled. "Well, I am relieved to know that I have not been the inadvertent cause of unhappiness for you by my marriage. Will your father now set about making another match for you?" she asked in sympathy.

"No, for I am strong enough to hold out against him now. I am his only child. He has no one else to leave his property to, and in any case, at this point I know almost as much about the estate and farming methods and dealing with the tenants as my father does. He knows he can safely entrust it to my care."

"You do not think you might regret your single state once your father is no longer alive?" Claire asked in real curiosity.

"I don't expect so, but if I did, a woman of property will never lack for suitors."

"You would not object to being courted for the sake of your estate?"

"Since my sole reason for marrying would be to produce an heir to inherit the estate after me, I could scarcely object if the other party to the contract had his own interests to advance also."

Claire felt that the introduction of such idealistic concepts as mutual affection and esteem as the basis for marriage would be dismissed as irrelevant by the practical Miss Winward, so she held her peace.

"Lady Hollister, would you extend my thanks to Sir Egon after I have gone, for extricating me from a situation that I was powerless to change?" Miss Winward asked as the men returned to the drawing room. "I should feel a trifle awkward broaching the subject with him myself."

Concealing her amusement at the unusual request, Claire willingly gave her promise. As she observed her husband's approach, the full realization came to her that she now knew the reason for his hasty marriage. This afternoon he had mentioned a letter from his grandmother and a birthday celebration. She'd be willing to wager her wisdom teeth that Lady Hollister had told him of Miss Winward's presence at Belhaven and her hopes for a match between them. He had obviously lied about when he received the letter in order to strengthen the story that his marriage was unrelated to the situation at Belhaven. The mystery she had sensed about his actions was now at least partly explained.

Egon bestowed a smile on his bride, though she saw that his eyes remained uninvolved. "Have you and my grandmother been getting acquainted, darling?"

It was his grandmother who answered him. "Actually I needed to discuss something with Clothilde, Egon. Your bride and Miss Winward have been getting acquainted."

Claire wondered if she detected a touch of irony in Lady Hollister's voice or if she were reading too much into it in view of Miss Winward's revelations just now. Egon included all three women in his smile, not a whit disconcerted that their conversation might have touched on matters he would prefer to keep dark.

Lady Hollister requested that the ladies favour the company with some music. Mrs. Blyden was the first to oblige with an aria from *Le Nozze di Figaro* that Claire privately thought her ill-equipped to handle. She did rather better with a couple of popular ballads, though Claire found her voice basically uninteresting and thin despite being well-trained. No one else seemed to sense a lack in her performance, and Egon's reaction was one of unalloyed admiration.

Claire rested a thoughtful glance on her husband's smiling face as he rose to seat Mrs. Blyden when she returned from the pianoforte. An easy audience? Tone deaf? Or merely besotted with his cousin's beautiful wife? He caught her eye on him and his smile became mocking in character. Claire's eyes flashed to Lady Hollister's face, but the old woman was busy persuading Michael to accompany his wife in a duet. She chided herself mentally for caring whether Egon endangered his masquerade as a doting husband by his blatant admiration of Mrs. Blyden. She was being well-paid to do a job of acting, and her responsibility ended with her own performance. She bestowed a sweet, killing smile on the brute she had married and prepared to listen to his cousins.

The young pair gave a spirited rendition of some comic ballads. Their voices blended well and the performance was well-received by all. Claire did her best to keep her real enthusiasm for the young couple's singing from being discernibly different from the polite applause she had produced after Mrs. Blyden's uninspired performance.

When her turn came, Claire got up willingly enough but reminded Lady Hollister, "I did warn you that my voice has not really been trained, and I fear I do not play the pianoforte at all."

"Claire is shy about performing in public, Gran," Sir Egon said with seeming solicitude.

His bride gave him another sweet smile. "Not when the audience is predisposed in my favour, darling."

"As indeed we all are," Jack Blyden chimed in.

"Yes, you'll not find us a critical audience, Claire," said Lady Hollister, "and Jessica will play for you. She is an accomplished pianist."

Claire prayed she would not disgrace Signora Fellini, who had been her singing teacher for the last few months, as she conferred briefly with Jessica before singing two lovely old Italian compositions by Bononcini. She knew her voice was a rare gift; indeed, her speaking voice was largely responsible for her ability to earn her own living on the stage, but so far she had only sung snatches of tunes as dictated by the roles she had played. She had never sung for her contemporaries during her season with her aunt, so even this small audience was a new experience. Only once during her performance did Claire really look at her unwilling bridegroom. Her glance clashed with his, intent, unsmiling, enigmatic. Conscious of a thrill of danger, she wrenched her eyes away and was careful to avoid looking again at Egon until she had finished.

Claire's singing was most flatteringly received by her husband's family. "That was lovely, Claire," Lady Hollister said with her rare smile. "I knew I wasn't mistaken in the musicality of your voice."

"Yes, Egon, you really should find a good singing teacher for your wife," said Mrs. Blyden, turning to the man seated beside her on a settee. "The vocal quality is there, and training would increase her range."

"I naturally agree about the quality of Claire's voice, but what if said teacher should convince her she could have a career as a professional singer?" Egon asked on a whimsical note. "I might wake up one morning to find she'd left me to join the Italian Opera Company."

Claire kept a faintly amused expression on her face during the laughter and joking suggestions from his cousins on how to keep his wife that followed her husband's light remark, but amusement was not a component of her thoughts just then. Mrs. Blyden had succeeded in surprising her. Just when she had decided the beautiful woman was a natural predator, the kind of female who had no loyalty toward her own sex, she proved herself capable of real generosity toward one who might be considered a competitor for male admiration. As far as Egon was concerned, he still seemed determined to wage a private war with his unwanted bride, though such an attitude posed a constant danger to the success of their mission. It crossed her mind to wonder if he had partaken rather more deeply of the port after dinner than was advisable, but he showed no signs of inebriation, and she did not know him well enough to make a guess at either his capacity or propensity for alcohol.

Claire contributed little to the conversation in the few moments before the welcome sight of Boynton carrying the tea tray signalled the approaching end of the strangest and most unnerving day of her life. The level of tense awareness between herself and Egon had climbed steadily from the moment of their meeting outside the church this morning. Even here in his grandmother's drawing room, surrounded by other people, she was conscious of his attention — his hostile attention — focused almost constantly on herself, and for her part, she was finding it nearly impossible to keep her own mental energy from straying to his person with disconcerting frequency and very much against her will.

Lady Hollister asked Mamzell to pour out the tea, saying as she rose from her seat with the aid of her ebony cane, "I believe I'll forgo tea tonight. No need for you young people to retire at this hour, but at my age, late nights must be the exception rather than the rule. Claire, my child, breakfast is served at nine, but if you wish something brought to your room, you have only to tell Estelle when she waits on you tonight. And now I'll say goodnight, everyone."

"I think I shall follow your example and retire early tonight also, ma'am," Claire said, seizing the opportunity to escape. "The long drive, plus a wealth of new experiences today, has left me rather fatigued."

As she said a general goodnight, Claire planned to let her eyes sweep around the room casually, but her glance tangled immediately with her husband's as he said softly, "I'll be up shortly, darling."

She managed a weak smile, but alarm widened her eyes as Egon got to his feet. He may have intended to convey solicitude as he accompanied his wife and grandmother to the door and kissed each one on the cheek, but Claire saw it as additional harassment and had all she could do to prevent herself from jerking away from his touch. Michael's voice proposing a game of billiards floated out the door after them, and she found herself praying Egon would fall in with his cousin's suggestion.

Claire's nerves were twanging like harp strings as she gave her arm to Lady Hollister until they reached the staircase. She barely took in the matriarch's comments on the evening just passed and her polite wishes for Claire's healthful repose. Hopefully, her responses made sense and were suitable to the occasion, but she could recall none of them by the time she reached the partial haven of her own suite.

Claire now knew she could hope for no better than a partial sanctuary and limited privacy at Belhaven. The bedchamber of the green suite might be hers, but situated as it was between the dressing room and sitting room, it was unrealistic to hope for complete protection from Egon's disturbing presence. The word "protection" grated on her mental eardrum and she repeated the phrase, trying to substitute "isolation," but the truth of her unconscious choice was too strong to deny. She needed more than isolation from her bridegroom; she required protection from his fierce eye and wounding tongue, and it simply slayed her that this should be so. It made no sense that this antagonistic stranger, this brooding, unkind, and unlikable man should possess such power to hurt her and to arouse her to novel and unpleasant impulses of retaliation. Her own strong reaction puzzled and alarmed her because it struck at the basis of her understanding of herself. Either she didn't know herself as well as she had assumed or there was a new person inside her that she didn't yet understand and feared she might not like when or if she did.

Claire was unaware that she had been wandering aimlessly between the bedchamber and the sitting room as an accompaniment to her equally aimless mental ramblings until a soft knock on the sitting-room door brought her up short. Her hand fluttered to her throat as she called permission to enter.

To Claire's trembling relief, it was the maid Estelle who came tripping into the suite, wondering aloud why Madam had not rung for her. The need to deal with Estelle's practical concerns brought Claire to herself again, and she rather enjoyed the little maid's continuous stream of chatter, which consisted mainly of admiring comments on Claire's hair and wardrobe interspersed with snippets of household gossip. By the time the girl left, Claire was relaxed and smiling. She was just climbing into the big bed when Estelle called back from the sitting room that she would leave one branch of candles burning in there for Sir Egon.

This announcement wiped the smile off Claire's face as she blew out her candle and arranged the pillows more comfortably for sleeping. She could not have said how long she lay there between smooth sheets smelling faintly of lavender, her eyes staring through the window at the silver disk rising in the dark sky, her thoughts going endlessly around in the same unsatisfactory circles, but eventually she did drift off to sleep.

It was the sudden depression of the bed that physically altered her position rather than any sound that brought Claire to a state of total alertness. "Who's there?" she whispered, freezing into immobility.

"Only your husband, my pretty one. Whom did you expect?"

The soft voice only inches from her ear shot Claire into an upright position with the force of an arrow from a crossbow. "You have made a mistake, sir," she said icily. "I am not really your wife and this is not your bed."

"I've made many mistakes, and marrying you may prove to be the biggest, but you have made one too, my dear Claire, in thinking this is not my bed if I so choose."

"You gave me your word of honour not to try to make love to me; in fact, you boasted of your lack of interest in my dubious charms. Is this an example of the worth of a Hollister's word?" she hissed, putting all the scorn she was capable of into her denunciation.

Egon struggled up onto one elbow and peered up at her. Claire's face was invisible in the dark, but the moonlight silvered her white bedgown and revealed the rise and fall of her breasts beneath their thin covering. Her hair hung in one loose braid over her shoulder, the ends curling over the enticing fullness of her breast. "You extracted that promise before I knew what you really were —" he began.

"I did not *extract* any promise from you," she cut in furiously. "You were at great pains to let me know how much you despised me, and I am exactly the same person I was then."

"Yes, underneath, but I happen to find the top layer not altogether unappealing, and I can see no reason why I should not get everything I've paid for."

"You have already gotten exactly what you paid for, sir. My person is not included in our bargain, as you very well know."

"Then let us renegotiate, by all means," Egon said, wrapping his arm about her waist. "You'll not find me ungenerous. Name your price. One thousand pounds? Two thousand?"

The fumes of brandy were apparent to Claire now as her husband pulled her closer, but her rage had gone beyond the cautionary influence of fear as she spat out, "You are despicable, sir! I may be everything you think me, but I choose who comes into my bed, and I would not choose you for a million pounds. Now, take your hands off me and get out of this bed before I start screaming and bring the whole house down upon you. That would put a quick end to any hope of inheriting Belhaven."

Egon pulled away from her. He sat on the edge of the big bed. "I can see that I have underestimated your dislike of me, my dear. You are certainly a worthy adversary. *Mes hommages*, Claire, and goodnight."

There was barely enough light to see that her husband swept her a very low bow before disappearing into the deeper gloom near the door to the dressing room. Claire remained poised tensely until the soft snick of the door latch reached her ears; then she burst into tears.

CHAPTER 9

Life looked a deal more promising when Claire awoke to bright sunshine in the morning. Last night's stormy bout of weeping had been violent but short-lived, perhaps the inevitable culmination of a nerve-racking day of accumulating strains. She had fallen asleep immediately after the cathartic storm passed over and had known nothing more until a gentle awakening to sunshine and a feeling of renewed energy.

Her waking thought was that she had won a vital victory in the undeclared war with her husband, though she had been too frazzled emotionally to take in that fact when he had vacated her bed last night. It would be an advantage to know whether his capitulation had been from fear that she would carry out her threat to expose the falseness of their union or was the result of a belated nudge from his conscience when he finally understood that she had meant every word of her prohibition of a conjugal relationship during the term of their temporary marriage. Whatever the cause, she was intensely grateful to have the most crucial doubt removed. She now felt competent to deal with Egon on an equal basis.

On the heels of this fleeting satisfaction her eyes flashed to the dressing-room door, to be partially reassured by its closed innocence. Egon might still be sleeping off his over-indulgence, in which case caution must be her byword. After a minute or two of indecisiveness, during which she had to battle a return of yesterday's tension, Claire bounded out of the bed and ran barefooted across the Aubusson carpet to put her ear against the door. A welcome silence greeted her, but it was a thick door. She gnawed on her lip, but ignorance was tantamount to insanity. How could she proceed with her morning routine, not knowing whether her husband might appear at any moment to rake her with those mocking eyes of his? There was no key for the door; she had digested that unpalatable fact before she had changed for dinner last night.

Another long moment of indecision crawled by. Claire's toes were curling as her feet grew cold in a spot where the centre carpet didn't reach. Tentatively, she took hold of the knob and inched the door open. There was only the tiniest creaking noise as it moved inward. Emboldened by the lack of any responding sounds from within the dressing room, she continued to push the door inward until she could see the unoccupied daybed. With all danger of detection over, Claire satisfied her curiosity by walking into the small room.

A bowl of scummy water and the crumpled towel on the washstand gave mute proof that Egon had arranged to have shaving water brought up to him at an early hour. Except for his black evening shoes placed beside the armoire, there was no visible sign of yesterday's discarded clothing in the small room. Somehow it did not surprise her to discover that he was neat in his personal habits. It had struck her that his was a controlled nature, and military men were probably neater than most, of necessity. Her eyes returned to the cot, which had been made up by an inexpert hand, giving rise to speculation about his motive in doing so. As she improved on her husband's amateurish efforts, Claire's conviction grew that Egon was determined to preserve the impression that theirs was a normal marriage. Though it was common practice for husband and wife to have separate bedchambers, he obviously did not wish it known that he was sleeping in the dressing room.

Back in the middle of the bed, her arms around her knees in a loose embrace, Claire let her eyes wander about the attractive apartment. The carpet was very handsome, with its large floral pattern executed in soft colours. One of the lighter greens in the pattern had been chosen for the wall colour. The plastered ceiling, with its lovely oval-shaped designs in the corners that repeated the central motif, was painted creamy white, as was the wide carved moulding around the top of the walls. Individual pieces of furniture were beautifully inlaid with several kinds of wood veneers, but there were few of them. An enormous armoire that reigned in solitary splendour on the wall that backed the sitting room, two bedside tables, and an exquisite dressing table with a carved and painted mirror to match were the main pieces in addition to the magnificent bed. A single small chair, its back and seat upholstered in the same green-and-white print as the bed curtains and cover, stood between the two long windows, and a painted screen was placed across an inner corner to conceal the washstand from view. Though not overly large, the bedchamber seemed spacious and serene, thanks to a lack of clutter. One beautiful landscape in a gold frame over the white-painted mantel contributed to the sense of serenity Claire felt in the room, with its soft green expanse of meadows and trees under a light blue sky.

Claire's idle musings were interrupted by the appearance of Estelle with morning chocolate and another maid carrying hot water. The enticing smell of the chocolate wafting toward her reminded the new Lady Hollister that she had scarcely eaten anything since attaining this exalted status. Suddenly she was ravenous.

A half-hour later, Claire entered the breakfast parlour, a bright chamber on the east elevation of the house, to which she had been conducted by the helpful footman who had discovered her trying to find her way back to the main dining room. She smiled her thanks for his assistance and paused just inside the door, victim of a sudden shyness.

Egon looked up and saw her. "There you are, darling, just in time to make a liar out of me after I have told everyone you never sleep well the first night in a strange bed. You look blooming, and you are wearing the pink dress that is my favourite."

He hadn't missed a beat! Claire scarcely knew whether to jeer or cheer his unabashed gall when she considered the note on which they had parted, but as her husband pushed back his chair and came forward to escort her to the table in the wake of greetings from all those present, she found somewhat to her surprise that she was no more embarrassed by this first meeting than was Egon.

"You put Kean and Kemble to shame," she whispered as he kissed her cheek with the air of a devoted husband. She regretted the flip comment when she saw a muscle twitch in his cheek. What was the matter with her that she could not keep her tongue between her teeth when Egon made those two-edged remarks? The fastest way to lose the advantage she felt she had gained last night would be to test the limits of his self-control. She was suitably subdued as she slid into a seat next to Jessica and returned the family's greetings, avoiding her husband's eyes.

She needn't have worried that Egon meant to continue their private war. He didn't look her way again after urging her to try the famous Rye herrings. Claire needed little persuasion to sample most of the kitchen's offerings as she set about repairing the omissions of her wedding day. All the men were at table, but Jessica was the only other woman present. She explained to Claire that Melissa and Lady Hollister never ate breakfast in company.

"Miss Winward and Mamzell were here until a moment ago, when they went to see about sending off a message to Fourways."

"Does everyone call Mademoiselle Ducroix 'Mamzell'?" Claire asked, *sotto voce*.

"Well, *I* have not dared to do so to her face as yet," Jessica admitted, "but all the cousins do. I gather your husband began to call her this when he came here to live as a child, and now all the grandchildren use that term. They are all very fond of her. Michael says she is a 'good fellow,' always ready to intercede with Lady Hollister when they have fallen from grace."

"Yes, I have seen that Egon too is very attached to her," Claire murmured. She exchanged small talk with Jessica while Egon's cousins brought him up to date on changes that had occurred in the neighbourhood since he was last in Sussex.

Claire had eaten her fill and was enjoying her second cup of coffee when Michael turned to her with a smile. "Do you ride, Cousin Claire?"

"Why, yes." She returned his smile and waited while he addressed her husband.

"How about taking Claire to see something of the area today, Egon? We could start with Winchelsea and perhaps amble over to Rye if the weather holds fair."

"I'm afraid Gran has already put in a bid for my time on the estate today," Egon said with what sounded like regret, though his bride was not fooled, "but I'd be grateful if you and Jessica were to show Claire around a bit. Would you like that, darling?"

"Very much." Claire's smile was all for the young couple.

"That sounds like a good idea, and I'll offer my services as additional guide and escort," Jack Blyden said easily, "so Cousin Claire won't feel she is playing gooseberry to a pair of newlyweds."

"How very kind of you, Cousin Jack," Claire said into the little pause that followed. "I shall feel myself honoured to have three guides." She knew by the cold look in her husband's eyes that he was displeased that his blond cousin had included himself in the exploring party uninvited, but he must be aware there was nothing she could do to prevent it without being uncivil.

Egon rose. "I'll see what is in the stables that is suitable for a lady's mount."

"Claire is welcome to take Melissa's hack, Gypsy, who is of a gentle, biddable disposition," Jack said to Egon.

"Oh, but I could not rob Mrs. Blyden of her horse!" Claire protested.

"Melissa woke up with a bit of a headache this morning," Jack explained. "She has already said she would not be riding today. She will be pleased to lend you the mare, Cousin Claire."

Claire glanced to Egon for guidance and took her cue from his casually expressed gratitude to his cousin for making Gypsy available to his wife. She echoed his thanks rather more warmly and left the small dining parlour with Jessica to change into her habit.

Claire lingered over her changing for a few minutes in case Egon wished to communicate with her or give her any instructions, but he did not appear to see a need for any private converse before sending his wife off with his relatives for the day.

Jessica was quick to express her admiration of Claire's appearance when the latter re-joined her by the side entrance nearest the stables. "Oh, Cousin Claire, what a dashing habit, with all the military braiding and epaulets! And I have never seen anything so vastly becoming as that tall visored hat tilting over one eye. Mama wouldn't let me have a black habit made, though I begged and pleaded for one."

Claire smiled in sympathy with the other's wistful tone. "Well, I daresay she might have considered black not entirely appropriate for a girl in her first season, and in any case, the russet-brown colour you are wearing is a perfect foil for your hair and eyes. If that was your mama's choice, then you were fortunate to have such excellent taste at your disposal. Besides," she added in a practical spirit, tucking her crop under her arm as she donned her gloves, "you have the rest of your life to wear black if you choose, now that you are a married lady."

"So I have." Jessica smiled at her new relative. The smile widened to a grin as a thought occurred to her. "Melissa will be pea green with envy when she sees your habit. She has nothing to compare with it."

Claire chuckled and swept her skirts over her arm as they started walking toward the stables together. "I am pleased that my riding dress meets with your approval, Cousin Jessica, but you will not convince me that Mrs. Blyden's appearance is ever less than perfection. I am persuaded she looks breathtakingly beautiful in everything she puts on."

"Oh, yes," Jessica agreed without envy, "but she will covet that habit all the same."

Claire did not comment on the obvious satisfaction in the younger girl's voice, but applied herself to getting better acquainted with her on the short walk to the stables.

Egon was there with the other men. He did not turn from watching the saddling of a coal-black mare with two white stockings when Mr. Blyden gave a slight whistle at the sight of Claire and delivered himself of an elaborate compliment on her appearance.

"Thank you, Cousin Jack," she said warmly to punish her husband for a lack of interest. "Is this beauty Gypsy?" She moved over to pat the horse's velvet nose, and laughed as the horse nuzzled her.

Though his attention still seemed to be taken up by the mare, Egon inserted himself between his wife and cousin in the instant before Jack could carry out his obvious intention of assisting Claire to mount, and it was her husband who actually tossed her up into the saddle. Their glances met, and her newly acquired *sangfroid* deserted her under that burning dark regard. She lowered her lashes, contending with a rising annoyance at her inability to remain cool and self-possessed in his presence. So engrossed was she in this futile activity that she failed to hear his question.

"I asked if you would like the stirrup shortened further, Claire?" he repeated with heavy patience, bringing her curling thicket of lashes upright again.

"Yes, please, just a bit. Thank you, that is perfect." She accepted his deft deployment of the folds of her skirts with outward composure and an unwelcome inner awareness of the warmth of his hands on her ankles even through the leather boots.

By now Jessica had been similarly assisted by Jack Blyden, and the men had vaulted into their saddles. Egon gave Gypsy's reins into his wife's hands and stepped aside to wave the party off.

"Do you know anything about Winchelsea, Cousin Claire?" Michael asked as the four riders set off abreast across the field at the end of the lane.

"Only that it was one of the Cinque Ports in the Middle Ages and played a part in the country's defences before the days of the Royal Navy."

"That is really about all there is to know, because Winchelsea has been deteriorating ever since. And that is New Winchelsea, of course. The original port town was flooded by the sea around the middle of the thirteenth century."

"But it is a charming little place, for all that," Jessica put in. "The streets were laid out straight and parallel, with others crossing at right angles. There are still lovely old buildings and vistas in the town, though it is actually little more than a village these days."

Claire listened to Michael's retelling of the destruction of the old town by the relentless rogue tides of long ago, his tale of the immediate rebuilding on the present higher site augmented by his cousin from time to time. Her eyes roamed over the gently undulating landscape through which they rode. Fortunately, Gypsy was a soft-mouthed joy to handle, leaving Claire free to enjoy the scenes around her while sparing a minimum effort to controlling her mount. When they came to the steep ascent leading to the Strand Gate, one of the three gatehouses remaining from the rectangular walled town of the thirteenth century, Claire's companions instructed her to keep her eyes straight ahead until they had gone through the gate. Once there, she turned at their bidding and beheld across the marshes the enchanting vision of Rye rising above the water-laced levels, tenacious on its cliff with its face still to the sea, though the fickle sea had long since deserted the town and silted up its harbour. Her enthusiastic reaction to the sight pleased her proud guides, though Michael hastened to point out that he considered it would have been more romantic if her first glimpse of Rye had come on a day when the mists rolled in from the sea.

"Today the air is so clear the town looks sharply etched against the sky, but on such days it seems almost to float above the mist."

Claire's eyes sparkled with interest. "It must look like something out of a fairy tale then, complete with spectral tower. What is that squarish stone tower called?"

"That is Ypres Tower — pronounced 'Wipers' by the natives," Jessica replied. "It is the keep of a twelfth-century castle built by the Earl of Kent, William de Ypres."

"Except for Dover Castle, there is no older fortification still standing in the five ports," Michael said as they prepared to go up the sleepy high street of Winchelsea, so unlike the usual bustling high streets of other towns. As they admired the simple old houses set in quiet green squares with their fine old trees, Claire's guides explained that Winchelsea had also been a bustling, self-contained world in the Middle Ages, able to support all the necessary trades within its walls, even including six goldsmiths and jewellers. It had had a violent history of fierce raids by the French and stalwart defences of the coastline by its citizens until after the defeat of the Spanish Armada, when it ceased to be a fighting port and sank into unimportance and, eventually, decay.

The party dismounted and wandered around the ruined church dedicated to Thomas à Becket, whose impressive proportions in such a small place testified to Winchelsea's former importance. Jack pointed out the tree in the church square under which John Wesley had preached his last open-air sermon in 1790, and Jessica insisted that Claire must drink from St. Leonard's well, for it was said that no one who did ever strayed far from Winchelsea without wishing to return. A middle-aged woman called Mrs. Cogger, who was drawing water from the well, produced a tin cup from which Claire and Jessica drank. When asked if she had been born in Winchelsea, she told them her husband's family had been there in an unbroken line since the building of the new town.

The riding party dropped into the Salutation Inn for a late nuncheon. Hours of being outdoors on a crisp October day had given Claire a splendid appetite and she was easily persuaded to partake of the native Sussex dishes recommended by her companions, although she was less pleased to learn that the delicious pie she was eating was made of the little wheatear birds, the "Sussex ortolans" that the shepherds caught in turf traps and sold for a penny each. She felt no qualms about sampling the eel pudding, redolent of bacon and herbs, that her host explained was rolled in a suet blanket and boiled in a cloth. The local version of apple pie with which they finished their meal she declared the most luscious she had ever devoured, with its surprising addition of an egg and cream mixture poured in under the crust when the pie was nearly baked.

Claire enjoyed her sightseeing expedition with Egon's hospitable cousins, though she knew her body would pay the next day for the unaccustomed hours in the saddle. On their way back to Belhaven, Jack Blyden laughingly urged her to canter Gypsy for a bit to give his cousins a chance to bill and coo. Claire had seen no evidence of that activity on the young couple's part, quite the opposite actually. Michael treated his bride with the casual care one would expend on a younger sister whose company was endured rather than desired, but she gave the black mare a nudge and rode a little ahead, affecting not to see the annoyance that suffused Michael's face at his cousin's words, or that Jessica was gripping her bottom lip tightly with her teeth. She judged it more politic to ignore any undercurrents, even if it meant giving Mr. Blyden an opportunity to embark on a flirtation.

Claire's months as Clairisse Deschamps had taught her much about men's behaviour toward women they found attractive. She had not missed the measuring looks or the admiring ones sent in her direction by Egon's handsome cousin last night or today, nor was she meant to. With no wish to be unfair, she had already set him down as a congenital philanderer, the rapid conclusion partly produced by the fact that the man's own wife was such a rare diamond. Sooner or later he would make an attempt to engage her cooperation in a flirtation, at the very least. Better now, when neither Egon nor Lady Hollister was present to disapprove. Claire's mind was functioning admirably as she listened with grave attention to Mr. Blyden's fulsome compliments on her person, her sense of fashion, and her riding ability. She permitted no emotion to disturb the serenity of her expression and made no encouraging response to any of his overtures. After a few moments her continued silence appeared to disconcert her companion a trifle, whereupon his attitude became less admiring and more measuring.

"How did you and Egon meet?" he asked abruptly when his praise of her seat and elegant posture on Gypsy had met with nothing save an unsmiling murmur of acknowledgment.

"A mutual friend introduced us."

"In London?"

"Yes." Claire made an admiring comment on the peaceful farm scene through which they were passing, aware that she and Egon had not worked out a detailed story to account for their courtship.

"You could have known each other only very briefly unless you met before my cousin joined the army. Was that the case?" he persisted when she remained silent.

"No." Claire made a mental note to report the conversation to Egon at the first opportunity, so they might at least avoid telling different stories if questioned.

"A case of love at first sight, in fact?"

She detected the faint sneer in his voice and turned an innocently inquiring gaze on him. "Do you not believe in love at first sight, Cousin Jack?"

"Oh, of course, of course. 'Whoever loved that loved not at first sight?' and all that."

Claire smiled at him sweetly and gradually pulled Gypsy back into a walk, allowing Michael and Jessica to catch them up.

It was past mid-afternoon when the riding party returned to Belhaven. Jack Blyden assisted Claire to dismount while Michael performed the same service for his bride. Claire was not altogether unprepared when her knees buckled initially. She steadied herself with her two hands pressed stiffly against Mr. Blyden's chest, a move that served the equally important function of keeping him at arm's length when he would have enfolded her in his arms under the guise of holding her upright. She laughed at Jessica's expression of concern at her involuntary little gasp of discomfort and shook her head.

"It's all right, Jessica. I knew I would pay for all this exercise after not having ridden in some time."

"You'll feel better after soaking in a hot tub," the younger girl said. "Take my arm on the way to the house."

"Thank you, but I believe I'll try to walk off some of the stiffness in the garden before I go inside."

The young women set off together, leaving the men at the stables after a shining-eyed Claire had expressed her gratitude to them for her lovely day. Claire was mentally accommodating herself to her various aches and twinges as they walked slowly toward the house, and Jessica too was quiet. They didn't exchange more than a half-dozen words before their paths separated as Claire veered off in the direction of the gardens, but her parting smile for the younger girl was warmly friendly.

There was a good-size rose garden enclosed by a rosy-pink brick wall at the back of the house that Claire had only glimpsed on their walk to the stables that morning. Now she set off for it, entering through a wooden gate in the wall beyond a neat herb garden that still scented the air in late October. She slipped inside the gate and paused in delight.

There were beautiful public gardens in London, but, living in the city, one forgot the pleasures of one's own private patch of earth, shaped and planned to satisfy a personal taste. She gazed around her, her eye traveling past the late roses and dahlias to the fruit trees trained against the brick walls and on to the tall hedges that beckoned invitingly. She strolled along the gravel paths, her aches forgotten until she bent to drink in the scent of an occasional outstanding specimen that riveted her eye. The sun was still warm, though the air had grown cooler in the last hour. A delicious sensation of privacy and peace stole over her, a feeling she tried to prolong by refusing to dwell on the contrasting wariness that must accompany her every word in company at Belhaven.

She wandered into an area defined by high hedges, though she did not think it could be a formal maze because the paths were wide. There were rosebushes here too, pink ones, surrounding a small fountain in the intersection of two paths. She rambled at will, supremely content to be alone in this beautiful setting, until a woman's soft laugh ended the idyll. Her steps slowed even more, and she hesitated near the intersection she was approaching, unwilling to give up her precious privacy. She glanced through a small gap in the hedge in time to see Mrs. Blyden decrease the space between herself and Egon to a few inches as she spoke too softly for Claire to comprehend her words.

Claire subdued a sudden impulse to disturb their intimacy — why should she care that Mrs. Blyden seemed to possess the same flirtatious nature as her husband, to put it no higher? The answer was, of course, that even an appearance of interest in the beautiful Melissa on Egon's part would expose their own show of marital bliss for the sham it was. She walked on, knowing the couple was too engrossed to notice her crossing their path at this distance. Her own walk led to the back of the house, where she could see a glassed-in conservatory or succession house. She was still a fair distance from this intriguing structure when a door opened and Lady Hollister stepped out. She was hatless, though she wore a dark shawl over her shoulders. Before Claire could announce her presence, Lady Hollister had turned away from her and started off down another path between the hedges. It took a split second to calculate that Lady Hollister's present path would cross the one where Egon and Melissa Blyden stood, though not at the same intersection. Claire nipped back the way she had come and headed for the unconscious pair, who had not moved from the spot where she had seen them.

Mrs. Blyden was about to present Egon with flowers for his buttonhole when Claire tapped her on the shoulder and said pleasantly, "My job, I believe, Cousin Melissa."

Egon had seen her approach, but Melissa had not, and she jumped back, startled. Her eyes widened as Claire took the posy from her slack fingers.

"Goodness, you do rather creep up on people, Lady Hollister," Melissa said, quickly recovering her aplomb.

"I'll remember to clatter a bit the next time, Mrs. Blyden," Claire replied with a sweet smile.

"I hope you enjoyed my ... horse on your outing today, Lady Hollister," Mrs. Blyden returned, ignoring any implications in Claire's remark in favour of launching her own attack.

"Oh, indeed I did. Gypsy is a wonderfully trained lady's mount, and I thank you most sincerely for your generosity in lending her to me. I hope your headache is better?"

Mrs. Blyden's large blue eyes had narrowed somewhat, but Claire's response had been so genuine that she returned a civil answer to the effect that she was quite recovered, adding, "However, I could do with a cup of tea about now, so I'll say goodbye for the moment, unless you are coming in, Egon?"

"In a moment."

Mrs. Blyden sauntered off with a mocking little smile directed at the baronet. The silence behind her lasted until her graceful figure disappeared from view; then Egon said in heartfelt accents, "I cannot tell you how gratifying it is to find you share the jealousy — or do I mean possessiveness? — of all new brides, my dear Claire."

Claire looked up briefly from the flowers she held. "I am about five seconds ahead of your grandmother," she said.

And, indeed, Lady Hollister's cane could now be heard tapping along the gravel path behind Egon. Claire would have enjoyed tossing the wilting posy aside, but Lady Hollister's keen eyes would be bound to spot it, so she shrugged and proceeded to pull the stems through her silent husband's buttonhole.

"Ever the loving bride, eh, my pet?" he whispered in her ear, putting his hands lightly on her hips. When she stiffened, he chided, "If a thing is worth doing at all, it is worth doing well."

A reluctant smile curved her lips as she noted the gleam of amusement in his eyes.

"I trust I don't intrude?" Lady Hollister's cool clipped tones announced her arrival.

For a second Claire had lost sight of the motive behind their playacting, and she started slightly. Egon slid his arm around her waist and turned her to face his grandmother, smiling gaily at the watchful old woman. "Of course not, Gran." As his grandmother's equally bright dark eyes rested on the flowers in his lapel, he added, "Claire has been stealing flowers, Gran, and must be firmly dealt with. Shall we turn her over to MacDougall?"

Lady Hollister permitted an indulgent softening of her thin lips as she considered. "Since it is a first offense, I would recommend leniency. MacDougall has been my head gardener for forty years, my dear," she explained for Claire's benefit, "and he is a czar in his realm, tolerating no interference from anyone, myself included."

"When we were children, we were convinced that MacDougall knew every plant on the estate personally. In fact, Mike claimed he had names for all of 'em and swore he'd heard him talking to the flowers by name to encourage them to grow. He would come after us with a stick if we trampled any of the seedlings in our games. I don't know how many times I was called a 'reet hellion' and given a lash across the back of my running legs."

"No more often than you deserved," Lady Hollister said calmly, and her grandson's grin broke wide and infectious.

In this reminiscent vein, Egon was a different person from the sarcastic man of the world who alternately taunted and tempted her. Claire tore her fascinated eyes from his animated countenance and addressed his grandmother. "Whatever Mr. MacDougall's faults, he has created a garden of rare beauty here, ma'am."

"Yes, it has often been my solace in my later years," Lady Hollister replied seriously, her gaze fixed in space for a moment before she pulled the shawl a bit closer about her shoulders. "It is growing chilly. I believe I will go inside now. It is nearly time for tea in any case."

The young couple turned to accompany her back toward the house, adopting her slower pace.

"Did you enjoy your outing, Claire?" Lady Hollister inquired.

"Oh, yes, ma'am. Winchelsea has a sleepy sort of charm, and I was fascinated by the sight of Rye in the distance, though we did not have time to go there."

"You'll find Rye vastly different, always bustling with activity. Egon will no doubt take you there one day."

When no immediate offer was forthcoming from her husband, Claire said, "Meanwhile, ma'am, may I beg your indulgence to absent myself from tea this afternoon? I have not ridden in a good many months and I am feeling rather awkward and stiff."

"Then what you need is a good long soak in a hot tub," Lady Hollister said kindly. "We will excuse you from tea today. I should tell you that Miss Winward left for her home this afternoon and charged me with making her adieux, though I have prevailed upon her to return with her father for the dinner party that we shall give on my birthday the day after tomorrow."

Claire murmured suitably and left the others at the side door to go up to her room.

CHAPTER 10

Claire learned from Estelle that Belhaven boasted its own bathing chamber that Lady Hollister had had built on the ground-floor level, and she repaired there for the most sumptuous and satisfactory soak of her young life. The generous-size bathing room was tiled in its entirety; plain white tiles made up the background on the floor and walls, but other tiles decorated with grape vines and leaves and bunches of fat purple grapes climbed up the walls at each interior corner and marched in horizontal bands around the room at ceiling and chair-rail level. An enormous stove completely covered with blue-and-white-patterned tiles like nothing she had ever seen stood in one corner and drew the eye like a magnet. Estelle explained that the ancient contraption came from the Netherlands. Its modern purpose was to heat water to mix with the cold water that actually ran into the large tiled tub from a spigot affixed to its surface and connected to pipes that ran behind the walls. The used water drained away into another pipe with mechanical magic.

Claire accepted these marvels in a spirit of purring pleasure and proceeded to luxuriate in an atmosphere of lilac-scented steam until her quiescent conscience was reactivated by a sneaky recollection that even with the departure of Miss Winward, there remained four other females in residence, whose claims on the bath must be considered valid under the demands of fair play. She left the beautiful bath chamber wrapped in a green velvet dressing gown and a mental cloak of conscious rectitude that covered a real reluctance to bestir herself for at least another hour. She used the back stairs

Estelle had shown her and succeeded in gaining entrance to the green suite without meeting anyone in her dishevelled state.

Claire had congratulated herself too soon, however. She had barely closed the door behind her when her husband strolled out of her bedchamber, a sheet of paper in one hand.

"I thought I heard someone come in," he said, lowering the hand that held the paper he had apparently been glancing at. His eyes made a lazy tour of her person as she stood near the hall door, startled and self-conscious.

Claire was only too aware that she stood at a decided disadvantage at the moment, *en négligé*, with the hair she had piled carelessly on top of her head for her bath half-tumbling down her back and clinging in damp strands about her neck. She could not know that her skin was delicately tinted and dewy fresh from her recent ablutions, or that her present state of undress dissolved the social barriers erected by correct costuming, immeasurably heightening her natural attractions in a man's eyes. She did know she was acutely uncomfortable under his deliberate inspection, a reaction she suspected he fully intended, and it took an act of will to keep her fingers from dragging her wet hair away from her neck or checking the tightness of the gold cord that served to confine her flowing dressing gown at the waist. She imposed stillness on her body and met his gaze calmly when it returned to her face, saying in an attempt to dispel the tension that had sprung up between them yet again, "Yes, I am just returning from my bath."

"So I see. Did you enjoy my grandmother's version of Roman decadence?"

Her lips curved naturally. "Very much. I approve of Lady Hollister's idea of decadence." For the life of her, Claire could think of nothing to add to bridge the chasm of awkwardness that yawned between them. He was blocking the door to the bedchamber, and her instinct warned her that physical movement on her part was not advisable. She was not some schoolroom miss who could be gaily provocative behind her shield of innocence, nor was this a conventional situation or a stage role with her next speech already written for her. She was still seeking an innocuous opening gambit when Egon rescued her.

"You did not seem surprised earlier when Gran announced that Miss Winward had departed," he observed unexpectedly.

"Because it was not a surprise to me. She told me last night that she would most likely be leaving this afternoon."

"Miss Winward told *you* she would be leaving?" His brows winged upward.

"Yes." Claire took a careful breath and came farther into the sitting room, relieved that his attention had switched from her person to her conversation. Now to keep it there. "She also asked me to convey her grateful thanks to you…" She paused, and he took his cue with mechanical precision, but those black brows were now drawn closer together.

"Thanks to me — for what?"

"For marrying and thus releasing Miss Winward from a promise she had made to her father five years ago. I imagine I need not tell you what that promise was?"

"No, although I haven't known until now whether the girl was a willing participant five years ago or even knew of the marriage scheme. At the time, I was in no humour to prolong the agony, and wasted no time in taking off for parts unknown. No man likes to be told when to marry and whom to marry, with a gun pointed at his head."

Claire chewed this over for a moment. "But you did not escape in the end, did you?" When Egon's thin cheeks remained grooved and his mouth stayed firmly compressed, she went on slowly, articulating her thoughts. "You merely exchanged one unwanted bride for another in the end."

"Have you forgotten that a divorce was part and parcel of the marriage we contracted?" he asked in silky tones.

"Of course, how stupid of me! I fear I was still thinking about the original plan to marry you off." Claire spoke quickly to erase any impression he might have received that she thought of her marriage as anything other than a temporary expedient.

"Claire, about the divorce," Egon began, looking less decisive than usual, but Claire did not let him finish.

"Naturally, I shall accommodate myself to your wishes in the timing of the divorce, but I fear I cannot discuss it just at the moment," she said with a pointed look at the enamelled porcelain clock on the mantelpiece. "Estelle will be here any second now to help me get ready for dinner."

As Egon's eyes drilled into hers, seeking whatever mysterious answers he sought to unasked questions, Claire fell back on stage technique as she concentrated on projecting an image of worldly self-assurance, not an easy feat when one took into consideration her vibrating nerves and the fact that she felt mentally naked under his scrutiny.

A light tap on the sitting-room door heralded Estelle's arrival and released Claire from the hypnotic spell Egon seemed able to cast over her at will. She resisted the need to babble a welcome to the girl, who was curtseying respectfully to Egon, her snapping black eyes full of interest and far from demure.

"Shall I come back later, ma'am?" she asked Claire.

"No, stay ... Estelle, is it?" Egon responded with a polite smile. "I was just leaving to speak with my grandmother. I'll be back in time to change, my love," he threw over his shoulder to his bride as he got himself out of the room with swift purpose.

There was a strange man in the drawing room when Claire and Egon joined the family before dinner. He rose from a chair near Lady Hollister's as they entered.

"Claire, my child, may I present Mr. Dawkins, my solicitor? This Lady Hollister is my grandson's bride, Mr. Dawkins."

Claire accompanied her greeting with the generous smile that was natural to her, aware that behind Mr. Dawkins' spectacles a pair of shrewd ice-blue eyes were taking stock of her with equal interest as he stated his pleasure in the acquaintance in an uninflected voice that gave away none of his thoughts. After several minutes of trifling conversation, she was none the wiser as to whether Mr. Dawkins concealed a favourable or critical impression of her under his noncommittal manner, though there was no doubt in her mind that the active intelligence revealed in his eyes would have made some preliminary judgment.

Mr. Dawkins' appearance was unprepossessing. His stature was moderate but his narrow, slope-shouldered frame was unimpressive, and a nondescript collection of features kept his countenance free of any distinctions. His cranium was perfectly round, bald at the top, the back and sides covered by a semi-circular fringe of coarse grey hair. Only the shallow-lidded eyes were assertive in a smooth-skinned face that was a continuation of his bald head, its contours also rounded. His dress was conservative, and his person was neat as a pin.

As the talk eddied around her, Claire wondered idly what Lady Hollister's attorney was making of herself beyond what was readily apparent, an attractive and poised young woman with a well-modulated voice. Four years ago, she would never have dreamed of applying such complimentary terms to herself on her most optimistic day, but her stint on the stage had done much for her in this regard. Would Mr. Dawkins discern, beneath the hard-won self-confidence, her discomfort with the anomalous position she occupied in this gathering? Though she felt increasingly at home with each hour she spent among the present inhabitants of Belhaven, every now and then would come a reminder that she was here under false pretences. None of Michael's and Jessica's friendly acceptance or Mamzell's kind welcome was really meant for Claire Yelland, but for Egon's wife. Even Lady Hollister, who might have been expected to resent her very existence on Miss Winward's behalf, had been graciously accepting of her grandson's unexpected bride.

Claire's brief spell of mental absence was brought to a halt by a tiny nip at the back of her waist, administered by her husband as he passed behind her. As she turned involuntarily, her startled eyes were inches away from his mouth as he bent to whisper in her ear.

"Stop mooning about like the Melancholy Dane or you'll have the company wondering if I beat you in private."

"You'd like to," she retorted with a quick flash of spirit that was rewarded by a glimpse of white teeth as Egon tossed her a devil-may-care grin before proceeding to deposit his empty glass on the silver tray Boynton had left on the tea table.

After another delicious dinner, the ladies retired to the drawing room, where they were not left for very long to console each other with conversation before the men re-joined them. Lady Hollister proposed to set up a table of whist, since Mr. Dawkins had a strong partiality for that particular form of recreation.

"Jack, Melissa, you will make up the table?" she asked, the command evident though well-concealed beneath the trappings of politeness.

Melissa Blyden chose not to recognize it as such, stating to her husband in an undervoice that was perfectly audible to Claire, on his other side, "I meant it when I said I had no intention of ever sitting down at the same card table as your grandmother again, Jack." She resumed her conversation with Egon, leaving it to her spouse to explain glibly that his wife begged to be excused because her headache had crept back in the last hour.

"Very well, we'll excuse you tonight, Melissa, and if you wish to retire early, we shall understand," Lady Hollister said, graciously granting a royal dispensation. "Egon, will you oblige us instead?"

"Perhaps Mamzell would like to play tonight?" suggested her undutiful grandson.

"Have you been away so long that you have forgotten that Clothilde is entirely lacking in the concentration necessary to make a card player?" Lady Hollister demanded.

Claire blinked at this forthright evaluation, but, far from being offended by it, Mademoiselle Ducroix turned reproachful eyes on Egon. "Fie on you, *mon mauvais*. You know that to play whist is of all things the most disagreeable and unsettling to me. It brings on my palpitations."

While Egon tried to placate the Frenchwoman, Claire turned to Lady Hollister, who was regarding the scene with a tolerant cynicism, and said diffidently, "If there is no one else you would prefer, I would be happy to play, ma'am."

There was a tiny pause during which Egon opened his mouth and closed it again before Lady Hollister said with a gleam in her eyes that put Claire on her mettle, "Thank you, my dear. We shall be delighted to have your participation."

"What do you say, Cousin Claire, to taking on the older generation together?" Jack Blyden proposed with a joviality she thought a shade overdone.

"We shall cut for partners in the accepted fashion," Lady Hollister replied, promptly putting him in his place.

Claire thoroughly enjoyed the next hour. She was paired with Mr. Dawkins, which suited her very well. Six months of exposure to all kinds of men having aided her in reaching the prosaic conclusion that the handsome Mr. Blyden was destined to become a pest, she regarded every denied opportunity as a boon. It meant she could keep her powder dry that much longer. And if she had overestimated her own cardplaying capabilities, the present partnership arrangement guaranteed that any misplays on her part would redound to Lady Hollister's benefit, a situation infinitely preferable to being the cause of the matriarch's undeserved defeat.

As matters fell out, Claire could not put a foot wrong that evening. She was doubly blessed with an abundance of good cards and an occasional challenge to her skill that she was able to meet successfully. Mr. Dawkins was as astute a player as she would have guessed him to be, and the partnership prospered. Lady Hollister was a formidable opponent, but Jack played erratically, not surprising since a portion of his attention seemed to stray repeatedly to the rest of the party, who were engaged in conversation, with the exception of young Jessica. She remained at the pianoforte playing softly, for her own pleasure primarily, though occasionally someone would request a composition. Once or twice, unconnected fragments of talk that drifted over to the game table seemed to indicate that Egon was being questioned about his years in the army. Claire felt a fleeting twinge of regret that she had not been privileged to hear anything of her husband's experiences in the Peninsula or Belgium, but then, the two of them had not so far managed to sustain a discussion on any subject that did not directly relate to the deception they were practising on his family. Dwelling on her inability to communicate with Egon would fast undermine her concentration on the card game, however, and Claire did not desire to come under the gimlet-eyed scrutiny of her hostess for inattention.

Actually, it was Lady Hollister's grandson and partner who suffered that fate. She called him to task for reneging, suggesting in her precise tones that his attention was not sufficiently on the game.

"I humbly beg pardon, Grandmother, but how can a man hope to concentrate on his cards when Cousin Claire sits there nibbling on her bottom lip so invitingly while she plots our destruction?"

Claire kept her countenance by dint of will, but the look she sent her cousin-in-law before dropping her eyes spoke volumes. How like a certain type of man to claim the woman tempted him!

"That remark went beyond the line of what is pleasing, Jack. You know I do not tolerate personal references in my drawing room," snapped Lady Hollister.

"Again I beg pardon, ma'am, and yours, cousin, though I had no intention of offending."

Claire could hear the note of sullenness in Jack's voice, but she maintained her air of detachment, merely signalling acceptance of the apology with a slight movement of her head.

The rest of the game passed without further incident. Jack's competitiveness increased markedly, but it was too late to substantially reduce the large lead built up by Claire and Mr.

Dawkins, and this pair emerged the decided victors when the score was tallied.

"You play exceedingly well, my dear, especially in view of your extreme youth," Lady Hollister observed to Claire as they were about to re-join the rest of the company for tea.

"My father was fond of all card games, ma'am, especially whist. He taught us the rudiments at an early age."

"Us?"

"My brother and myself."

"Egon did not tell me you had a brother." Lady Hollister's dark eyes flashed quickly to her grandson, sitting stony-faced on the sofa beside Mrs. Blyden, before returning to Claire.

"There has been no opportunity as yet for Jeremy and Egon to meet. Everything happened so quickly." Even in her own ears the explanation sounded feeble, and Claire did not dare to look at her husband. It was his own fault, she thought, whipping up some defensive indignation, for his tacit refusal to decide on a story to tell together at Belhaven to account for her history. She could not be expected to read his mind!

In the next few minutes, Claire considered she owed her deliverance from being subjected to a detailed exploration into her background and antecedents to the fact that Mr. Dawkins engaged his hostess in a lively post-mortem discussion of the whist game just concluded. In her relief at being spared — though for the moment only — she did not immediately question that her good fortune was a matter of sheer accident until she glanced over at Mr. Dawkins and was greeted by that very proper gentleman with the suspicion of a wink before he turned an attentive face to his hostess, who was vigorously defending her play of a certain hand that he had called into question. A little glow of warmth spread inside her at this display of disinterested kindness on the part of a stranger. It helped balance her husband's avoidance of her. Egon had not spared her the smallest part of his attention since the end of the card game.

In the short time before Lady Hollister retired, Claire noticed that she was not the only new bride being neglected that evening. Jessica left the pianoforte and drifted over to join the group when the tea tray arrived. She smiled at her husband and took the seat next to him. His acknowledging smile was a mere stretch of the lips, gone in an instant as he turned to ask Egon a question. When the tea was being passed around, Michael carried a cup to Claire and remained in the chair near hers. Claire thought she detected a hurt look on the young girl's face as she accepted a cup from Jack, mumbling her thanks and falling silent thereafter. Michael's conversational overtures since coming up to Claire were of the most trifling nature and, she thought, somewhat forced as well. She grew thoughtful and her own responses dwindled to mechanical civility. Again this evening she seized the opportunity to say goodnight when Lady Hollister rose to leave, and again she heard Michael propose a game of billiards to the men. This time, the rest of the women decided to have an early night also and they left the room together. Tonight Egon did not escort them to the door or place an ostentatious kiss on his wife's cheek.

Claire's rest was undisturbed by any midnight visit from her husband. She had not really expected another attempt to claim a husband's right after the decisive confrontation on their wedding night, but she could not be completely easy in her mind. This was not to be wondered at, considering that she was separated only by an unlocked door from a near-stranger who just happened to be bound to her by the closest of all human ties, albeit most unwillingly. She wished with all her heart that she understood Egon better, but his mind remained

162

an enigma to her seeking intelligence. At one moment charming and carefree, almost boyish in his enthusiasm, he could change on the instant into a brooding, moody creature who delighted in lashing out at her. It was her own misfortune that she could not seem to remember she was simply playing a part for hire so that she could allow his scorn to wash over her unabsorbed. The truth was that his contempt for her as a person hurt badly.

As Claire prepared for another day of consorting with her husband's family, who did not know she was not really one of them, she puzzled over her reaction to the man she had married. From the first moment of meeting his compelling gaze and realizing that it held censure, she had burned to reverse his judgment of her as a loose woman, but why this one man's opinion should matter when that of others did not was a riddle she had been unable to solve. She was not in love with him; she rejected that horrifying theory the instant it crossed her mind. One could not fall in love with a man who looked at one with contempt, for heaven's sake — not if one was a rational being! Moreover, one could not love a person one didn't really know or understand, especially when what one did know of that person was not particularly to his credit, even though the same person could on occasion exhibit an endearing warm-heartedness toward people like Mamzell, who obviously could see no fault in him.

Having thoroughly muddled her original clear rationale, Claire wisely abandoned unprofitable introspection in favour of getting on with her job, which was to play the happy bride before her select audience at Belhaven.

Mr. Dawkins took his departure directly after breakfast, which he consumed with fastidious perseverance, putting away a remarkable amount of food for someone his size. He was correct and formal until the end, when his manner toward Claire unbent sufficiently for him to express his pleasure at having had the opportunity to play whist with a young lady of rare aptitude and his hope for future meetings. This was conveyed as he shook hands with those who had escorted him to the front door, where his hired carriage was waiting.

"You've made another conquest, Cousin Claire," Jack Blyden declared as the post chaise moved off.

"I liked Mr. Dawkins too," she replied simply.

The men were going riding, but she declined their invitation to join them, citing the various aches she had acquired the previous day in excuse.

"Did you hurt yourself yesterday?" Egon, who had had nothing to say to her beyond a syrupy greeting for the benefit of his relatives when she had entered the breakfast parlour, turned to his wife in some concern.

Claire gave him a reassuring smile, pleased that the concern had sounded genuine. "No, nothing like that, I assure you. It is no more than the natural stiffness in one too long away from an exercise, but I think I shall just ramble about the grounds this morning. They are so invitingly lovely."

Egon did not urge her to accompany the riders, nor did he offer to stay behind and show her over the estate. Claire told herself there was no surprise in that. He had avoided her company yesterday also. If he did not find it difficult to reconcile an aversion for her society with the role of devoted bridegroom, then she would not trouble her head over it either.

Claire was returning to the house after a pleasant stroll through the spacious well-tended grounds of Belhaven some two hours later, when, emerging from a peach and cherry orchard onto a level lawn once more, she spotted a small boy

164

aimlessly kicking a red ball. The child was too well-dressed to belong to the village, but no attendant was in sight.

"Hello, young man. Who are you?" she asked cheerfully.

The child had been too absorbed in his own pursuit to hear her approach. He looked up in surprise, and the ball dribbled toward Claire, who picked it up. "My name is Cyril Blyden. What's yours?"

"I am Claire Hollister, and I think I must be your cousin." She should have guessed that this beautiful golden-haired child must belong to Melissa and Jack Blyden, who were nothing if not spectacularly good-looking.

"I shouldn't think you could be my cousin," he answered gravely, "because I have a cousin Dolly and a cousin Kitty, and they are just babies."

"Ergo, cousins must be babies?" Claire smiled at the solemn little boy. "They can be big too, did you not know? As a matter of fact, you have four grown-up cousins staying at Belhaven right now."

"I have?" Big blue eyes widened and he looked intrigued. "Who?"

"Do you know Mr. Michael Dunston and his wife?"

The child nodded. "Mr. and Mrs. Dunston, yes. I made my best bow and shook hands the other day when we arrived to visit Great-Grandmother Hollister."

"Well, they are your cousins Michael and Jessica, and I am your cousin Claire. How do you do, Cousin Cyril?" She extended her hand and the little boy put his in it, remembering too late about the bow, an oversight he rectified as soon as Claire released his hand.

"That was very well done, Cousin Cyril," she said admiringly.

"You said four cousins. That is only three."

"The fourth is my husband, whose name is Egon, Sir Egon Hollister."

"So I have cousins Michael and Jessica and Egon and Claire," the youngster repeated. "Do Dolly and Kitty have grown-up cousins too?"

"Probably, but I do not know precisely who they might be as yet. I am new to the family, you see, because I married your cousin Egon." When the child, who seemed to possess a methodical mind, opened his mouth for further enlightenment on the complexities of family relationships, Claire said to distract him, "Shall I throw the ball to you?"

"Girls can't throw balls good," Master Blyden said with masculine scorn. "My nurse never throws it straight."

"Well, here is one girl who can throw straight. Move over there." Claire waved him back, and, smiling suddenly, the little boy scampered to the rear. She put the red ball right into his surprised hands, but he managed to hang on to it, laughing delightedly.

As the ball came back to her, thrown quite strongly, Claire called out, "Bravo! How old are you, Cyril?"

"I was four years old on my birthday in September."

"Only four?" She pretended amazement. "Four-year-olds can't throw that far. I'll wager you are at least six."

"No, I'm not!" The child's initial indignation changed to earnestness. "I never tell lies, Cousin Claire — that is, almost never. I am truly four years old. You may ask my nurse."

"Where is your nurse, by the way?"

"Reading in the kitchen garden." Cyril indicated the area to his left as he threw the ball back again.

"Shouldn't you be there with her?"

"My ball ac… ci… dent… ly went over the wall and I had to go fetch it."

Claire eyed the height of the brick wall and grinned to herself. Some accident. A nurse must be an awful hindrance to an adventurous little boy. She deliberately threw the ball farther the next time, enjoying the sight of the sturdy youngster giving delighted chase. She was sending him farther back each time, with some idea of working their way back to the nurse, when she spotted the top of a man's hat moving along the other side of the garden wall. It looked to be a grey beaver like the one Egon had been wearing when he went riding earlier. Suddenly an imp of mischief took possession of Claire, and she acted on the instant. Taking careful aim, she let the ball fly toward the wall. "Here it comes, Cyril," she called out.

The boy headed backward on a dead run, but he wasn't going to catch this one.

Claire had barely time to regret her impulsive action before the red sphere descended, knocking off her unsuspecting victim's hat. She put her hands over her mouth to stifle laughter and then removed them as Egon came through the gate carrying ball and hat. He stopped short at sight of the little boy, who was almost upon him. Dropping the ball, he put out a hand to save the child from crashing into him full-tilt.

"Oh, dear, I am so very s— sorry, Egon. Did I hurt you?" Claire sent her voice ahead of her as she approached the pair examining each other in wary silence.

"You threw that ball?" Egon looked dumbfounded, and Claire struggled to subdue the laughter bubbling up inside her.

"I … I'm afraid so," she confessed with abject meekness.

"We were playing catch-the-ball. Cousin Claire can throw it almost as far as my papa does," the boy informed the frowning stranger.

"Can she indeed?"

"It … it was an accident," Claire lied, desperately trying to keep a straight face in the presence of the dawning suspicion on her husband's.

"Was it, by George!"

"Egon, I'd like you meet Master Cyril Blyden," Claire said, hastening to give his thoughts a safer direction. "Cyril, this is my husband, who is your cousin Egon."

Egon flashed her a look that promised a reckoning in the future before he turned to acknowledge the creditable bow being executed by young Master Blyden.

The next few minutes while the missing nurse came bursting out of the garden looking for her charge and the man and boy took each other's measure left an impression of everyday normality in Claire's mind. After the high drama of the past forty-eight hours, the little group that wended its way back to the house, with the chattering child the clear centre of attention and indulgence, carried a welcome air of hominess about it. This impression might be spurious, but it was a sign that lives were not always lived at fever pitch or on the brink of crisis, and it went some way toward restoring Claire's mental balance to a more serene state.

CHAPTER 11

Sir Egon Hollister eyed the sturdy little figure trotting along beside him with amused interest. The child was almost too pretty to be a boy, with big eyes of deepest sapphire and soft gold curls covering a finely shaped head, but there was no suggestion of delicacy or timidity about his person, quite the reverse. There was an eagerness about him that bespoke an adventurous soul and a hint of mischief, almost of conspiracy in the smile he gave Claire. Obviously he was already well-practiced in eluding authority in the harassed person of his nurse, who scolded him for dirtying the knees of his nankeen trousers and escaping from the garden the moment her back was turned. As young Master Blyden offered the tale of a ball accidentally lost over the wall and his subsequent meeting with Claire, which naturally delayed his return from forbidden territory, his matter-of-fact delivery raised the excuse to the level of a reasonable explanation. A child to be reckoned with, Egon decided as his eyes met Claire's in swift understanding before Cyril reclaimed her attention.

Egon took the opportunity this afforded him to study his wife without her knowledge. She and the little boy seemed to be dealing comfortably together on a person-to-person basis after an acquaintance of a few minutes' duration. How nice to be a four-year-old male and free of the conventions that bound one of nine-and-twenty! He could envy the child his ease of manner with Claire. Egon became conscious of a strong desire that his own dealings with her could be so uncomplicated. Unfortunately, it was far too late to achieve that desirable state. Too much had happened between them.

Egon had been prepared to dislike Clairisse Deschamps on sight for her potentially disastrous hold over his cousin Geoffrey, but he had been unable to do so. It was not that he had found himself physically attracted to the actress, though he had thought her voice and eyes beautiful, but there was a disarming simplicity about her manner, an absence of affectations that was rare in the sort of woman who lived off her sensual appeal to men. This had had the curious effect of making him despise her the more for the way she had chosen to live.

None of this had been clear to him on that fateful night when he first met Claire and later rescued her from the Earl of Mostyn. His own problem, the seemingly impossible task of re-establishing communication with his grandmother without acceding to her plan to marry him to Miss Winward, had been uppermost in his mind then. It was only after he'd conceived of the brilliant notion of hiring a temporary wife, a notion he now suspected was inspired by Lucifer himself — who was surely laughing in his beard in the hottest corner of hell — that he began to crystalize his impressions of the actress. Her manners and speech did not disgust him when he took her driving and startled her with his outrageous proposition. If her appearance was a bit extreme for a young lady of refinement, he was in a mood to regard that as an additional reason to enjoy thrusting her down his family's throat. He had rushed through all the arrangements for the marriage, driven by resentment and a bitter spirit of retaliation.

It wasn't until the morning of his wedding day as he paced back and forth in front of the church that the long-range implications of his mad scheme had begun to penetrate the haze of anger in which he'd been acting. He found it hard to believe that he'd been stupid enough to think he could marry a woman and promptly divorce her and still meet his grandmother's requirements for her potential heir. The truth was that he'd been too furious to care about consequences until that moment. He'd been within a hair's breadth of calling the whole thing off when Claire had appeared in her own persona. The first sight of her had given rise to two opposing thoughts — that he could pull it off with this woman posing as his wife, and that, on the other hand, he would be an egregious fool to endanger his crucial emotional non-involvement by tying himself to someone as attractive as she was unsuitable.

Well, he had stupidly gone through with his ill-conceived plan, and thus deserved to be punished by being chained on an emotional seesaw ever since. His contempt for Claire had begun when he realized she was not from the lower classes, and thus could be excused for using every possible asset to seize a chance to rise out of grinding poverty, but had been gently born and had elected to barter her reputation and virtue for a materially more comfortable life than the genteel poverty in which her family probably lived. His contempt for his own moral weakness had grown apace when he found himself in her bed trying, against all honour, to coerce her acceptance of him as her lover on their wedding night. It was no defence to claim she tempted him. She did, but he was honest enough to concede that it was not her actions, which had been coolly and politely in accord with their agreement, but her lovely person that drove him wild with desire.

Claire exuded a more subtle sensuality than Clairisse Deschamps. It was all mixed up with the natural sweetness of her temper and the warmth of her smile and the incandescent glow of eyes like dark molten amber, eyes that could look almost mournful when her face was in repose. Those eyes were also eloquent of accusation whenever he said something deliberately unkind, but this was one means by which he kept reminding himself that she was a clever actress, with those lovely eyes fixed on the main chance. He also saw the necessity of staying away from Claire as much as possible under the nearly impossible circumstances of their being ostensible newlyweds, if he hoped to be able to keep his hands off her in accordance with their agreement.

He had been greatly tempted to seize upon his grandmother's idle suggestion that he take Claire to see Rye. Michael and Jack were high in their praise of her horsemanship, Mr. Dawkins was looking forward to another chance to partner her in a whist contest — even this small child was obviously revelling in the company of his charming new cousin, while the person with the best claim on her attention stood back from the competition. There was no doubt in his mind that he would find her a delightful companion on an outing, but to what point? Such an imprudent course would make the inevitable parting more wrenching for him. She had made it abundantly clear that she did not wish to have him as a lover, no matter how generous he was prepared to be. Was his conceit of himself so great that he could not accept that he apparently appealed to her as little as Lord Mostyn had? There were any number of similarly circumstanced and equally attractive women in London, who would welcome his attentions with enthusiasm. All he had to do was sit out another few days of the wretched charade he had brought upon himself before he could remove from Sussex forthwith and begin to sample some of the delights that Claire's proximity had given him a hankering for.

Life was certainly well worth living at present. Once he had feared that Belhaven was lost to him; now, thanks to Claire, he had renewed hope in that direction. He realized that if Gran made him her heir, he would be unable to initiate a divorce during her lifetime, but even that might not be an insuperable obstacle. If Claire were willing to wait, he would be happy to set her up in a little house of her own and settle a modest annuity on her until they were free to dissolve the marriage. He would still be able to produce her if his grandmother summoned them to Belhaven on occasion. It was a lot to ask, but she would be in no worse case than she had been in last week, on the open market, as it were. Of course, she would be unable to marry during this period, but the chance that any of those aristocratic sprigs who dangled after her in her role as Clairisse Deschamps would offer marriage was remote indeed. That sort of infatuation almost never led to the altar.

Egon had all but convinced himself that the deception he and Claire were embarked on would end with satisfaction to both parties when his sombre gaze was drawn to her laughing face as she held the ball just out of the small boy's reach for a few seconds before turning it over to him. Cyril had been teasingly bouncing and catching it just out of her reach until she had suddenly darted forward and scooped it up. When she assumed that expression of demure mischief as she had after knocking his hat off, her husband had all he could do to refrain from catching her in his arms and kissing her breathless.

At that moment she looked up, and the fierceness of his expression drove the laughter from her face. Once more, Egon felt he had been needlessly cruel to a child. With a muttered excuse, he left the nursery party at the side door and went off in another direction.

"Oh, pray excuse my unannounced entrance, ma'am," Claire said on discovering Lady Hollister sitting behind a large desk in the room Mamzell had pointed out as the library sometime after lunch, when the members of the household had scattered to their various individual pursuits. "I was told I might find some writing paper in here." She would have gone out again, but Lady Hollister made an imperious gesture beckoning her inside.

"Do not hover in the doorway, child, as though you were afraid of me. You're not, are you?"

"No, ma'am. Should I be?" Claire asked with real interest.

One of her infrequent smiles crossed the lightly lined face of the chatelaine of Belhaven. "I should hope not at your age, though I admit I have never discouraged a healthy fear in the youngsters, my grandchildren first, and now my great-grandchildren. I find it a useful aid to discipline and the development of good manners."

"I am persuaded you are right, ma'am." Claire's sunny smile broke, setting lights in her eyes. "I met a delightful member of the youngest generation this morning, Master Cyril Blyden. How many great-grandchildren do you have?"

"Three at present. Has Egon given you a coherent picture of his family — his father's side of the family?"

"Not very comprehensive, I'm afraid. Just the odd reference to various cousins."

"Very remiss of him. Well, since a number will be present tomorrow for my birthday dinner, I shall take it upon myself to categorize them for you now. It will spare you some measure of confusion when you meet everyone at once. Sit down here." When Claire had obeyed, Lady Hollister continued in the manner of a lecturer. "My husband, who was Sir Matthew, and I had one son, also Matthew, Egon's father, who died at sea with his wife when Egon was only nine. We had two daughters also. Caroline, the elder, married John Blyden and they produced four children. Jack is the eldest; he and Egon are of an age. Then there is Geoffrey, who is still a bachelor, and Maria and Emily, both of whom are married. Emily is Mrs. Nelson Smyth-Thomas and the mother of an infant daughter, Dorothea, known by the silly sobriquet of Dolly. Maria has been married just a few months to Lord Darcy, the fourth baron. Caroline is now widowed. My youngest child is Arabella, whose husband is Sir George Dunston. Michael, at six-and-twenty, is the eldest of four children. Alice is Mrs. Derek Blayde, and they have an infant daughter, Katherine, regrettably called Kitty by her doting parents. My youngest grandsons are still at school and will not be here tomorrow, of course. Anthony is at Cambridge and George is at Eton. And there you have the whole family to date."

"I shall try to remember who belongs to which branch, ma'am."

"All in good time. You cannot be expected to keep them straight at first," Lady Hollister said with indulgence.

A touch of mischief appeared in Claire's smile as she proceeded to rattle off the married names of Lady Hollister's daughters, their children, spouses, and grandchildren.

"An impressive feat of memory," said Lady Hollister, "and a partial explanation, I would venture to say, for your proficiency at whist."

"Yes, ma'am," Claire agreed, feeling like a vulgar show-off. "A good memory is an advantage."

"Tell me about your family, Claire. Are your parents recently deceased?"

Here it comes, Claire thought in dismay, wishing she knew what tale Egon might have told his grandmother already.

As if she had divined the reason for her hesitation, Lady Hollister prompted, "Egon has had almost nothing to say on the subject of your family except that he has only met the aunt with whom you have recently made your home. I believe you said you are from Northumberland?"

"Yes, Lady Hollister. My family has long been established in the border country in the Cheviot Hills. Do you know the area at all?"

"Only from passing through on my way to Scotland once, when I was much younger. I remember that the scenery was spectacular, with first the hills and then the mountains of Scotland, and that the weather was dreadful, interminably cold and wet." The old woman shivered in remembrance.

Claire smiled. "The winters are long and harsh, it's true, but the swift-flowing burns and waterfalls are wild and wonderful, and spring, though late, is lovely in the north. The inhabitants are a different breed also, fierce and stubborn and taciturn. Our home was not large and luxurious like Belhaven, but it was solidly built of grey stone, and really quite comfortable, while the views over the hills, looking toward the rugged mountains of Scotland, were magnificent."

"Were? Does your brother not live there now that your father is dead?"

"Unfortunately, no, ma'am. My mother died when Jeremy was born. I was a bit over two at the time, and my father's elder sister came and lived with us until she died when I was seventeen. Jeremy was away at school then, a small school in the north. My mother's sister brought me out the next year. After my season, I returned home to keep house for my father. He was a strange man, well-educated, with a poetic bent, given to quick, strong enthusiasms, but not ... not steady, I fear. He was never really at home on the land and could never make it pay. His many business ventures and investments over the years were mostly unsuccessful. I knew we were in financial difficulties, but I never knew how bad things were until ...

until my father went bankrupt and committed suicide last year."

Lady Hollister raised her head and looked Claire straight in the eye. "That must have been a very difficult time for you and your brother," she said with masterly understatement.

"Yes, ma'am, it was. We lost the estate, of course, but my father had had the foresight to secure an apprenticeship for Jeremy with a large bank. I had no dowry … so I came to London."

"To your aunt," Lady Hollister finished for her, and Claire did not correct her misreading of the situation. "Who is this aunt who brought you out? Would I know her?"

"I shouldn't think so, ma'am. She lives rather quietly in Curzon Street. Her name is Mrs. Martin Smedley, and she is a childless widow."

"But she is about to go back to the north country; I remember now." Again Lady Hollister finished with an assumption, and again Claire remained silent, hating herself for the untold lies and furious with Egon for abandoning her to her own devices.

"Egon must have seemed like the answer to a prayer to you," Lady Hollister hinted broadly.

"He did rather," Claire replied with perfect truth.

"My grandson is worthy of a woman's devotion, Claire. I am not saying he is a plaster saint, mind you, but his impulses are generous, his feelings are loyal, and he is a man of honour."

Claire's smile was gentle. "I had reached a similar conclusion, ma'am, and I do not believe I should find a plaster saint at all appealing." She sat quietly and withstood the matriarch's searching look.

"I believe Egon has chosen well," Lady Hollister said after a long moment, and Claire knew that she had been approved.

She fought to keep at bay a pervasive sadness that Egon had not chosen her at all.

"Thank you," she said softly.

"Did Egon tell you that I intended him to marry Miss Winward?" Lady Hollister rapped out, the momentary softness gone.

"No, but Miss Winward did. She also told me she has no real interest in marrying at all, but had given her word to her father some years ago to accept an offer from Egon."

Lady Hollister's slanting brows, which were a feminine version of Egon's, shot up, then drew together. "She never gave me a hint that she was personally unwilling to marry my grandson."

"From our rather brief conversation, I received the impression that Miss Winward is a woman of her word and one who would not let personal preference keep her from performing what she perceived to be her duty."

"I admired her strong-mindedness and her well-bred reserve, but I have come to appreciate that such a woman would not do for Egon. He needs someone with a warmer nature."

"I think so too," said Claire, wishing she were in truth that person.

Claire left the library with a few sheets of pressed paper and an unhappy conviction that she and Lady Hollister would have dealt famously together had she been Egon's true choice for his wife. She retreated to the sitting room in the green suite to pen a long letter to Sadie, taking pains to set down only what would ease her dear friend's anxieties about the mock marriage. She described the beauties of Belhaven in great detail and included a short word sketch of all the temporary and permanent inhabitants, laying stress on the kindness of her reception by Egon's family, including his formidable grandparent. Of her husband she said very little, because what was there to say? It would scarcely gladden Sadie's heart to learn that Egon did not cherish the same high regard for her darling's sterling character as the Mullins family did, nor could she confide the shaming fact that his opinion of her morals was so low that he had actually tried to treat her like one of his light-o'-loves, believing her only stipulation would concern the amount of money that would change hands during the transaction.

When she had finished her letter, Claire was restless and decided to go on down to the drawing room. It was too early for tea, but there was nothing to read in the suite, and she did not wish to interrupt Lady Hollister a second time to seek out a book from the well-stocked shelves she had caught brief tantalizing glimpses of earlier. She had heard the sound of music when she passed the drawing room on her way upstairs after her interview with Lady Hollister. In all probability it had been Jessica playing. She would go in and chat with the girl before the others drifted in for tea. Jessica was a sweet-natured girl, generally quiet in company, but eager to be friendly. Claire sensed that the younger girl was not quite happy. She might be entirely mistaken, and even if it were true, there was no reason to suppose she could do anything to alleviate the situation, but she could at least let Jessica know she stood ready to be her friend.

The drawing room was silent and empty when Claire entered. Jessica must have gone up to freshen her appearance before the rest of the family assembled. As she came slowly into the large rectangular apartment, Claire saw it from a different perspective today, devoid as it was of the distracting human presence. The proportions were gracious and it was a bright room, courtesy of the four long windows looking out at the

179

gardens at the back of the house. The plaster ceiling was delicately patterned. A diamond motif formed the central design element and the background for a chandelier of surpassing beauty. Claire guessed it to be of Venetian manufacture as she approached to get a closer look at the exquisite flowers formed of blown glass that held the candles. Most were clear crystal but some were of an arresting deep rose shade. It would seem that the room's beautiful appointments had been selected to complement the chandelier. The large carpet incorporated the design elements of the ceiling against a deep rose background. The walls had been painted a lighter rose-pink shade above the chair rail, and in combination with the bright white woodwork gave a happy tone to what was actually a formal reception room. A floral-print fabric with a deep rose background covered the seats and oval backs of a handsome set of gilded chairs. A pink-and-white-striped pattern was used for the upholstery of the sofas and on the seats of armless side chairs. Claire travelled slowly around the room, admiring the beautiful and unusual flower arrangements on several tables. Someone at Belhaven had a real flair for creating exuberant riots of massed colour — Mamzell perhaps? The fireplace was made of pink marble, and she wandered up to examine the elaborate gilt-and-porcelain clock on the mantelpiece. It was probably made by Sèvres, and being of the marvellous hue called "rose pompadour," was a perfect accent for this lovely room. She ran the tip of an admiring finger lightly over the smooth porcelain.

"Pricing it, Lady Hollister, or are you merely myopic?"

Claire stiffened, but had herself in command as she turned toward the source of the lightly uttered insult. "Neither, Mrs. Blyden, merely admiring. This is a lovely room," she added, offering an avenue of escape that the beautiful young woman in the doorway elected to spurn as she strolled into the room.

"Yes, it is. The dowager Lady Hollister has excellent taste and the wherewithal to indulge it. I wouldn't count on taking possession in the very near future, though. Despite the cane, the old woman's health is excellent."

"I am happy to hear that." Claire continued to regard the other with a tranquil expression that did not waver under the mocking little lift of one golden-brown eyebrow. Goaded by her failure to rock Claire's composure, Mrs. Blyden continued her attack, assuming a judicious air.

"Yes, Belhaven should certainly qualify as a source of consolation."

Against her better judgment, Claire took the bait. "Consolation?"

"Why, yes. It must have been a bit of a blow to realize that your *beaux yeux* were not solely responsible for Egon's whirlwind courtship, but all this —" she waved a hand that took in the splendid setting — "should go a long way toward making up for any disappointment on the personal side."

"I fear you have lost me, Mrs. Blyden," Claire said, her face a careful blank.

"Oh, come, Cousin Claire; you cannot expect to gull all of us into accepting that a woman who plays such a brilliant game of whist could be so dim as to fail to draw the correct conclusions from the recent presence of Mr. Dawkins at Belhaven."

Claire shook her head slightly. "I am persuaded I may call upon you to draw them for me, Mrs. Blyden."

"Jack certainly didn't swallow Egon's hoaxing tale of finding Lady Hollister's invitation on your return from a wedding trip. The timing is a bit too-happily fortuitous, fortunate for you, that is, not for Jack. He should have known she always meant

Egon to have Belhaven. Why else go to such lengths to get rid of me five years ago? Mustn't let a taint of the shop corrupt the aristocratic Hollister blood."

At that moment, a slight stir in the doorway brought Mrs. Blyden's bitter tirade to a halt. Mademoiselle Ducroix had evidently stopped short just inside the room, and Cyril's nurse had caromed into her. Claire didn't hear the explanations and apologies that ensued, and she was only dimly aware that Mrs. Blyden had left the room with the nurse in a swish of blue skirts. Her mind was trying to make sense of the beautiful Melissa's insinuations. Her eyes met the concerned gaze of Mamzell, hurrying forward.

"Do not distress yourself, *ma p'tite*. Melissa was unkind just now, but I think *peut-être* it was disappointment that made her so, *tu comprends*? One fears that Jack is not the most satisfactory of husbands, and to see Egon again, so charming, so *distingué*, she begins to think it might have been otherwise."

Claire's forehead was furrowed in an effort at concentration. "Was Egon in love with Mrs. Blyden at one time?" she asked bluntly.

"They were — how do you say? — affianced, but just for a short time." Watching Claire's face, Mamzell hurried on. "You did not know? *Ma fois*, why is it that I cannot learn when to *fermer la bouche*?" She struck her forehead with the heel of her hand in a theatrical gesture. "It was finished long ago, *p'tite*. Egon was very angry, *tu comprends*, when Lady 'Ollister say she will cut off his allowance if he marry the daughter of a mill owner, but then Melissa decided she wished to marry Jack instead, so it would not have done in any case, *n'est-ce pas*? It was a very long time ago, and *tout le monde* can see that Egon is in love with you *maintenant, tout a fait boulversé*. You must not dwell on the past. It is over, *fini*. You are to believe that, *chérie*."

"Yes, of course, Mamzell." Claire spoke to comfort the anxious and earnest little woman with the generous heart. She even produced a little smile. Still, it was a profound relief when she heard the tinkle of china that meant Boynton and tea were arriving.

Claire was absent in spirit from the family gathering that afternoon, though she did her best to conceal this. The item of past history she had just learned put a different construction on Egon's attentiveness to Melissa Blyden. Observing them together when Mrs. Blyden slipped into the drawing room and took the chair next to Egon about halfway through the hour, Claire could now see his gallant attendance as the persistence of a long-denied love. It was mostly Melissa who sought out his company, and Egon's manner toward her was not overtly flirtatious, as was Jack Blyden's toward herself whenever his grandmother's attention was fixed elsewhere, but, Claire concluded sadly, that most likely was a measure of how much more important the woman was to him than just a willing partner in a passing flirtation. Mrs. Blyden's unprovoked attack on herself earlier must have been the result of frustration and despair at realizing that she could not go back and undo the mistake she had made in throwing Egon over for his cousin. Claire felt sorry for her, trapped in an unhappy marriage, sorry for Egon, who had lost the woman he wanted, and sorry for herself that she had ever set eyes on that intelligent and brooding face of his that could flash into laughter and youthful high spirits when least expected. She must overcome the morbid fascination the man exercised over her enslaved emotions if she was to come out of this unhappy imbroglio with a shred of dignity to her name.

It was a physical impossibility for Claire to choke down any of the Madeira cake Mamzell had insisted on setting at her elbow. Even the cooling tea felt harsh passing across the back of her throat, which seemed to close up against it. She longed to get right away from Belhaven, but she was bound by her bargain with Egon to remain until he wished to leave. One would think in a house as large as this one that people could coexist without ever coming into contact with each other, but the truth was that it was almost impossible to secure even a few moments of privacy without having to account for one's time. They were shackled by the conventions of mannerly behaviour.

Egon had been sending thoughtful glances her way for the past half-hour and had even directed one or two remarks to her, something he had not been in the habit of doing the past two days, since their skirmish on the battlefield known as the marriage bed on their wedding night. Claire did not think she could bear to be cross-questioned and put under a microscope by that probing intelligence in her present state, but in a few moments everyone would begin to melt away to dress for dinner. It would be a simple matter for him to waylay her in their sitting room.

She was no better than a craven coward where this man was concerned, she thought in disgust, cudgelling her wits for a way to avoid a meeting. She was bound and determined not to go back to their quarters right away, at least not until she could be reasonably certain that Estelle would be there waiting for her.

CHAPTER 12

Claire shivered a little in the cool damp atmosphere of the conservatory. She'd dismissed the library as a temporary refuge, thinking any member of the household might wander in there at any time. The chances seemed much better that she would have this place to herself at this hour. It had been no problem to linger in the drawing room on the pretext of finishing her tea when people had begun a general exodus. After Michael, who had stopped to scoop up a final slice of cake to hold him until dinner, winked at her and disappeared through the door, she had waited another minute or two before heading for the conservatory. If anyone asked for an accounting of her time, she would explain her detour as a sudden wish to explore this interesting appendage to the house, she decided with a little upward thrust of her chin that was intended as a courage builder.

The conservatory was not at its best at this early-evening hour. The sole illumination was provided by the remnants of daylight left behind by the sinking sun. As Claire wandered slowly down one side, everything within was bathed in a murky green gloom that suited her mood. She noted an abundance and variety of vegetation, but no specimen, however exotic, was likely to divert her thoughts from the complicated situation she had landed herself in at Belhaven.

Claire was barely halfway through the tour when someone tapped her on the shoulder. Having been too self-absorbed to hear any sounds outside of her own head, she jumped half a foot and let out a squeak of alarm. Whirling to confront the smiling figure of her husband's cousin Jack, she gasped indignantly, "Good heavens, do you always sneak up on people like that?"

"Every chance I get, if my victims look as pretty as you do with sparks in those gorgeous cat's eyes," he drawled, pleased with himself.

It would have given Claire enormous satisfaction to wipe the smug look off his handsome face with the palm of her hand, but the tenets of civilized behaviour held her back. She said dryly, "I shouldn't imagine such tactics would increase your popularity with the fair sex, Cousin Jack."

"Popularity with the fair sex has never been one of my problems, Cousin Claire."

"Well, it is about to become a problem if you followed me out here with the idea of embarking on a squalid little flirtation," she snapped, abandoning the restraints of good manners. She could not see that her forthright speech had had much effect. He looked at her a bit more searchingly, but that irritating self-confidence was still apparent in his voice and manner as he decreased the distance between them to an uncomfortable proximity, shaking his head slowly.

"You have not convinced me that your prim speeches reflect your true sentiments, Cousin Claire. Those slumberous yellow eyes and that glorious mouth belie your words."

"The words that spring to mind at the moment, sir, are 'egotistical' and 'insufferable.' Is that plain enough for your understanding? Now, let me pass, please. There is really no more to be said in this context."

She had succeeded in eradicating his complacent smile, but the calculating expression that replaced it gave her pause. Escape became Claire's chief aim, but she made the strategic error of trying to brush past him.

"Not so fast, Miss Pickles and Prunes," he said on a sneering note, catching her by the elbow and whirling her around into his arms. "I think you owe me a little compensation for my pains, so I'll collect now."

Some instinct told Claire this man would welcome the excuse to hurt her that any struggling on her part would provide him. She stood perfectly still within his grip and disciplined herself to ignore the cruel pressure of his mouth on hers, willing herself elsewhere mentally. The hateful interval seemed to go on for an eternity, but she fought to remain totally unresponsive, though the ache in her neck from being bent backward was nearly intolerable. She was becoming afraid she would faint before the smothering pressure finally abated, but the blessed release and her cold steady anger gave her the necessary dignity to present him with a blank mask when he shoved her away from him at last.

"You have had your tawdry little revenge, sir, but even a cretin like yourself could not claim to have enjoyed it."

"Up to your old tricks, I see, Jack."

Egon's crisp interruption drove the colour from Claire's cheeks, but it had the opposite effect on Mr. Blyden, who gritted his teeth and faced his cousin with what aplomb he could call upon as he put up a languid hand to flick an imaginary speck from his lapel.

"It would be in better taste to give some slight warning when you are about to commit the solecism of intruding upon a tryst, coz," he declared with a mocking bravado that made Claire long to hit him.

Egon was unmoved by these heroics. "That won't wash this time. I heard too much. Your technique wants mending, Jack."

"I'd love to stay and exchange notes with you on this fascinating topic, but I fear it would put the lovely Claire to the blush, and I would hate to offend her when we have just passed such an enjoyable time together. *Au revoir*, Claire."

Claire wrenched her eyes from Jack Blyden's jaunty exit to glance uncertainly into her husband's dark face. Did that muscle twitching in his cheek mean he was not so unmoved by this scene as he had appeared?

"Did you arrange to meet him here?"

"No." A stubborn streak in her makeup prevented her from elaborating or offering excuses.

"Then why did you come out here?"

"I wanted some privacy, but I might as well have drawn a map with my path marked in red," she replied in some exasperation.

"When you did not appear in the suite, I set off to find you."

"Well, you succeeded. What did you mean when you implied that you had seen — or heard, rather — too much to believe your cousin's implications?"

"Just what I said. I heard most of what passed between you as I approached."

"It did not cross your mind to rescue me from his clutches?"

"I was not absolutely sure you wished to be rescued."

"Heaven forbid that you should commit a *faux pas* when you come upon your wife in a compromising position," she said with some bitterness.

"Why didn't you resist his embrace?"

"He would have liked that, and I was not in the mood to afford him any masculine enjoyment. Now, if you have finished the inquisition, I would like to go upstairs and get ready for another happy family dinner."

"Wait, Claire, I'd like to explain. You could not possibly know what my relationship has been with Jack. Suffice it to say that anything I ever had over the years turned out to be precisely what Jack coveted most. That has been the story of our lives."

"And does that not apply equally to you?"

He was frowning. "What do you mean?"

"The beautiful Melissa," she said, staring squarely into eyes as dark and unfathomable as midnight.

Egon was silent so long that Claire's glance wavered, and she made a movement to step around him. For the second time in ten minutes, a man prevented her escape from his disturbing company by grabbing her arm. Egon did not attempt to embrace her, however. He simply held both her arms above the elbows in a non-threatening grip. "I don't know what you've been told," he began, "but there is no reason to conceal the past from you. You seem to be discovering all the family skeletons anyway."

A little smile flickered across his mouth. It really was a quite beautiful mouth at times. Claire looked away, painfully aware of that throbbing tension between them again. She forced herself to concentrate on her husband's words.

"Melissa's brother was at Oxford with me. I met her at her father's home over five years ago, fell tail over top in love, and promptly proposed. My grandparents had raised me after my parents died. When I brought my fiancée here to meet them, I was shattered to find they did not intend that their heir should contract what they considered a *mésalliance* by bringing a mill owner's daughter into the family. I stood out against them in a fine fit of righteousness, determined to live on my small inheritance, only to discover before a sennight had passed that Melissa had changed her mind and now preferred Jack. My grand gesture went for naught. That is the whole story. You already know the rest — about the plan to arrange a marriage with Miss Winward. At that point, I lit out and had no contact with any member of my family until I returned to England last month. Now you know all the past history."

She shook her head, looking at him with sad and sympathetic eyes. "Except that it isn't past for you as far as Melissa Blyden is concerned, is it? I am very sorry, Egon."

"You are wasting your pity," he said, giving her a slight shake. A gentle smile transformed his face in the shadowed conservatory. "I promise you I am no longer in love with Melissa, but it is a welcome change to inspire some kinder thoughts from you. Sweet Claire. Kind and gentle and wise Claire." His voice sank to a caressing whisper.

"I … I must go and dress or I'll be late for dinner." Claire's breathing was becoming difficult and she attempted to break free, but Egon's hold tightened just enough to prevent it.

"Claire, I don't want you to remember Jack's kiss. Remember mine instead."

She should have run for her life at that point, but Claire stood mesmerized by her husband's nearness and the new note in his voice. Egon pulled her to him very slowly, his seeking eyes holding hers prisoner. His lips were warm on hers and very gentle. Claire sighed and surrendered to the solace of that kiss. Soon, however, nameless, hitherto unexperienced waves of feeling swept her whole being in the embrace of his hard-muscled body. Time and place, problems and personalities all dissolved in that racing tide of feeling. A force beyond Claire's comprehension drove her to meet and match his ardour. She was mindless and breathless, quivering with sensation when Egon finally ended the embrace. Despite the need to draw breath, something inside her protested dumbly at the ebbing of the charge of emotion that had flowed between them. For another second or two he held her with her face turned into his shoulder while he steadied his own breathing; then he put her a little away from him with his hands on her shoulders to gaze solemnly down into dazed eyes.

"I wasn't prepared for that," Egon admitted.

The mists cleared from Claire's eyes and her mind as she took in his uncertain expression. What had she done? How could she have revealed...? "Oh, no!" she moaned, pushing against his chest to gain her release. "Why did you have to do that?" she said shakily; then she spun about and fled without giving him a chance to reply.

It took some planning and a modicum of luck, but Claire managed to evade any close association with her husband for the rest of that evening. It was necessary to call upon all her training to present a picture of a carefree bride enjoying herself in the midst of her husband's family. Fortunately, two powerful motivating forces — the desire to uphold her end of the bargain she had made with Egon and the desperate need to recover her own dignity in the aftermath of the revealing scene in the conservatory — operated to overcome the dragging depression of spirits that would have left her cowering in her room otherwise. Though she made sure she was never alone with Egon, she noted his solicitous regard for her comfort and convenience and was grateful for it on one level. On the deepest level, she cringed with internal humiliation that he must indeed have divined her foolish feelings and was moved to pity her.

Music was again the form that the evening's entertainment took, and Claire was happy to lose herself in performing. Despite a firm resolve not to watch her husband, she could tell that her singing greatly pleased him. The approval in his eyes tonight was balm to her smarting soul. The time passed smoothly enough, though at a crawling pace that set Claire's teeth on edge. She was drained of emotional energy by the time the company dispersed for the night, but contrary to her fears, she dropped into bed and fell asleep within minutes of coming upstairs.

The morning dawned cloudy and cooler than the brilliant autumn weather they had been experiencing since her arrival in Sussex. Michael and Jack both decided to ride over to their respective homes to keep abreast of what had been happening in their absence. Egon accepted Michael's invitation to accompany him. Michael and Jessica were residing near his parents' estate, a distance of ten miles from Belhaven, so they expected to be back for lunch. Jack, on the other hand, would need most of the day to accomplish his mission. Claire was forced to dissemble her pleasure at seeing him take himself out of her orbit for a long stretch of hours. He had been somewhat free with purring little jabs at her last night that had brought a speculative gleam to his wife's eyes and a look of fastidious distaste to his grandmother's face after a while.

Melissa had the headache again and planned to remain in her rooms that morning. Claire and Jessica offered their services to Mademoiselle Ducroix for any outstanding housekeeping chores in preparation for additional overnight guests after the birthday celebration. The Frenchwoman accepted their assistance in freshening the existing floral arrangements and creating new ones from the flowers MacDougall reluctantly sent up to the house from the cutting garden. By late morning the three women had accomplished this pleasant task, and Mamzell waved her helpers off with instructions to take the air into their lungs and stretch their legs before the threatening rain should prevent it.

"A brisk walk through the orchards sounds like a perfect antidote to standing in one spot for hours doing the flowers," Claire said. "Shall we, Jessica?"

"Well, Michael and Egon might be returning soon."

"Before lunchtime, do you think? It is only a bit after eleven now."

"Oh. Very well, I'll get my shawl and meet you at the side door directly."

Claire was pensive as she waited for the younger girl by the entrance. Jessica had seemed somewhat subdued this morning, responding rather mechanically to the other two women. More than ever Claire was convinced that something troubled her. It was not in Claire's nature to walk by a person in trouble without making a push to help, and she tackled Jessica on the subject when they had walked for better than ten minutes with Jessica's share of the conversation limited to monosyllabic agreements to Claire's observations on the serene beauty of the grounds.

"Is anything the matter, Jessica?" she asked point-blank, stopping to look at the forlorn little face with its drooping lips and unhappy, evasive brown eyes.

"No, of course not. What could be the matter with a new bride? Belhaven is a lovely place to visit. I am having a wonderful time." Her voice faltered at the end after a bright beginning.

Claire was silent for a moment, mulling over the possibilities inherent in the girl's answer. She had been told in civil terms to mind her own business, and she was going to do just that, but it couldn't hurt to make one last stab at uncovering the problem. "As it happens, I can envision a number of problems that might beset a new bride," she said softly. "Have you known Michael long, Jess?"

"We met in late May, near the end of the season."

"And when did he offer for you?"

"Two weeks later, just before my parents took me back home to Somerset. We were married late in August."

"And did you see much of him during the period of your betrothal?"

"Nothing at all, actually. Everything happened so fast that Michael and his father had to set about finding a place for us to live, and then the house needed some urgent repairs, so Michael stayed in Sussex to supervise the work."

"In other words, you only knew him for a fortnight. Essentially you were marrying a stranger. It takes time to become quite comfortable with one's husband, I imagine."

"Oh, it's not that, Claire," Jessica said. "Right from the beginning I felt completely at home with Michael. We liked the same people and laughed at the same things. I was not coerced into accepting him, or anything of that nature."

"I see. I thought myself that you appeared to be a well-matched couple when we first met."

Claire walked on, saying nothing more, and after a moment the younger girl said on a wistful note, "You have such poise, Claire, and self-confidence. So does Melissa. I imagine it comes from being beautiful."

Claire gave a negative shake to her head. "I am not beautiful in any classic sense, Jess, but I am comfortable with my own looks and with myself as a person. And so should you be. You are a very pretty girl and a nice person. Michael obviously knew this within two weeks, or he would not have popped the question so quickly."

"But now he's sorry he did."

Claire stopped and faced her friend, who retreated rapidly.

"I shouldn't have said that. Pray forget I did." Jessica began to walk on, but Claire caught up with her and stopped her with a hand on her arm.

"But you did say it, Jess, so it must be bothering you. Why do you imagine Michael is regretting your marriage?" She stood quietly, waiting for the small, slight girl to overcome her hesitation.

Jessica was clasping her hands together in front of her and twisting her fingers. "I was very nervous on our wedding night, and … and I fear I acted like a baby. It … hurt so much, you see, and I cried and couldn't stop crying. Michael became very upset and kept apologizing until I screamed at him to stop. Then he got very quiet and dignified and said he would not trouble me again. And he hasn't!" she wailed, coming to an abrupt end.

"You mean you haven't … not since your wedding night?"

"No. He hasn't come to my room once, and I don't know what to do about it. I mean, I cannot boldly ask him to come to me if he doesn't wish it. How could I? I was counting on this visit to Belhaven to change things after I found that we had been given a suite with only one bedchamber. But … but Michael never comes upstairs until he thinks I'm asleep; then he sleeps on that stupid little cot in the dressing room, and to make matters worse, that wretched Jack caught me by surprise in the garden the other day and kissed me, and Michael saw him. Now he is barely speaking to me. What can I do, Claire?"

Claire stood in appalled silence at what her probing had uncovered. Obviously poor Jessica considered her a worldly-wise woman to whom nothing so humiliating could happen. She stared at the ground, wondering what the girl would think if she knew her chosen confessor had threatened to crush her own bridegroom's skull on her wedding night. As Claire swallowed against hysterical laughter, Jessica said timidly, "Even if I could somehow find the courage to bring this out in the open, Michael might just push me away. Lately it seems he cannot even bear to sit beside me!"

The misery in the young girl's voice galvanized Claire's scattered mental faculties into working order. "Jess, I am persuaded Michael doesn't wish to hurt you. It is only a guess on my part, but I would say that his patience may be wearing thin and he is finding it difficult to be near you constantly when he feels he cannot touch you. He would probably welcome frankness on the subject from you, but I appreciate that you feel unable to speak of this," she added hastily as the girl's eyes dilated with alarm. "Therefore, you must focus your attention on indirect means to the same purpose.

"I gather tonight's dinner is going to be very festive, and Mamzell told me Lady Hollister has engaged some musicians to play at dinner and later for impromptu dancing if enough people desire it. Michael will have to dance with you, hold you. It's up to you to turn this to your advantage. There will be all sorts of things to drink also. They say alcohol diminishes inhibitions. We'll see that Michael's glass is kept filled during the evening, but the single most crucial point is that you go upstairs together. If he seems determined to play billiards till dawn, then you'll simply have to swoon in his arms or something so he'll have to carry you up to your room."

"It sounds a bit ... devious," Jessica said doubtfully.

Claire's laugh was spontaneous and genuine. "So it is, but the straight path to an object is not always available. These tactics may not succeed tonight, Jess, but you will wear him down in time. I am persuaded Michael is no happier than you at this stalemate."

The two had been walking where their feet carried them without paying much heed to their surroundings. They had just crested a hill, on the other side of which lay a stretch of ornamental water, fringed on the banks by plantings and shrubs set around much of its perimeter. One huge chestnut tree at the water's edge spread its branches in a wide circle. One main branch extended out over the lake for some considerable distance. On a sunny day, it must be an enchanting sight, but the clouds had melded together in the last half-hour, and rain seemed imminent.

"Goodness, look at the sky. I didn't notice how black it was getting while we were in the orchard," Claire said. "It's time we turned back if we have any hope of avoiding a wetting."

Jessica was standing quite still. Now she held up a hand. "Hush … listen. Do you hear a faint whimper or something?"

Claire listened as directed for a moment and said doubtfully, "I hear something, but I'm not sure what it might be — a strange bird call perhaps?"

"It sounds more like a child's whimper." Jessica put her hands up to her mouth and called, "Halloooo!"

This time an unmistakable answering call came back, and the two young women began to hurry down the hill, calling out as they went.

"It's Cyril!" yelled Claire, who had outdistanced Jessica. "He's up in the tree." She stood as close to the edge of the water as she could get and looked up with an assessing eye. The child was no more than ten feet above her, but he was perched on an alarmingly narrow limb that branched off from the main one that reached out over the water.

"How did you get way out there, Cyril?" she asked in a matter-of-fact voice. "You must be a very good tree climber."

"I was chasing a lost kitten, and it came up here," replied the little boy on a sob. "I came up the tree to get it, but it jumped to another branch and then went down again. And now I cannot get down."

"Certainly you can," Claire argued cheerfully. "All you have to do is move backward along your branch until you come to the big one. If you like, I'll come up and help you down when you get to the big one."

"I can't go backward," cried the child. "Every time I try, the branch makes a scary noise."

Jessica had come up by now, and the two exchanged a look of dismay. There was no possibility that the narrow branch would take any extra weight. Claire made another attempt to calm the child's fear. "Cyril, perhaps the strange noises have stopped. Will you try again to move back toward the big branch?"

The boy gulped and nodded. As the girls peered anxiously up from below, he unwrapped his arms from the limb and prepared to try to inch backward. With his first movement, the branch creaked ominously and he froze.

"That's all right, Cyril. Don't try going backward anymore. We'll get you down another way." Claire turned to the frightened Jessica and whispered, "Run, Jess, as fast as you can, up to the stables and bring back some of the men — and a rope," she added aloud as Jessica left on the instant.

Another creaking noise, louder this time, brought her eyes back to the child. "Did you move again, Cyril?"

"N-no, but my arms are getting awfully tired, Cousin Claire."

Claire attempted to gauge the distance the boy would have to crawl backward before he could drop into her arms, but she feared the branch would break before he could come close enough. If that happened, he would drop into the water. If she lunged for him, she could pitch headfirst into the lake herself. There was the additional grim possibility that the falling branch might hit her before she could catch Cyril. Even as she speculated on how long it might take Jessica to return with help, the branch gave a loud splitting sound and the child cried out as he nearly lost his perch in the dipping of the branch.

That ended speculation for Claire. Still with her eyes on Cyril while she murmured soothing noises, she was casting off her heavy shawl. She'd keep her shoes on — no telling what the bottom was like.

"What are you doing, Cousin Claire?"

"I am going into the water, love, to catch you." She sat on the bank and started to ease her way into the water. "Ohhhh!" she gasped. No matter how one tried to prepare oneself for the shock of cold water against one's skin, it remained one of the nastiest sensations one could experience. She slid forward, clamping her teeth against another exclamation. It took courage to give up her precarious seat on the bank, but her hesitation was wiped out as Cyril began to cry in earnest. She went into the water with the slick speed of an eel and found to her unutterable relief that she was able to stand up when she had manoeuvred her way to the spot beneath the sobbing child.

"Cyril, my pet, listen to me. Open your eyes. I'm right down here below you. Let go of the branch and drop down, and I'll catch you."

"I don't want to jump in the water, Cousin Claire."

"I know, dear. It's cold," she agreed in the same cheerful voice, "but, you see, that branch you are on is going to break soon, and when that happens you will fall anyway. The problem is that if the branch hits me when it falls, I shan't be able to catch you. Can you swim, love?"

"No, but my papa is going to teach me next summer."

"Well, then, you don't wish to have to swim today before you have learned properly, do you?"

"N-no."

199

"You don't really have to jump, you know. If you just keep holding on with your hands while you swing your legs off the branch, your legs will be almost down here near my arms already. Then you'll just let go, and I'll catch you. Will you do that for me, my love?"

"Y-yes."

"Good boy." Claire was praying madly, incoherent, wordless prayers, as she continued to coax the frightened child into releasing his illusory hold on safety. Inch by cautious inch he moved one leg off his perch, and then everything happened in an instant. As the branch tore, he lost his hold and fell into Claire's upraised arms with an impact that drove her under briefly. She kicked backward strongly off her feet, and none too soon, for the falling branch grazed her shoulder, tearing her dress. She was conscious of Cyril's choking sobs and a stinging pain in her shoulder as she struggled to get upright again. How long had it been since Jessica had gone for assistance? There was no hope of climbing out of the lake without help; the bank was too steep here. She was casting her eyes around, seeking a spot where the edge was more accessible, when she heard a shout from the top of the hill. Her relieved brain shut down operations immediately; thinking was too difficult in the numbing cold water.

Claire watched in an unconnected daze as Egon splashed into the water beside her and took the child from her arms. One of the stable lads was carrying a rope, but it was Michael who leaned over the bank and took Cyril from his cousin. She was vaguely aware that Jessica was wrapping the boy in Michael's coat while the men tossed the rope to Egon. Claire was too cold by now to do anything for herself. Egon, muttering under his breath, knotted the rope about her waist and she found herself boosted from behind and hauled up onto the bank like a bundle of wet wash. She never actually saw Egon's exit from the lake because Jessica was insisting on wrapping her own warmed shawl around her friend's shivering form. Suddenly Egon was there beside her, shrugging back into his coat, and the next thing she knew, she was being carried in his arms.

"I can walk," she protested feebly, more from duty than desire.

"Not in those hampering wet skirts, or I'd let you," he said shortly. "You need all the warmth we can muster between us. That was a very brave thing you just did, Claire."

"There was nothing else to do. The branch was about to break."

"I gather the imp gave his keeper the slip again, but what in God's name inspired him to climb out on a limb that overhung the water?"

"He was chasing a kitten," she replied as if that explained everything, and her husband must have agreed, because he said nothing more.

Egon was breathing rather heavily when the straggling party breasted the hill and saw the gig coming toward them, driven by a stable hand. "That was good thinking, Dudeney," he said. "I'll take it back to the house, and you can send someone for it. Do you think you can hold Cyril on your lap, Claire? You both need to get warm and dry as soon as possible."

In short order Claire was seated in the gig, holding the shivering child close. Egon drove off before she had finished delivering her thanks to Jessica and the rescue party.

"You can thank everyone later. Warmth before manners at this point. Hold on, this next part is going to be bumpy until we get back to the gravel."

And bumpy it was. At times Egon had to steady her with a hand on her arm, for her arms were holding the now-quiet little boy close.

"That water was damned cold," Egon said after emitting a sneeze as they reached the gravel path.

"Not as cold as Northumberland burns," she said through chattering teeth.

"Are you really from Northumberland?"

Claire turned and stared at him. "Of course I am."

"There's no 'of course' about it. I don't know what is true and what isn't, from what little you've told me about yourself."

"I haven't lied to you, Egon. I just haven't told you the whole truth. Ours was a pure business arrangement. There was no need for you to know the story of my life."

"Would you tell me now if I asked nicely?"

There was only the briefest hesitation before she said, "Yes."

Egon's eyes were darkly serious. "Thank you. Here we are. First things first." He dropped the reins and jumped down from the gig, striding around to the other side.

"Down you come, young man," Egon said, holding up his arms to the bedraggled little boy.

CHAPTER 13

Claire heard a knock on the sitting-room door. She glanced at the mantel clock as she entered from her bedchamber. Almost time for tea. Where had the day gone? She must have dropped off to sleep after all, though she had protested that she did not wish to lie down upon her bed after she had warmed her bones in the tub and enjoyed the luxury of having her hair washed by Estelle.

Egon had come in to report that Cyril had been bathed, fed, and popped into bed for the rest of the day, over his vociferous objections. His mother had said at lunch that he had been asleep within ten minutes, protests notwithstanding. Food had been sent up to Claire on a tray also. When her husband entered she was wrapped in her green velvet dressing gown, sitting on a footstool and drinking tea in front of the fire. Egon's eager step had slowed on catching sight of Estelle kneeling behind her mistress, carefully brushing out the half-dry mane. His words had been prosaic enough, but the look in his eyes had been as warming to her spirit as the fire at her back. A little smile tugged her lips upward as she recalled her ingratitude in wishing at that moment that her devoted little handmaiden might vanish in a puff of smoke.

That had not happened, of course. After making his report, Egon had added the weight of his persuasion to Estelle's exhortation to her mistress to retire to her bed until teatime. With the mental reservation that she would get up as soon as her hovering attendants left her alone, she had allowed herself to be persuaded into her bed and between the sheets.

And the result was that she had slept half the day away, but she certainly felt marvellously refreshed. She tossed her hair back over her shoulder and pulled open the door.

At the sight of Melissa Blyden, Claire's smile lost something of its spontaneity, but she kept it fixed on her lips as she stepped back. "Come in, Mrs. Blyden. I must apologize for my appearance. I actually fell asleep."

"You and Cyril," Mrs. Blyden said with a little smile. "He's still fathoms under." She came slowly into the centre of the room and turned to face Claire with less than her customary self-possession. Her hands were linked loosely in front of her delicate muslin gown of buttercup yellow that looked as if it had just left the hands of the presser. Claire felt at a decided disadvantage, but that was nothing new. There could not be many women who would appear to advantage beside the exquisite Mrs. Blyden.

"I came to thank you for saving my child's life," Melissa said, her deep blue eyes grave.

Claire squirmed in embarrassment. "It was nothing so dramatic as that, Mrs. Blyden, and I was not the only person involved in rescuing Cyril, you know."

"If you had not been on the scene this morning, Cyril would have drowned," Melissa said, quietly insistent. "Jessica cannot swim, and the men would not have reached him in time."

"I too am very thankful I was there this morning. Cyril is a rather special child, so bright and friendly and adventurous, and he was very brave during the whole ordeal, despite being badly frightened."

Melissa smiled with real charm this time. "I hope you will excuse my partiality if I say I agree with you; he is indeed rather more advanced than most children his age." Her eyes fell beneath Claire's smiling regard, and she seemed to gather her thoughts together as she looked up again. "That was not my only reason for seeking you out, perhaps not even the most important reason. I was abominably uncivil to you yesterday — not that those tame words convey the whole sense of what I did. I wanted to injure you, and I'm afraid I said what I thought would hurt you most. I would not blame you if you found it impossible to forgive such conduct, but I do apologize most sincerely." Blue eyes searched amber-brown ones as Melissa paused to draw a difficult breath.

Claire could appreciate what it cost this proud woman to apologize to her. Trying to ease the situation, she said gently, "Please, let us try to forget that it happened, Mrs. Blyden. I think I understand."

Melissa's soft mouth twisted momentarily into a wry grimace. "I wonder if you do. Frankly, I doubt anyone who was not married to such a man could possibly comprehend what it is really like to have to sit back and watch his manoeuvres to attach every attractive female who crosses his path. One would think I'd be used to it by now," she finished bitterly.

Claire stared. "Are you referring to your own husband, Mrs. Blyden?"

"Of course. Who else?"

"Oh. From what you said yesterday, I fear I rather jumped to the conclusion that you were still in love with Egon and —"

"I was never in love with Egon Hollister," Melissa said.

"B-but were you not betrothed to him?"

"Yes. I liked Egon very much indeed from the moment we were introduced, and I was flattered by his attentions. It was very heady stuff for a girl who would not ordinarily be received in the upper echelon of society to be courted by an attractive man who belonged to that class and stood to inherit a title to boot. I was thrilled to accept his offer, and we might have made a fairly successful match of it had I not met Jack." Melissa stared off into the middle distance, her mouth a tight line of repression. "There are times when I wish I had never met him, but I did, and that's the end of it. Or rather, that was the beginning." Still staring at an inner vision, Melissa lifted her shoulders and dropped them in a fatalistic shrug. "Sometimes I wonder: if I had known at nineteen what I now know of his nature, would I have had the sense to run back to Egon before it was too late? Probably not. I fell in love with Jack, and that was all that mattered."

"I … I don't believe he means anything by … by his little flirtations," Claire offered in an awkward attempt at comfort.

"Oh, no," Melissa agreed, "but it has gradually been borne in upon me that he'll never change, and they are more than little flirtations if the woman of the moment can be persuaded beyond that point. That's why I was so annoyed with you yesterday. With that cool self-possession of yours, you give very little away, and I could not be sure that your hasty marriage really meant anything to you."

Claire stared into speculative blue eyes, amazed that she had not been as transparent as she had feared.

"There was no excuse for trying to cast doubt on Egon's affection for you, Claire. I am really ashamed of myself for trying to hurt you simply because I had been hurt. I don't say this just because you saved Cyril. I knew last night that you must have spurned Jack's advances, and I was already regretting my actions then."

"You did?"

"Jack was behaving like a spoiled child after dinner, which is always an indication that he did not get his own way. Jessica is afraid of him, you are a match for him, and Miss Winward doesn't appeal to him. At least the rest of this visit should pass smoothly, for all the other guests tonight are family members."

"I … I'm glad," Claire said inadequately. Melissa's weary candour aroused compassion for her unenviable situation, but that pride of hers would reject any expression of it on her part, she was certain.

"Thank you, Claire. You are more forgiving than I deserve. I will offer one small excuse, if I may. Ordinarily I would not have attacked you like that, but I am increasing again and have not felt myself lately. Also I cannot forget that it was when I was expecting Cyril that Jack first began to cast his eyes at other women. I am not looking forward to the next months. Jack covets beauty in all forms and has a real aversion to anything that is ugly. He came to avoid me during the last months before Cyril was born, after I grew awkward and grotesque."

"You could never be that," Claire assured her, "and I think it is not uncommon that men become very nervous of their wives during this period, and afraid of hurting them. Also, some may experience a strange sort of guilt because they are responsible for their wives' condition. It will be worth it, though, when you produce another beautiful child like Cyril."

Melissa had listened with a questioning look to Claire's earnest words. Now her enchanting smile flashed out. "You sound like an old and wise grandmother, which is incongruous when you are standing there looking like a schoolgirl with your hair hanging down your back. I do thank you for your kindness, Claire. I think Egon is a fortunate man. I hope you appreciate that you are fortunate too, my dear. When I knew Egon five years ago he was a carefree, likable young man, nothing more. Now I sense a solid strength and maturity in him. How wonderful to have that strength always at your back.

Before I go, I should say in Jack's defence that he really does love me in his own fashion, and he is a marvellous father to Cyril; in fact, he is very good with all creatures that are young and helpless, animals and children."

After Melissa left, Claire was pensive as she wound her hair into a simple chignon and slipped into the rose-coloured cotton for tea. Melissa had really unburdened her soul to one who was a near-stranger, perhaps because the potential tragedy for her child had stripped away some of the pride she generally paraded to cloak her disappointing marriage. Hopefully, she would not regret having let her hair down when her relief for Cyril's safety settled into a more normal state of mind. Claire had been uncomfortably conscious of the animosity she had aroused in Egon's former fiancée, though she had misconstrued the cause, and she would have liked to believe it was permanently ended.

As Claire was slipping a fresh handkerchief into the embroidered wristband of her sleeve, Estelle came in and proceeded to scold her mistress for not ringing for her. She tut-tutted at the plain coiffure and was only dissuaded from pulling it apart by Claire's promise that she might have a free hand at creating a new one for the dinner party.

Melissa Blyden's visit had made Claire a bit late for the afternoon tea ritual. As she approached the drawing room, a mixed chorus of voices accompanied by the tinkle of china floated out to her. She knew she would be the focus of attention and prepared to treat the next few moments as if this were her first entrance in a play, with her opening speech looming as the most significant hurdle to get past before she fell into the rhythm of the performance.

Actually, she got past the initial awkwardness quickly, thanks to Egon, who came to meet her and escort her into the room.

He smiled at her and said with a teasing inflection, "Melissa tells me that the young lady who spurned the idea of resting on her bed after her adventure slept the afternoon away."

Claire went a delicate pink and admitted her weakness as Lady Hollister declared, "There is no denying nature. Our bodies demand to be restored, no matter how much our intellects or our wills would have it otherwise. You look none the worse for your cold ducking, my dear Claire."

"Oh, no, ma'am. I am perfectly fine. I only hope Cyril will not suffer any untoward effects."

Melissa spoke up then. "I popped into the nursery just before coming here and found Cyril in perfect health and tearing spirits, sitting up in his bed playing with his toy soldiers. He has already forgotten the bad fright he had and is rather regarding the accident as a lark by now. I don't fear any lingering consequences for him. Poor Grimstead, his nurse, is the one whose suffering is likely to be prolonged. She is heaping coals of fire upon her head for allowing him to escape her custody again."

"Grimstead is getting too old to have the complete care of an active child," Lady Hollister said.

"Perhaps he needs a male attendant," Michael suggested. "Someone who would encourage his adventurous spirit."

"It doesn't want encouragement!" Melissa cried. "Heavens, that is the problem. He is too adventurous for a four-year-old."

"But you would not wish to suppress a boy's natural thirst for excitement and new worlds to conquer, Melissa," Egon said, entering the discussion. "His father ran wild over his own estate and here at Belhaven too."

As if on cue, Cyril's father came striding through the door, still wearing buckskins and top boots, though he had shed hat and gloves. "What is all this about Cyril falling into the lake today?" he demanded of his wife. "They were full of the story down at the stables when I rode in just now. Did Claire really save his life?" The concerned parent glanced from Claire, who was disclaiming any such heroics, to Melissa, who gave him a rapid description of the morning's incident, her story augmented once or twice by Jessica.

Jack listened in horrified silence until Melissa finished her tale with a picture of Cyril as she had left him a half-hour before. "You do not think we should summon the doctor to look him over?"

Melissa shook her head. "It is not necessary, really, Jack. He hasn't even a sign of a sniffle or a cough."

Jack came over to Claire then. For the first time in their brief acquaintance, that challenging look of the male hunter that raised her hackles was absent from his countenance. He held out his hand and she put hers in it, meeting his serious gaze somewhat warily. "I am eternally in your debt, Claire, for my son's life."

Claire read gratitude and apology in his serious expression as he raised her hand to his lips and pressed a kiss on her fingers before turning to accept the glass of sherry that Egon was holding out to him. He thanked the others for their part in rescuing his son, downed the sherry in two quick swallows, and begged the company to excuse him so that he might run up to the nursery to satisfy himself as to Cyril's present state of health and happiness. "Coming, Melissa?" he asked, holding out his hand. His wife put down her teacup and excused herself to accompany him upstairs.

Lady Hollister stared after the departing couple for a thoughtful moment before returning her attention to her eldest grandson, who had resumed his seat next to his bride. "Tell me, Egon," she said out of the blue, "where do you and Claire plan to live?"

Claire returned her eyes to her cup to hide her surprise at this abrupt change of subject, but Egon replied with no hesitation. "I thought I'd ride over to Hollister Place tomorrow, Gran, to assess just what needs to be done to make it habitable for us. I find I have very little recollection of the estate. It has been many years since I have been there."

"You won't find it as derelict as you may have supposed," Lady Hollister replied over Claire's mounting confusion. "Your grandfather had the roof repaired the year before he died. There is an elderly couple there who see to the house and report any new problems. I had it cleaned thoroughly about a year ago, but I warn you the grounds have been badly neglected of late. You and Claire are most welcome to remain here while you are bringing it into order."

Claire continued to sip her tea while her husband thanked his grandmother for her kindness. Watching them from under her lashes, she was struck anew by the family resemblance. It was more than the eyes and the slant of their brows. Lady Hollister must have been a handsome woman in her youth. With those thin cheeks and sculptured jaw, her face would have been too angular for conventional prettiness, but the lovely eyes must have dominated her face, and the obvious look of intelligence and presence, for want of a better word, would have made her stand out in any group of ordinary young ladies. There was a mental kinship between Lady Hollister and her grandson that she became increasingly aware of as this visit lengthened. At their first meeting she had sensed the wariness and tension in the air, though she had not known then of the long estrangement between the pair. That must have been quite a scene five years ago when two determined personalities clashed head to head over something of vital importance to each. The breach seemed to be healing rapidly, but the *détente* was based on deception. Couldn't Egon see how hurt Lady Hollister would be when he dissolved his marriage? How could he calmly speak of future living arrangements with his bride, knowing that he intended nothing of the sort? She would not have believed him capable of such callousness toward someone he obviously loved. His cavalier attitude toward herself had been understandable, given the unfortunate impressions of her character and morals he had received from the circumstances of their meeting, but his behaviour toward everyone at Belhaven, with the possible exception of his cousin Jack, had been considerate, even affectionate in some cases. Despite her best efforts, Claire could not quite keep her glance free of reproach when Egon smiled at her, though she shaped her lips into a responsive curve for the sake of the others present.

It took longer than usual to complete Claire's toilette on the evening of Lady Hollister's birthday dinner. Estelle had taken her mistress's casual promise to allow her a free hand to create a suitable coiffure quite literally. Upon learning that afternoon that Claire planned to wear a gown of black lace for the festivities, she had begged Mademoiselle Ducroix for some black ostrich feathers, which she produced triumphantly as she set to work removing the pins that anchored the heavy knot of hair. She prattled along, composing a pianissimo accompaniment to the deft movements of her fingers as she rolled and pinned the hair in curls atop the crown. Along with a description of the frantic activity taking place in the kitchen as the staff prepared an elaborate dinner for the influx of guests coming to celebrate with Lady Hollister, she dropped snippets of information about that lady's daughters and various other family members who would be arriving within the hour. Claire produced an occasional murmur of encouragement, but very little that reached her ears penetrated her mind, which was overfull of impressions received during the four days of her stay at Belhaven, a chaotic mass that resembled the complicated patterns and disorder of a tangled skein of yarn.

Under different circumstances, she'd have enjoyed getting ready for the festive evening ahead. She admired the strong-minded matriarch and liked the members of Egon's family she already knew, even including Jack Blyden, now that his attentions had ceased to be a problem. If she were really Egon's wife, she would be looking forward to meeting the rest tonight. As matters stood, however, she felt a complete fraud every time she encountered Lady Hollister's penetrating dark eyes, and this uncomfortable state would be compounded with each new relative presented to her this evening. A kind of anticipatory dread of the ordeal before her must account for the strange sense of excitement that was making her stomach behave oddly. She didn't feel sick exactly, but she was shaky and far from herself as she submitted to Estelle's ministrations like an automaton. The odd sensation had increased each time Egon looked at her as he had been doing all day, a warm glance so full of intimacy that it seemed to isolate the two of them even in a crowded room. Almost from the beginning of their association, she had recognized the danger inherent in the enforced intimacy of this false situation. She had been in control on their wedding night, but the more they were thrown together, the greater had grown her fear that her own developing attachment would betray her common sense. She would have to watch her step very carefully tonight.

Claire sighed and stared unseeingly into the mirror.

"Do you not like the style, Lady Hollister?" Estelle queried anxiously. "I think those long ringlets cascading over your ears from the knot at the crown are most becoming to you, and the black feathers are exciting against the tawny colour. Turn this way and look at it in profile," she urged, pressing a hand mirror into Claire's hands.

Claire returned to the present and obediently followed her handmaiden's directions. She was able to assure Estelle with complete honesty that her hair had never been dressed more becomingly. She agreed that the upswept style made the most of her heart-shaped face and displayed her profile to great advantage. A mild suggestion that one plume might be sufficient was vetoed strongly by the artist, and Claire subsided meekly, thanking the proud abigail instead for her efforts.

It was discovered that the bandage Estelle had applied to the lacerated shoulder after Claire's bath that afternoon was visible beneath the low-cut bodice of the gown. This necessitated the careful removal of the gown so the bandage could be replaced by a smaller version that did not spoil the line of the dress. It was a time-consuming procedure, not without some attendant discomfort for the patient. By the time the gown had been donned again and some necessary repairs made to the elaborate coiffure, Claire was a trifle pale and shaky. She acquiesced to the application of a bit of rouge over her cheekbones and this aid to nature was being added when a knock sounded on the dressing-room door.

Before Estelle could reach the door, Egon, tall and elegant in black-and-white evening dress, entered the bedchamber. He took a few paces forward and stopped at sight of his wife sitting before the dressing-table mirror.

"My word, aren't you beautiful tonight!"

She needn't have bothered with the rouge after all, Claire decided *en passant* as she met her husband's eyes in the mirror. One admiring look from him and she coloured up like a schoolgirl. She laid down the hare's-foot brush and rose from the bench, turning with one sinuous movement to face him.

"Thank you, Egon. May I return the compliment? You are very elegant tonight also." She was pleased with the casual tone she had achieved, a triumph of acting when she considered that her pulses were thrumming under his continued regard. She was also conscious of a beaming Estelle, well-satisfied with this first reaction to her artistic efforts.

Egon was also aware of the maid's presence, for he looked at her and said with a little smile, "Thank you, Estelle. You have achieved wonders with Lady Hollister's hair. She looks even lovelier than usual tonight. Are you quite ready, my dear? It is growing late," he added pointedly to his wife.

"Yes, all ready as soon as I find my handkerchief," Claire said, taking her cue. "Oh, thank you, Estelle." She accepted the matching lace reticule the abigail handed to her and smiled a dismissal. "That will be all for tonight. The company will probably stay downstairs till quite late tonight, so don't wait up for me."

"Very good, my lady." Estelle curtsied and took her reluctant departure, her eyes lingering on the long velvet case in Sir Egon's hands.

When the door to the sitting room had closed softly behind the abigail, Egon opened the case and held it out to his wife. "My man Henley arrived this afternoon. I had him retrieve some of my mother's jewellery from the bank in London. Will you wear these tonight? If you don't care for them, I also have pearls with me."

Claire hoped her eyes weren't starting from her head as she gazed at the magnificent necklace and earrings of rubies set in gold filigree glowing up at her from their box. "Oh, they are beautiful! I'd love to wear them to the party. Thank you for lending them to me, Egon."

She took the earrings from the case that he still held and turned to face the dressing-table mirror as she inserted them. Before she could reach for the necklace, Egon had taken it from the box and come up behind her to fasten it around her neck. She stood perfectly still, hardly daring to breathe as his fingers brushed the sensitive skin at her nape. She could feel her heart hammering beneath the black lace, and heat rose into her cheeks once more while the delicate operation was underway.

Egon did not step back when he had done up the clasp, but stood staring into her eyes in the glass. Claire remained frozen in place until he gripped her shoulders to turn her toward him, whereupon she let out an involuntary gasp of pain.

"What is it? What is wrong?" he demanded, removing his hands.

Her breath quivered back as she gave a tremulous laugh. "Your hand gripped my shoulder where the tree limb cut me this morning. It is nothing, really; it hurt for only a second."

The concern deepened in his eyes. "Why did you not tell me you were hurt at the time? Exactly where is this cut? Who took care of it?"

"It is nothing serious, I promise you, Egon, not deep at all. Estelle bandaged it for me after my bath. The edges of the cut are together and she put basilicum salve on it before bandaging it."

"I'd better see it. I have had a deal of experience with wounds inflicted in battle. Is it the right shoulder?"

"Yes, but she just rebandaged it so it wouldn't show above my gown. It was healing nicely already, truly, Egon. I looked at it in the mirror. It is growing very late. If we keep your grandmother waiting, she'll want an explanation, and it will be most embarrassing in front of all her guests."

"Dammit, who cares a fig for that? I have seen men lose limbs because wounds were neglected."

"Do not exaggerate," Claire said calmly. "I have told you it is nothing serious. You may satisfy yourself on that score later if you wish, but now it is high time we put in an appearance downstairs." She gathered up a black lace stole from atop the bed and headed for the sitting room, relieved to be in command of the situation once more. Egon followed reluctantly, assuring her in no uncertain terms that he meant to have a look at that shoulder before she was a day older.

Claire smiled serenely and kept walking toward the stairs.

CHAPTER 14

As Sir Egon and his bride neared the drawing room, it became apparent from the steady drone of sound emanating from the large apartment that the usual chorus had been enriched by a number of new voices. The baronet had been unusually quiet in the wake of the discovery that Claire had been injured during her heroic rescue of his cousin's child, but he'd been covertly studying the calm profile of the woman who had been his wife for less than four full days. He'd been trying to conjure up the feelings of contempt, self-loathing, and incredulity that had tormented him during the dry ceremony in the musty church office that had united them, and was intrigued to find that the impressions had become memories from which the emotional accompaniment had departed. In four short days, it had ceased to seem incredible that Claire was his wife.

Admittedly, he did not know what went on behind that lovely face, though he'd made several fascinating discoveries about her nature, including this most recent one of the existence of a smiling stubbornness that refused to give way before the automatic exercise of masculine domination. He now knew she possessed more than a female's share of physical courage and a quiet steadiness of purpose that demanded respect. There had been never been any doubt that he was dealing with a person of superior intelligence, although he had been inclined to regard it merely as self-serving shrewdness during the negotiations that took place before their arrangement had been completed. There seemed to be so much more to Claire than lay behind the pretty face of the young women with whom he had associated in the past. He

218

was fired with a burning desire to learn all there was to know about her, however long it should take.

"Don't be in a twitter about meeting hordes of people tonight, Claire," Egon said impulsively, taking her hand and placing it on his arm, enjoying the sensation of her wrist cradled securely between his arm and his ribs. "I'll be right beside you."

"Oh, I am not really too nervous," she said, smiling at him. "I pretend I am making my first entrance in a play and have only to say the right words in the right manner, and then everything will go swimmingly."

"But what are the right words when there is no script?"

Claire replied seriously, "Social situations are fairly conventional, requiring only polite formulas in response. I always pray that I will not be called upon to come up with anything original, though," she confessed, her smile becoming impish, "as poetic inspiration is not my forte."

"I can't believe that," he replied with a smiling gallantry that caused her lashes to flicker momentarily.

Just then, a jovial voice accosted them before Egon and Claire had crossed the threshold. "I've a bone to pick with you, Egon, you sly dog! Why did you not tell me you were about to tie the knot when we met in London last week?"

Even before his cousin's dapper figure had separated itself from the crowd milling about, Egon felt the consternation that flooded through Claire in the sudden clutching of her fingers on his arm. She froze, and he nudged her forward unobtrusively, angling his shoulders to shield her somewhat while she mastered her panic as he turned to greet Geoffrey Blyden.

"Perhaps because it was none of your affair, my lad," he riposted, adopting his cousin Jack's drawl. "Not that I was given much opportunity to interject news of my own heart's desire into our conversation, which you may recall was taken up almost exclusively with talk of yours." He felt Claire's swift intake of breath at this rash remark, but he'd been talking to gain time for her. "However, I shall be delighted to present you to my wife now. Darling, this fashion plate is my cousin Geoffrey Blyden, though I am persuaded I need not identify him, since the resemblance to Jack is so marked. Geoff, this is Claire, my wife."

Claire had removed her hand from the false haven of her husband's arm, and she stood composed and elegant as she held out her right hand to the young man with the charming smile. "How do you do, Cousin Geoffrey?" Her voice and smile were subdued, Egon saw, but her eyes met his cousin's unflinchingly.

Geoffrey's own smile flattened and his glance sharpened. "Have we met before, Lady Hollister? Or should I say, Cousin … Claire?"

"I shouldn't think so, old man," Egon said smoothly, in a move to bring his cousin's attention back to himself. Claire's composure was being threatened by Geoff's puzzled study. Egon amplified this denial as keen blue eyes swung toward him. "Claire has been living very quietly in London with an aunt who is something of a recluse."

"Yet you contrived to meet her," Geoffrey said slowly, his eyes traveling back to the silent young woman.

"Ah, but I have the devil's own luck, my lad," Egon began, then broke off to stare across the room. "Sorry, Geoff, but Gran is beckoning us. No doubt she wishes to present Claire to my aunts."

"We'll talk later, then," Geoffrey said, unsmiling now as he bowed to Claire.

Egon could feel his cousin's eyes boring into their backs as he and Claire crossed the room to where his grandmother sat enthroned on the sofa surrounded by a number of persons, some of them still strangers to him. "Courage, my love," he whispered out of the corner of his mouth as they drew near. "I did not recognize you on our wedding day without your disguise."

"But your cousin knows me better than you did at that point, and I cannot disguise my voice." Claire's answering whisper was despondent.

"Well, he's not likely to make any public announcement of his suspicions," Egon said bracingly. "I'll speak to him later and explain everything, if it should be necessary."

There was no time for more, as the bridal pair was soon engulfed by Egon's relatives, who appeared genuinely happy to see him safely returned from the wars and were pleased to welcome Claire into the family. In the few minutes before dinner was announced, Claire was presented to Egon's aunts, the widowed Mrs. Blyden and Lady Dunston, whose thin cheeks and decided jaw proclaimed her relationship to Lady Hollister, though her colouring was not so dark as Egon's. Sir George Dunston proved to be a hearty, red-faced gentleman of expanding girth and expansive manner, who patted Claire's hand paternally and predicted that she was just what the family needed; he was glad to see his nephew possessed the same eye for beauty and discriminating taste that his own son had demonstrated in bringing Jessica into the family. Of the younger generation, two of Egon's three female cousins were present with their spouses; only Maria, Lady Darcy, whose husband's estates were in Lancashire, had been unable to attend her grandmother's celebration. Michael's younger brothers were also missing from the gathering, it not being thought desirable to interrupt their schooling in midterm for a jaunt to the country.

Throughout the entire ceremony of introduction, Egon had kept Claire at his side with a casual arm about her waist, certainly to lend her physical and moral support, but also simply because she did not object. It was pleasant just to be near her, breathing in the faint perfume of her hair, his hand resting against one curve of what he now knew to be a perfectly proportioned body. He was not so blinded by sensual pleasure, however, that he missed Geoffrey Blyden's continued scrutiny of his wife. In an automatic reaction, Egon unobtrusively moved to place his body between Claire and Geoffrey each time the latter circulated about the room on the periphery of the group surrounding his grandmother. Not that this would make any difference ultimately. There would be ample opportunity in the course of the evening for Geoff to make the connection between his cousin's tawny-blond bride and his own favourite brunette actress if that was where his suspicions were tending, but Egon acted instinctively to lend Claire what protection he could until she had herself in hand again. Actually, he decided with possessive pride, his bride was demonstrating a convincing *sangfroid* as she smiled and conversed easily with various members of his extended family. No one could have guessed from her polite answers and interested expression that her mind was running on two tracks at present. He would not have known from looking at her that there was a nerve in her body, but he could feel her trembling slightly beneath his hand and was convinced that she drew comfort from his touch as she concentrated on charming his relatives by the too rarely used device of listening to them with wholehearted attention. An aching tide of tenderness rose in him for the lovely girl who had borne so much in the past few days with an uncomplaining gallantry and an exemplary determination to carry out her part of their infamous bargain in the face of great difficulties, most of them put there by him.

The now-familiar longing to take Claire in his arms had him in its grip again, but for the first time its source was his heart rather than his loins. The potential problems posed by Geoffrey's appearance seemed as nothing. He had survived the Peninsula fighting and the carnage of Waterloo. He was now back in the midst of his family, happily augmented by Jessica and Melissa and the husbands of his female cousins, and at his side was the loveliest girl in the world. *My cup runneth over.* The words flashed through his mind as he gazed at Claire listening sympathetically to a tale of her infant daughter told with expressive grimaces and gestures by Michael's sister, Alice, while her husband, Derek Blayde, shook his head in laughing protest. Suddenly, Egon became aware of his grandmother's intent stare and he smiled fully at her.

"Have I told you yet that you look wonderful tonight, Gran, in your party pink?" he asked, leaning toward her. "I'll challenge any man who says you are a day over sixty."

Snapping lights appeared in Lady Hollister's dark eyes and she displayed a fine set of teeth, all her own, in a startled laugh whose rarity brought all eyes to her. Ignoring Sir George's hearty, "Hear, hear!" she fixed her now-grinning grandson with an admonishing look and said accusingly, "You did not learn to tell flattering lies at Belhaven, Egon, so I must assume it is the pernicious influence of the military on your character. It's more than time you returned to your home."

"Hear, hear!" Sir George said again.

Egon glanced around his expanded family circle and was warmed to the core to see that, with two notable exceptions, there was a genuine sense of welcome being extended to him.

Jack, of course, wore his usual mocking expression, but it was the rigid set to his cousin Geoffrey's features and the dislike in his eyes that gave him pause. Obviously, Geoffrey had guessed the truth of Claire's identity. He would have to take him aside for a private talk before the men re-joined the ladies after dinner. It must wait until then because Boynton was approaching to announce dinner now. Egon could only hope that Gran had not placed Geoffrey next to Claire at table, or his poor darling would find her appetite deserting her. Before he could warn her, his grandmother took his arm and indicated that they should proceed in to dinner.

Egon found on entering the dining room that he had been placed opposite his grandmother in the role of host. Claire was between Mr. Winward, a somewhat tactless choice in view of that gentleman's recent disappointment, and Sir George, who would provide his own entertainment. Geoff was seated on the same side of the table as Claire, where he could neither see nor speak with her, for which little mercy Egon was duly grateful. As long as he could delay their meeting until he had spoken to Geoffrey, he would be able to smooth his cousin's feathers and spare Claire some distress.

Unfortunately, matters did not fall out the way Egon intended. His grandmother chose the forum of her birthday dinner to announce that she intended to make her eldest grandson her heir. Egon's eyes flew to Claire, to find her smiling gamely but with a hint of sadness in her amber eyes. He knew her well enough by now to interpret this as a reaction to the deception she saw as promoting his grandmother's choice of himself. He yearned to speak to her ear alone, to tell her not to look so sad, to explain that he now knew that Gran had never meant to leave things any other way, no matter whom — or whether — he married. Instead, he was forced to smile and receive the good wishes of those present and say all that was proper to the occasion.

Rather than being able to have some time alone with Claire to set her mind at ease, he was forced to possess his soul in patience as she filed out with the rest of the ladies, eyes downcast and still with that subdued look about her. Egon sighed and turned his attention to the immediate problem of correcting whatever wild impressions Geoffrey might have taken into his head about Claire's presence here. He frowned heavily as the thought crossed his mind that the truth might actually be wilder than anything Geoffrey had envisioned.

Over the next half-hour, Egon was stymied in this purpose also. Mr. Winward cornered him immediately to reassure him that he had taken no offense at the failure of his long-cherished scheme to unite their two families through marriage. He explained conscientiously and at considerable length that it seemed his daughter had not really been interested in promoting the union and had in fact been relieved to have an end to the plan. Egon was forced to listen to a lecture on the inability of the female of the species to know her own mind or communicate this knowledge to the more rational half of the population. Knowing it was important to Lady Hollister to keep on good terms with her old neighbour, Egon controlled his impatience and heard the man out before delivering himself of the formal expression of their esteem and friendship that his grandmother would expect of him.

This exercise in restraint cost him the opportunity to speak to Geoffrey and, what was worse, he received the decided impression that this suited his cousin's book at present. It was impossible to catch his eye during the time the men devoted to their port, and his duties as host precluded pursuing his cousin out of the room when he gave the signal to return to the ladies.

It was beyond doubting that Geoff would make a beeline for Claire. Egon would have to force his way into that conversation to rescue his wife from her disillusioned admirer.

Once again Egon was stymied in his objective, this time by the other half of the Winward family. Miss Winward must have been lying in wait for him, for she appeared in his path the moment he entered the drawing room. He resigned himself to the inevitable and helped her cut through the polite preliminaries to get to the heart of the matter, which was her unspoken concern that her volatile parent might have offended him by some intemperate comments on the failed marriage plan. By the time he had reassured her as to her father's diplomacy and the continued goodwill between the two families, his opportunity to cushion any blows for Claire was past.

From his position just inside the door, where Miss Winward had pinned him, he watched impotently while Geoffrey cut Claire out of the crowd and walked her to the corner of the room where the pianoforte stood. By the time Egon had surreptitiously signalled Mamzell to rescue him and had made his excuses to the two women, Claire had turned abruptly away from his cousin and was walking rapidly toward him, her eyes full of distress. They met in the centre of the room. Egon tucked her hand under his arm and whispered warningly, "Shhhhh, darling, all eyes are on us. Smile at me. Trust me to make matters right with Geoffrey."

"He recognized me, Egon, though I tried to deny it. He is demanding an explanation. I told him he would have to ask you."

"Quite right; now, smile," he said again, and she complied, though it was a tentative effort at best. "He is coming this way now. If anyone asks for us, we have gone outside to enjoy a cigar. Now, go talk to Melissa, who is alone for the moment."

Claire slipped away. As Egon followed her graceful gliding walk with his eyes, he felt his arm seized in no gentle grip.

"I wish to talk with you," Geoffrey said through clenched teeth.

"Certainly," his cousin drawled with immense affability. "Do you think you could remove your hand and take that ugly look from your face before the rest of the company perceives it and begins to speculate that we might be at odds?"

"I don't care what they speculate about," Geoffrey growled, but he let go of the other's arm.

"Well, you should, considering that this is your grandmother's evening," Egon snapped. "She would not thank us for introducing dissension into this happy occasion."

Geoffrey uttered an inarticulate snarl, but he nodded and smiled at his cousin Alice in the next second as Egon guided him through the crowd with a hand under his elbow.

"If we are missed, Claire will put it about that we've sneaked out for a smoke," Egon said. "Come into the library, where we should be undisturbed." He could feel his cousin's simmering anger and impatience, and he sighed with resignation as they headed down the hall. "All right, you may now open the budget and vent your spleen," he invited, closing the library door behind them. He strolled over to the desk, where two chairs were drawn up, and gestured to one. "Sit down."

"I do not wish to sit down," Geoffrey said, seemingly at a loss for the moment in the face of Egon's insistence on observing polite formalities.

"Well, I am more stricken in years than you, and I do wish to sit," Egon retorted, dropping into one of the chairs. He sprawled at his ease, eyeing the younger man not unsympathetically, and after a taut hiatus, his cousin turned and took the other chair.

"What black arts did you employ to induce Clairisse to allow herself to be paraded in front of the family as your wife?" Geoffrey began, going on the attack at once.

"Let me correct you on one point," Egon said softly. "Her real name is Claire, not Clairisse, and the only art I employed, if such it can be termed, was money."

"You mean you *paid* her to pretend to be your wife?" Geoffrey gasped. "Jack says you've been here *four* days … in the green suite … *together*." His nostrils flared.

"Again I must correct you on one point. Claire is not pretending to be my wife, she is my wife." Egon's voice was still soft and uninflected, but his words caused his cousin to slump in his chair. Much of the anger drained out of his face, to be replaced by perplexity.

"You actually paid her to marry you? Why would she do such a thing? Why would *you* do such a thing?"

"Claire did it for money, and I did it because if I had showed up at Belhaven without a wife, I would have been agreeing to my grandmother's terms that I marry Miss Winward."

"But … but this is appalling! How could Clairisse — Claire — lend herself to such an unsavoury scheme?"

"Perhaps you would not think it so unsavoury if you had ever needed money desperately," Egon suggested.

"But to go so far as to actually marry a stranger!" Geoffrey raised stricken eyes to his cousin's unrevealing face. "What kind of farce does that make of marriage? It's no better than selling herself — why, she's no better than Haymarket ware! And I thought her a model of virtue and —"

"That's enough!" Egon blazed. "The little you know does not give you the right to judge my marriage, and you'll take

228

back that insult to Claire right now unless you wish to have your cork drawn and your nose rearranged on your face!" He had sprung out of his chair and was fast approaching Geoffrey, his hands curled into fists and a look of sheer menace on his face.

Geoffrey blinked rapidly and his jaw dropped. "Why, you're in love with her!" he exclaimed, watching in growing astonishment as Egon pulled up short, all expression atrophied for an instant until a careful blankness spread over his features.

Suddenly, Geoffrey's air of disillusionment and anger fell away from him as he rose and said cheerfully, "Well, that's all right, then. While you are weighing whether to draw my cork or not, you might remember that *I* always did have a good opinion of the lady's character. You know, I thought she took a fancy to you right away — at least she seemed different, more serious, when she spoke to you... I am not expressing myself too clearly, am I?" he asked, still in that cheerful vein. "Oh, well, never mind. If Clairisse — Claire would not give me a chance, at least we've kept her in the family.

"They were starting to clear the furniture away to the walls for dancing when we left the drawing room. I aim to secure the first dance with my new cousin and offer her my belated felicitations. Coming?"

"Uh … in a moment. You go ahead." Egon stood in the same spot watching an insouciant Geoffrey stroll out of the library. The click of the door latch released him from the spell that had kept him motionless for the last two minutes, and he sank onto the chair his cousin had vacated.

He felt as if someone had delivered an unexpected blow to the solar plexus, knocking all the stuffing out of him.

Why had he needed Geoffrey to point out the obvious to him? How dull-witted could one man be? Of course he was in love with Claire, though he'd be hard-pressed to say when it had happened. He'd been uneasily aware of a rising desire to possess her bodily starting from the time they left the church office, a desire that had filled him with self-loathing, given his stated opinion of her morals. The urge to snipe at her had slowly given way to a stronger need to believe in her and a rising desire to stand between her and life's vicissitudes. Had he said *slowly*? Looking back on the recent past, it struck him as nearly inconceivable that his life could have changed so radically in four short days.

Soft strains of violin music reached Egon through the wooden door and jogged him upright once more. Determination sat on his serious countenance as he headed back to the party. Unless Claire had undergone a similar moment of revelation in the last ten minutes, the immediate future promised to be equally full of interest and peril. The path to Claire's affections was undoubtedly strewn with uncharted snags, some of them put there by his earlier unkindness toward her. It would not be easy to convince her that he no longer cared about her past mistakes, that what he had learned about her sweetness and strength during their stay at Belhaven had filled him with love and admiration, apart from the desire that had already existed. All was fair in love, though; he was going to take to heart Geoff's casually expressed belief that Claire felt some sort of attraction to him and storm the citadel of her defence against him. He rejected the memory of their wedding night when it arose to taunt him. That scene had happened aeons ago in another lifetime.

The scene that greeted him in the drawing room brought back memories of another kind, recalling the gay dancing parties that had taken place at Belhaven before his grandfather's health had failed. Boynton and the footmen had rolled back the carpet, exposing the beautifully polished parquet floor. His eyes sought and found Claire whirling by in Geoffrey's arms, her face smiling and serene once more.

The musicians his grandmother had hired were grouped around the pianoforte, and Lady Hollister herself was seated with Mamzell on the sofa that had been pushed against the wall at one end of the room. Mr. Winward was in close attendance, but almost everyone else appeared to be on the floor.

Egon headed straight for his grandmother and bowed, extending his hand. "May I have the pleasure, Gran?"

She smiled but said, "I gave up dancing years ago, Egon."

"Just half a dance, then," he persisted, taking her feather fan from her and handing it to a beaming Mamzell. He pulled gently, and after an instant's resistance, Lady Hollister allowed herself to be drawn forward.

"I've never waltzed," she protested. "It's too fast for me."

"It's the simplest dance imaginable, Gran, and we'll slow down the tempo." He signalled with his hands to the musicians and held out his arms.

Within a half-minute, Lady Hollister had caught on to the basic step and they began a stately progress around the room. The other dancers, hearing the beat change, gradually pulled back to allow them the centre of the floor. Egon smiled down at the straight-backed woman with the beautifully coiffed white hair that was so flattered by the deep pink taffeta of her gown, and the concentration on her face broke into an answering smile.

"It is quite pleasant to be moving in this fashion, though rather dizzying too. I wish your grandfather might have lived to learn the waltz."

"So do I. I'm sorry it's only I and not Grandfather partnering you tonight."

"Oh, you'll do in a pinch," she said with the slight smile that was typical of her. "You look very happy tonight."

"And so I should. Thank you, Gran."

"I hope it isn't just Belhaven?" She was not smiling now.

His eyes returned from locating Claire, watching them from a spot near the musicians. "Oh, no; it isn't just Belhaven," he said simply.

"I'm glad. I like your wife, Egon."

"Thank you, Gran; so do I."

Sensing that his grandmother was tiring a bit, Egon waltzed her back down the room to the sofa. As they left the floor, there was spontaneous applause from all the others in the room. Head high, Lady Hollister lifted an acknowledging hand briefly in a regal gesture. She accepted her fan from her companion and waved it slowly to cool her cheeks.

Egon tarried a moment to make sure she was all right, but she said firmly, "I am fine, my dear. Go take Claire away from Geoffrey. Let him find a girl of his own."

A few seconds later, Egon tapped his cousin on the shoulder and solemnly delivered their grandmother's message. Geoffrey grinned and relinquished Claire to her husband, who immediately pulled her a bit closer than was permissible on a public dancefloor. She smiled at him, tacitly allowing the liberty as he swept her down the room.

"Our first dance," Egon said after several minutes had elapsed in which he'd mutely savoured the heady pleasure of holding his wife in his arms.

Claire's eyes fell before the demand in his. "Yes," she said, adding, "You are a very comfortable partner."

He chuckled and whirled her into a complex turn. "I can think of more complimentary terms to describe my partner — a feather in my arms, a delight in my life."

"It isn't necessary to pay me flowery compliments. Actually, I'd rather you did not," Claire said, looking up at him gravely, and Egon realized with a pang that he had his work cut out for him to overcome her prejudices.

"But I like paying well-deserved compliments," he said lightly.

"Has anyone ever told you that you strongly favour your grandmother in looks?" she asked to introduce a less personal note into their exchange.

"Would you be disappointed if I said you were not the first to point out the similarity?"

"No, of course not. It … it was just the sort of observation one makes —"

"When one is trying to avoid a real conversation," he finished for her. "I quite understand."

"You … you must be very pleased at Lady Hollister's decision to leave Belhaven to you," she said in desperation.

"Yes, I love every stick and stone of the place, but, Claire, you mustn't look so grave. I am utterly convinced that Gran always intended to leave Belhaven to me, wife or no wife, so you must not feel you have been a party to a swindle."

"Oh, no, not that, but if she really intended to make you her heir, you need not have complicated your life by contracting a sham marriage."

"Believe me, darling, I would never have showed my face at Belhaven without a wife, either you or some other unknown woman. I do not regret it for a moment."

"But I do! I have felt like such a horrid fraud when everyone here has been so kind and welcoming to me."

The music was ending and Claire pulled back from him. Egon hurried to say, "Claire, please, you need not feel that way. We can make it true."

He was given no chance to explain his statement. Sir George came up at that moment to take Claire to his wife, who desired to become better acquainted with the newest member of the family. Again Egon had to exercise patience, and this time his frustration was aggravated by the knowledge that Claire was relieved to escape from his company. He was beginning to despair of ever achieving a modicum of privacy in which to discuss their own situation.

It would certainly not be at Lady Hollister's birthday celebration.

The evening was judged a great success by almost everyone privileged to be present. The musicians played for dancing for more than two hours, until those persons living near enough to drive home took their departure when the moon had risen high enough to aid them. Delectable food and beverages of all sorts were available throughout the evening, including a free-flowing champagne that was pronounced exquisite by the connoisseurs among the company, Mr. Michael Dunston for one. Lady Hollister stayed up until the last of the temporary female residents retired to bed, reluctant to end one of the increasingly rare occasions when most of her descendants were assembled at Belhaven at the same time.

Egon may have been unique in desiring to see the end of such a good party, but the need to be alone with Claire was mounting with each passing hour. There was so much that was unsettled between them, and he was driven by the admittedly irrational notion that time was running out on them. That was nonsensical, of course, but he was determined not to put off their talk for even one more day, even if Claire should plead fatigue.

And this was exactly what she did do when he indicated his intention of accompanying her upstairs. He noted the flash of panic in her eyes with regret. The last thing in the world he desired was that she should be afraid of him. "Remember that we agreed that I would look at that wound before the day was over," he said gently, and she ceased to argue, though fear did not entirely depart from her shadowed eyes.

As they reached the foot of the staircase after taking leave of the night owls, Michael appeared carrying Jessica in his arms.

"What has happened, Jess?" Claire asked in swift concern.

"Nothing serious. I just twisted my ankle a moment ago. I can walk on it, but all these stairs seemed so daunting."

Claire and Egon stood aside, voicing their hopes that a night's rest would do the trick for the ankle.

"Did Jessica wink at you as they passed us just now?" Egon asked his bride.

"It's most unlikely," Claire replied serenely. "It was probably an illusion caused by the flickering candles in the wall sconces." She made a comment on the dancing, and during the walk to their suite they exchanged impressions of the party they had just left.

"Shall I help you remove your gown? You will recall that you told your maid not to wait up for you."

She bit her lip and cast down her eyes, but turned her back in silent acquiescence. When Egon had dealt with the fastenings in like silence, he proceeded to slip the gown off the right shoulder. Before he could repeat this action with the left sleeve, Claire turned toward him, her left hand holding the loosened dress against her chest. Her voice was husky as she said, "I think you will be able to get at the bandage now."

Egon put a tentative finger under her shift and pulled it away from the bandage. "I'll try not to hurt you."

Claire turned to give him access to the area, decreasing the distance between them to inches. At Egon's quick intake of breath, she looked over her shoulder, her eyes dilated at the grim set to his features. "What's the matter? I thought it looked fine earlier this evening."

"Oh, it is clean enough and it had already begun to heal. It's the … the desecration of it. You have such lovely, smooth skin. That infernal branch!" He pressed lightly with a finger around the area. "Does that hurt?"

"Not really, no more than a natural soreness."

Claire stood perfectly still, seeming not to breathe as he replaced the bandage, but when his fingers continued to slide over her shoulder and slipped beneath the shift to begin caressing her breast, she shied away from him. "Please, Egon, that isn't wise. You really should go now."

"I'd say it is the wisest thing since the beginning of time, and I do not believe you really want me to go. Don't fight me, darling; admit that we belong together."

Eyes full of uncertainty searched his as Egon gathered her into his arms in a deliberate motion, taking care to keep her right shoulder free of pressure. Her resistance was less physical than mental as her eyes pleaded wordlessly for something… What?

Obeying the oldest instinct in the world, Egon abandoned thought and kissed his wife's beautiful mouth. He felt her resistance dissolve in the explosion of sensation that contact produced. Pleasure raced through his veins as he discovered that their first kiss in the conservatory had been no once-in-a-lifetime thrill. This was the effect Claire had on him. They stayed in that kiss until a mutual need to draw an unrestricted breath forced its cessation.

Egon released her lips to demand, "Can you deny that you belong to me after this, Claire? Admit it, darling."

Her eyes on his mouth, her voice a mere thread of sound, Claire capitulated. "Oh, yes, I admit it."

He kissed her again in thanksgiving, an infinitely pleasurable exercise, but he was becoming increasingly conscious of the demands of his body and the layers of clothing between them. "Don't move an inch," he whispered, raising his head.

This order had to be disobeyed because Claire's arms had wound themselves around his neck in the course of that marathon kiss. He managed to shrug himself out of his coat without moving his mouth out of reach of hers, so that he was able to take brief advantage of the sweetness of her lips during the ensuing contortions, but he could not get rid of the cravat without reluctantly dislodging her arms. "Be useful; unbutton my shirt," he commanded as he tossed jacket and neckcloth onto the chair between the windows.

Claire's colour had heightened, he noted with passing satisfaction, but her fingers automatically followed his instructions, though they fumbled in the doing. Meanwhile, he expertly dealt with her gown and shift. "No stays?" She shook her head dumbly and trembled as his hands took the measure of her slim waist with slow, caressing strokes.

"Good Lord, but you are beautiful!" As she stood there before him like Botticelli's Venus, with the discarded clothing tumbled around her shapely ankles substituting for seafoam and shell, a reminder of the men who had been before him seared into his brain to torture him as he compelled her nervous glance.

"Never in the history of mankind has one woman ever been more specifically designed and destined for one particular man," he told her, denying the others, expunging them.

Her eyes widened at the fierceness behind the soft words. As he picked her up and deposited her on the bed, which had already been turned down, they widened still farther, until they were enormous molten amber pools in her pale face when he blew out the candles.

Claire had not uttered a syllable by the time Egon joined her in the bed. When she stiffened as he gathered her into a full embrace, he murmured, "Do not be nervous, darling. I'll not do anything you don't wish." He kissed her lingeringly, and she obviously liked that, for he could feel her relax against him. His hands roamed over her smooth supple body, delighting in the curves and valleys encountered on his voyage of exploration. A bit surprised at her passiveness after the passion of her kiss, he firmly restrained his own desire in order to bring her along slowly, and he was well-rewarded as he felt her breath and body quicken under his touch and strain closer to him. He placed her hands, which had not left his shoulders, on his hips and whispered encouragingly when they began their own tentative explorations of his body. Her heightened arousal spurred him on, though he was unprepared for her initial shock at receiving a fully aroused male.

The greater shock was reserved for Egon, however, when it became obvious that Claire's virginity was still intact. For an instant, he was completely paralyzed. He groaned and started to withdraw, but Claire clung to him with all her strength. Sweat broke out on his forehead at the prospect of hurting her, but though her whole frame quivered as he drove through the barrier, she still clung and she did not cry out beyond a slight hissing breath. Instantly her body accommodated to his, arcing instinctively with his movements within her.

When Egon came back down to earth again, it was to the exquisite joy of knowing his first possession of Claire had been desired and welcomed. It would now be his greater joy to complete her initiation into the pleasures of the flesh available to those who loved. That of all the women in the world he should have found Claire without having done anything to merit her had to be a stroke of divine providence. He was filled with thankfulness, yet he remonstrated with her as he rolled onto his back and pulled her against his side. "Why didn't you tell me? I'd have prepared you better, been more gentle."

Claire was indignant. "I did tell you, and you refused to believe me."

Egon chuckled, and it turned into a yawn. "I beg your pardon, darling, but it wasn't a very convincing story from where I stood. Circumstances were against you. Lord, but I'm tired. It has been a very long day, and I promised Michael we'd be off at the crack of dawn to ride over to take a look at Hollister Place tomorrow."

"I thought you said that to appease your grandmother, who wished to know where we were going to live."

"I did, of course, but everything is changed now," he mumbled sleepily, pulling her closer to him so that he could bury his lips in the little hollow of her throat and savour the scent of her.

"Nothing about our bargain has changed, Egon. I agreed to a divorce whenever you wished to secure it," Claire said earnestly.

"Lord, darling, don't be a peagoose. A gentleman doesn't marry a virgin, seduce her, and then divorce her. What do you take me for? Besides," he added on another yawn, "in case I forgot to mention it earlier, I love you madly."

There was no sound in the big bedchamber while Claire digested this casual proclamation. At last she let out a sigh and asked timidly, "Do you really mean that, Egon?"

Silence greeted this request for confirmation. After a long moment, Claire raised her head and eased herself up on one elbow, the better to search her bridegroom's face, but there was nothing to be read on the face of the man beside her.

Egon was sound asleep.

CHAPTER 15

Claire did not stir when her bridegroom left her side in the morning. She did not see him pick up her clothing from the floor and drape it neatly over the dressing-table bench, nor did she hear the click of the door latch as he took himself and his clothing into the dressing room. She did not even move a muscle when, fully dressed for riding, Egon returned to the bed with a night rail he had found in the armoire. She was unaware that he stood looking down at her, a tender smile on his lips as he removed a black ostrich plume that had survived their lovemaking and now lay curled around one ear. Nor did she feel his lips brush hers lightly before he went out of the room once more.

Claire's obliviousness to this series of events could be explained by the fact that she had fallen into an exhausted sleep only just before dawn, after long hours of self-recrimination, tears, and soul-searching had culminated in a decision to leave Belhaven before her husband returned from his day at Hollister Place. Honourable man that he was, Egon planned to make their mock marriage real because, as he had plainly stated, one didn't seduce a virgin and then divorce her. But it was entirely her fault that matters had reached such a pass. True, he had wanted to make love to her, but that was when he believed her to be experienced. He had made it clear that it would not affect the decision to divorce. Last night he had tried to pull back when he discovered the truth, and she had not let him. That was the situation in a nutshell. Intentionally or not, she had tricked Egon into a position where he felt it would be dishonourable to pursue a divorce.

The question of her own motives had contributed most to the sleeplessness. Her conscience was clear up to the moment when Egon had examined her shoulder. She had not intended to let him make love to her, though she desperately wanted something to remember from her brief experience as the wife of the man with whom she had tumbled into love almost from the moment of meeting. He had been correct about one thing: he had seduced her with his eyes, his smile, and, above all, his tantalizing touch. Her good intentions had shrivelled before the magic power he exerted over her. The fact that she loved him did not excuse her conduct. She had been enough in the possession of her senses to listen carefully for a declaration of his love for her. It had not been forthcoming, and yet she had still thrown judgment to the winds and allowed herself to be possessed. The fact that judgment had failed her made it imperative that she not be found lacking in honour also. She must release Egon from any sense of obligation toward her in the only way possible.

This decision had not been reached without many tears of loss and longing, but it had permitted her the saving grace of sleep. When Claire awoke, the sun was already high in the sky and Estelle was rapping on the sitting-room door to the hall. It took only a second to see that Egon was gone, having left all neat behind him. She was struggling into the night rail he'd thoughtfully provided when the abigail entered with hot water.

Claire was unnaturally quiet as she got ready for what would be the most difficult day of her life, too self-absorbed to be aware of the knowing look Estelle cast at her upon seeing the wreck of the elaborate hair arrangement she had created for the birthday celebration. The practical difficulties in implementing the decision she had reached occupied her mind and were daunting to say the least. For one thing, the house was full of guests who had remained overnight. She could not expose Egon to the humiliation of having his bride run away in the full public eye. She frowned in concentration as she tried to recall if any of Lady Hollister's family had planned to stay past lunchtime. A casual question to Estelle satisfied her on that point. Even Jack and Melissa were planning to return to their home this morning. That still left Jessica and Michael on the scene, but perhaps Lady Hollister would oblige by making up some tale to account for her sudden departure.

Lady Hollister would have to know, of course. Even if it had not been necessary to apply to her for the funds to pay for a ticket on the stage, she could never have sunk to the depths of disappearing without a word to her kind hostess. Additionally, now that Egon had assured her that his grandmother had always intended to leave Belhaven to him, she felt she must make a clean breast of the affair to Lady Hollister for the good of her soul. The deception had eaten away at her conscience from the moment the people at Belhaven had become real to her. The problem was that this smacked of disloyalty to Egon. Thoroughly miserable before she even embarked on her great renunciation, Claire barely glanced into the mirror, though she thanked Estelle for dressing her hair so nicely.

Claire had no desire for food, but she slipped into the deserted dining room and found a pot of hot coffee on the sideboard, which she drank before screwing up her courage to approach Lady Hollister. She came into the main hall in time to bid farewell to most of the departing guests, only Sir George and Lady Dunston having left at an early hour. Geoffrey, who was escorting his mother to her home, surprised her and the others by giving her an exuberant hug before climbing into Mrs. Blyden's carriage, and Melissa kissed her on both cheeks in the French manner. Claire's stage training stood her in good stead as she fought to conceal her unhappiness at bidding a final goodbye to Egon's warm-hearted relatives.

Claire would have followed Lady Hollister back into the house when the carriages rolled down the drive, but a bright-eyed Jessica took her arm and stayed her progress.

"Do not go inside just yet, Claire. I've been waiting for you to appear all morning. I've been just bursting to thank you."

"Thank me — for what?" Claire's mind was so intent on her own problem that she stared blankly at the blushing girl before her.

"For your advice about Michael, of course!"

Claire's features warmed into a smile as she assimilated the added sparkle to Jessica's pretty face this morning. "I'm so glad, Jess, although it would have happened soon in any case. You two could not have continued to circle each other in that stiff fashion much longer. It is alien to your natures."

"I'm not so convinced of that as you. Michael really believed that I didn't want him to make love to me. He knows better now," she finished, the momentary cloud clearing from her brow.

"I take it your ankle is much improved this morning?" Claire asked slyly.

Jessica giggled. "All better," she confessed, "though I had to promise Michael I would not ride or go for a walk today."

"Then you are well-served," Claire said, assuming a stern look. "I almost lost my countenance last night when Egon asked me if you had winked at me on the stairs."

Jessica giggled again. "I trust you didn't give me away?"

Claire smiled and shook her head, but the introduction of her husband's name had brought her own unhappy situation to the forefront again. When Jessica asked if she'd like to sit in the garden and sketch with her, she begged off, explaining that she needed to talk with Lady Hollister about something. The girls parted on a casual note that Claire regretted, but she had no intention of casting any shadows over Jessica's lovely day even if she could have borne to confess the sordid situation between herself and Egon.

It was going to be difficult enough to explain to Lady Hollister. The full truth of this hit Claire only when she was seated in one of the chairs pulled up to the big desk in the library, facing her husband's grandmother across the desk a few moments later. Mademoiselle Ducroix had been closeted with Lady Hollister going over some household routines when the nervous young woman had entered and expressed a diffident wish to speak privately with the mistress of Belhaven. The energetic little Frenchwoman had jumped up instantly, proclaiming her willingness to give way to Claire's more pressing concern. Her rapid exit had been accompanied by an even more rapid stream of inconsequential chatter, none of which Claire had taken in in her perturbed state.

Noting the girl's pale cheeks, Lady Hollister had nodded to a chair. "Sit down, my dear. What may I do for you?"

Claire bit her lip and raised strained eyes to the calm, barely lined visage of the matriarch. "I ... I have come to beg a favour, ma'am. I must leave Belhaven — today."

At this terse statement Lady Hollister's slanted brows elevated fractionally, but her calm demeanour varied in no other fashion. "I see. Has there been some family emergency, your brother perhaps?"

"Yes." Claire seized the excuse like a drowning man, then shook her head. "No. I ... I do not wish to tell you any lies."

"That's as it should be. I do not wish to hear any. Suppose you tell me the truth instead. Why is it so important that you leave Belhaven today?"

"Because I must get away before Egon returns or ... or he will feel he should dissuade me, and I cannot allow that ... for his sake." Claire fell silent after this vague statement, perhaps under the impression that she had made all clear.

"You think Egon will not wish you to leave?" Lady Hollister probed delicately.

"Not exactly. I am persuaded he would welcome it, but naturally he will feel honour-bound to protest, so it is best that I go before he returns."

"Why would he welcome your departure?"

Claire sat there in miserable silence, gnawing on her lip with eyes cast down. Lady Hollister tried again. "Do you feel perhaps that this is something I have no right to know because it concerns only the two of you and your marriage?"

"Oh, no, ma'am. Actually, I feel you should know the reason, but Egon will disagree. And there's no denying he will see it as disloyalty, and rightly so, though I hope you will tell him for me that I would not have dreamed of betraying his confidence had he not assured me that you always meant to make him your heir, even if he did not marry the person you chose."

"When did my grandson assure you of this?"

"Last night at the party. That *is* the case, is it not, ma'am?" she asked, anxiously searching the unrevealing countenance across the desk.

There was a decided pause during which Lady Hollister looked rather forbidding; then she said with deliberation, "Yes, I would have to accept that assessment of the situation. Now, suppose you tell me what you think I should know, and then we will decide whether or not to tell Egon I know it."

Claire blinked and considered, then pushed her spread fingers into her hair in a gesture of confusion. "The truth is," she blurted, "that ours isn't really a marriage at all."

Lady Hollister sat very still, her opaque eyes never leaving the distraught girl's face. "Do you mean," she asked still more softly, "that you and my grandson are not married?"

"Not really," Claire repeated, then, realizing the purport of the question, added quickly, "Oh, we are *legally* married, if that is what you meant, ma'am?" Amber eyes were large and questioning.

"That is what I meant," Lady Hollister confirmed, permitting a slight relaxation in her jawline. "Now, perhaps you will be so good as to tell me what you mean by 'not really married'?"

"Well," Claire said reluctantly, "Egon paid me to marry him and come here as his wife."

"Then you are not from a Northumberland family after all?"

"Oh, yes, all that part is true. I haven't told you any lies, ma'am, but neither have I corrected a couple of Egon's statements about me that are not true," Claire replied with painful honesty.

If Claire had been less miserably conscious of her own iniquity, she'd have noticed the slight twitch of her auditor's finely cut lips before that lady inquired, "And what statements were those?"

"That I was living with an aunt in London when we met."

"There is no aunt who brought you out and has now returned to Northumberland?"

"Oh, there is an aunt who brought me out, but she is still living in London, only I wasn't living with her. Egon doesn't even know where I live."

"May one ask where you were living?" By now Lady Hollister was resigned to extracting information piecemeal from this jumbled tale.

"With my old nursemaid and her family." Claire sighed and said abruptly, "You may as well know the worst. I am a professional actress, and Egon hired me to play his wife."

"*An actress!*"

"I was afraid you would be very shocked at this." Claire's hands were tightly clasped in her lap.

It was inaccurate to state that Lady Hollister was shocked. She had lived too long to be still capable of being shocked by the foibles of her fellow humans, but she was certainly a good deal surprised at this latest nugget of gold extracted from Claire's incoherent story. "I am not at all shocked, my child, but I should be most interested to learn how it came about, your acting career, I mean." She listened with her customary attention as Claire explained her position after her father's death and told of her decision to accompany her brother to London. She did not interrupt the subsequent narration of her new granddaughter's unsuccessful search for respectable employment in the metropolis, only saying when the girl had finished her account with her good fortune at being hired by the management of Drury Lane Theatre, "I am curious as to why you did not seek asylum with the aunt with whom you had lived during your come-out."

"She hated having me then, but she had made the sacrifice for her dead sister's sake. She disliked my father intensely, and wrote such a ... an ungenerous letter after his death that I'd rather have starved in a ditch than ask her for shelter."

"You have had a difficult time since your father's death."

"Only at first, ma'am. I enjoy performing, and I have become quite adept at comedic roles, though I make no claim to being an accomplished dramatic actress."

"Would I have heard of you? We get the London papers."

Claire responded to the innocent interest in the old woman's voice. "I do not act under my own name, of course. My stage name is Clairisse Deschamps."

"And you were performing at Drury Lane when you and Egon met?"

"Y-yes, ma'am." The interest of her audience had caused Claire to forget for a few moments the reason for being in this room. Now her tones became dull again.

"May I ask, Claire, if you had any qualms about taking on the part of Egon's wife for money?"

"I beg you to believe that I would never have agreed to such an imposture, Lady Hollister, except that my brother was in dire need of a large sum of money, and I was at my wits' end. Frankly, Egon's proposition seemed heaven-sent at the time. I could see no other solution … and … and you know the rest of the story."

"Not perhaps all the rest," Lady Hollister said with a perfectly straight face, "but we are coming to the crux of the matter, are we not? Why do you now wish to back out of the agreement? You could do much worse with your life than marry my grandson. I would have thought him quite a good catch."

"Oh, but it was never intended to be a real marriage!" Claire cried, shocked. "Egon was to divorce me when the marriage had served his purpose."

Lady Hollister's brows drew together. "A divorce was to be part of the agreement? When was this to take place?"

"I don't know exactly. Egon told me practically nothing except that he had to be married in order to be considered as your heir."

"If that were the case, how would a divorce serve his purpose?"

"I was never quite clear on that point, ma'am, but my impression was that my part in all this was to be quite temporary."

"Your part." Lady Hollister paused and directed a searching look at the uneasy girl. "You'll forgive my asking so personal a question, but was your performance as my grandson's wife to include conjugal privileges?"

Claire's chin went up defensively. "One of my conditions for accepting the proposition was that it would not."

"Then would not an annulment have been preferable to a divorce?"

"That was always in the back of my mind too, ma'am."

"But you never discussed it with Egon?"

"He never discussed anything with me, Lady Hollister."

"Well, then, let us proceed to the present. Correct me if I am wrong. You have come to me today because you no longer wish to carry out your part of the agreement you made with my grandson, and you wish to seek an immediate annulment?"

Colour flooded Claire's cheeks. She opened her mouth, but no sound came out. As her tongue came out to moisten her lips, Lady Hollister asked softly, "Do I take it from your confusion that an annulment is no longer possible?"

Claire nodded, biting her lip fiercely.

A little line appeared between Lady Hollister's brows. "You said earlier that you wished to leave for Egon's sake. You still believe he wishes to divorce you?"

"Yes, ma'am, I know it."

"I would have thought that the fact that he consummated the marriage proved just the opposite."

"No," the girl said earnestly, "for he would not have done it had he known I was a virgin." As those slanted brows really escalated this time, Claire tried to explain. "You see, he never believed I was not a ... a fallen woman, and he always intended to divorce me, so he thought it would not matter if we ... if he made love to me. In fact, he had tried before, on our wedding night, despite our agreement, only I wouldn't let him. Last night when I assured him that what had happened made no difference to our agreement to divorce — it was only fair, after all — he said it made all the difference in the world to his honour and we were going to stay married."

"And quite right, too."

"No, ma'am, it isn't. You see —" Claire swallowed with difficulty, "at the moment he realized I was untouched, he tried to pull back, but I wouldn't let him, so you see, I really did trap him. *My honour* demands that I leave."

The two women, one old and wise, one young and vulnerable, looked into each other's eyes and reached a rapprochement based on respect for the integrity of the other's spirit.

"You love my grandson very much." It wasn't a question.

"Yes, I love him," Claire admitted painfully, "but I cannot bear to contemplate living with him when he does not love me."

"Has Egon never told you he loves you, then?"

Claire hesitated, then said with compulsive honesty, "After he said we were going to stay married because a gentleman doesn't seduce a virgin and then divorce her, he finished by saying in the most offhand manner imaginable that he loved me madly, but when I asked him a moment later if he really

251

meant that, he was *asleep*. So you *see…*" she finished on a despairing note.

"Oh, yes, I see." Lady Hollister nodded sagely. "In that case, you have made the right decision, my dear, and I will certainly assist you in leaving here undeterred."

"Thank you very much, ma'am. I hate to ask you for a loan for my stage ticket, but I have only enough money with me for vails for the servants."

"Do not let us speak of stagecoaches or even mail coaches," Lady Hollister said in peremptory tones. "My grandson's wife will naturally travel post chaise. I'll see to everything. One of the grooms will take you to the nearest coaching inn as soon as you are ready. I'll send Estelle up to help you pack. You may tell her that a family emergency has called you to London. Your brother is ill. Yes, that will serve. Normally, I do not condone dissimulation, but for the sake of sparing Egon the mortification of having people know his wife has run away, I am persuaded the Almighty will forgive us this infraction."

Claire winced at this representation but echoed dutifully, "Yes, ma'am."

"Come to see me before you leave, my dear. Now, I'll let you get on with your packing." The dowager lifted a dismissing hand.

A half-hour later Claire presented herself in the library once more, wearing the sage-green pelisse and hat in which she had arrived at Belhaven and a slightly bemused expression at the speed with which events had moved forward once Lady Hollister swung into action.

"Ah, here you are, my dear. That was very quick of you." Lady Hollister came around the desk with an envelope in her hands. "This will take care of your expenses on the trip."

"Thank you, ma'am. I will repay this as soon as possible."

"Nonsense. I shall present the account to your husband," Lady Hollister said with a gleam in her eye that Claire mistrusted.

She said timidly, "Do you not think it rather … irregular to expect a man to pay his wife's expenses when she leaves him?"

"If he is going to be as relieved as you believe at the separation, he should be happy to foot the bill," came the ruthless reply in bland tones.

"Y-yes, ma'am," Claire said, looking singularly unhappy.

Lady Hollister's eyes softened as she said gently, "I am not going to ask your direction now, my child, because I do not wish to lie to Egon when he asks me for this information, as I am persuaded he will. But I desire you to write to me within one week with the address. Will you promise me that you will do this, Claire? You are a member of my family, and I am entitled to be concerned for your wellbeing."

"Of course I shall, and thank you for … for everything." Claire's smile was tremulous as she stepped forward and briefly embraced the dowager, who looked surprised but not displeased by the spontaneous gesture.

It was early evening in London when a mud-splattered post chaise wove its way around the vehicles heading for the theatres and turned off onto Long Acre. A few minutes later, it came to a sweeping halt before a narrow yellow brick house in a neighbourhood unused to the presence of such lavish conveyances. The postilion jumped down and unstrapped some modest baggage before opening the door and assisting his passenger to alight.

An attractive and elegantly clad young woman well worth a second look stepped onto the pavement and thanked her escort. The second look had revealed smudges of weariness beneath light brown eyes and perhaps the faintest trace of tears on her smooth cheeks, but her smile was the kind that compelled a like response. The postilion touched his hat and accepted the gratuity she pressed into his hands after sounding the brass knocker on the door and depositing her small bags on the step. He lingered for a second until the door opened, and then strode back to join the impatient driver with a farewell wave for his passenger.

She, however, failed to note this salute, having already cast herself bodily into the surprised arms of the comfortable-looking woman who had opened the door. This dramatic gesture was preceded by a near-wail of "*Oh, Sadie!*" and accompanied by a fresh burst of tears.

CHAPTER 16

Egon and Michael arrived back at Belhaven just in time to change for dinner.

"It has been a long day, but worthwhile," Michael declared, kicking a stray pebble from their path on the way from the stables to the house. "Since Jess and I are leaving in the morning, it might have been months before I got the chance to see the old Hollister estate. Fascinating place to poke around in. It must have been larger than Belhaven at one time. Much older, of course."

"Yes. I gather the oldest wings were pulled down or fell down over the last two centuries. Even the part still standing must date from the Tudors — all those casement windows. It's strange that I have so little memory of living there. It will take a pile of money to make it really comfortable."

"But you'll have a pile of money, old son," Michael said, grinning at him.

"I only hope Claire won't think it gloomy, with all those small rooms and low ceilings."

"If you take my advice, you won't let her set eyes on the place until you strip away most of that covering ivy and the growth that has encroached over the years. Just let some light into the rooms and she'll call it picturesque instead of gloomy."

Egon laughed. "You could be right. The grounds have really gone to wilderness. Bringing some order to the unrestricted growth will be my first aim."

Egon was whistling when he entered the sitting room of the green suite a few minutes later. It was empty, so Claire must still be dressing. His pulses quickened as he headed for the bedchamber. Claire had been almost constantly in his thoughts today while he and Mike had inspected his grandfather's estate, her heart-shaped face with the high cheekbones that provided an inspired setting for the lovely wide-set eyes remaining a clear vision before his mind's eye. At times the picture had shifted to the last image he'd had of her deeply asleep in the bed they'd shared, her face sweetly young and somehow vulnerable, even after he'd removed that ridiculous black-feather earpiece.

In recalling their lovemaking today he had been struck sharply, though belatedly, by this vulnerability. Claire had initially impressed him as a young woman well in control of her life and emotions, so much so that he had found himself repeatedly tilting at that control and challenging it during the early part of their stay here. Her impersonal reaction to him as a man had stayed annoyingly constant until he had kissed her in the conservatory. That had been a revelation that had alerted all his hunting instincts. The fire beneath the ice had amazed and intrigued him, but then, many qualities about Claire had intrigued him from the beginning. It wasn't until he'd seen her floundering, as he had feared, in the frigid waters of the lake, trying to save Cyril, that his heart had leapt to a sudden painful cognizance of her importance in his life. Even then he had not known it was love he felt for her, but he had already determined that he would make their temporary marriage permanent before Geoffrey had obligingly put his feelings into words for him.

Claire had not yet stated her love for him in words, but he was convinced she reciprocated his feelings in full measure. That vulnerability that comes from being unsure of the loved one had been much in evidence last night when she had overcome her scruples and fears and given herself to him with such wondrous generosity. He knew it in his bones, but he wanted the words, and he was going to have them from her lips now.

Egon tapped briefly on the bedchamber door and entered, sparing a hope in passing that he would not discover the ubiquitous Estelle in attendance on her mistress. That particular hope was realized on seeing the room deserted, but a quick frown gathered on his brow as he noted the absence of light. Surely the candles should be lighted by now, even if Claire had lingered over tea with the other ladies.

His glance sharpened as a feeling of emptiness crept up on him. His searching eyes paused at the mirrored dressing table, its top bare of any feminine impedimenta; and now fear kicked at his heart, stopping the beat for a second and then sending it racing onward. He strode into the room and opened the large armoire. Empty shelves greeted him.

Fully alarmed by now, Egon was on his way out of the room when he glanced at the bed and stopped short. He moved forward slowly, against his will, to confirm what his quick eyes had recognized. In front of the candlestick and the bronze statue that Claire had brandished on their wedding night lay his mother's ruby necklace, encircling the emerald ring he'd bought for Claire after their wedding.

Egon tore out of the room without touching these tell-tale items, making for his grandmother's apartment.

The door was opened a crack by Elphick, Lady Hollister's long-time dresser, who looked askance at his demand to see his grandmother. "You know her ladyship isn't to be disturbed at her toilette for anything, Master Egon," she said flatly. She'd have closed the door on the words except that he'd put a foot there to prevent this. "*Master Egon!*"

"It's all right, Elphick, I'll see my grandson. Leave us alone until I ring," Lady Hollister called from her boudoir.

Egon closed the door behind the affronted dresser and strode into his grandmother's sanctum without a glance to right or left.

Lady Hollister was reclining against the rose-pink velvet cushions of an ornately carved chaise longue, wearing a dove-grey dressing gown of a sumptuous soft silk that flowed down over the sides. "I've been expecting you," she remarked, placing a bookmark between the pages of the volume in her hands as she closed and lowered it to her lap.

"Where is she?"

"I presume that peremptory demand refers to the whereabouts of your wife?" Lady Hollister queried. "You may sit," she added, indicating a boudoir chair covered in the same rosy velvet.

Egon ignored this. "Where did she go, Gran?"

Lady Hollister raised her lorgnette to her eyes and inspected the tautly controlled impatience on her grandson's dark countenance at her leisure before replying. "I was not made privy to Claire's ultimate destination, though I assume it to be somewhere in London. You would do better to curb whatever rash emotion has you in its command and prepare to exercise a rational judgment."

"I must find her; I am going after her," he flung over his shoulder as he started to leave the room.

"You will not do so tonight, however," his grandmother said, not raising her voice by even half a tone. "Claire left Belhaven shortly after midday. You could not catch up with her tonight even if you knew her destination. Do you know where she would go?" she added as Egon stopped his forward progress and turned back reluctantly. She waited patiently, never taking her eyes from his face, which was a battleground of conflicting emotions at present.

"No," he admitted at last, his shoulders slumping forward as some of the urgency drained out of him. He fixed burning eyes on the still figure on the *chaise longue*. "Why did you let her go, Gran?"

"Claire was a guest at Belhaven, not a prisoner," his grandparent replied tartly. "I do not know what you think I could do to prevent a guest from leaving if she so desired."

Egon's lips parted, but he apparently had second thoughts about arguing this point, for he closed them again. He walked slowly back into the room and sat in the chair his grandmother had indicated. "Obviously Claire apprised you of her intention to leave Belhaven. Did she tell you her reason for going?" The fire had died out of his eyes, leaving no trace of emotion on his countenance.

The older edition of that thin-cheeked face was equally unreadable as Lady Hollister replied, "Claire said her honour demanded that she leave you."

"Her *honour*!"

The white head nodded in confirmation, the dark eyes watchful as astonishment enlivened the young man's features briefly.

"How could a woman cite honour as a reason for *leaving* her husband?" He raked his fingers through his raven-dark hair, looking at such a loss that his grandmother took pity on him to the extent of amplifying her statement.

"Claire felt she had tricked you into consummating the marriage." She paused as a tide of red surged into Egon's cheeks and a muscle twitched therein.

"She did no such thing!" he snapped.

"She felt," Lady Hollister went on carefully, "that you would not have acted thus had you known she was a virgin. She also felt, rightly or wrongly, that she should have stopped you at that point so that you would not have felt that *your* honour compelled you to continue with the marriage instead of seeking the divorce you had planned."

The silence that followed on this statement was electric with strongly held feelings as the young man fought a desire to relieve those feelings with some sort of violent outburst. "Claire seems to have confided rather thoroughly in you," he said at last with masterly restraint. "Just how much did she tell you about our marriage?"

"The whole sorry saga, I should imagine."

His eyes probed hers. "Did she tell you how we met?"

"If you mean do I know she is an actress, yes. Claire told me the whole story, though she begged me to make clear to you that she never would have betrayed you — her word, not mine — by telling me anything had you not assured her that I always intended to leave Belhaven to you, despite anything I may have said to the contrary." There was a good deal of asperity in Lady Hollister's voice, to which Egon addressed himself.

"I only said that to ease Claire's mind. She was greatly troubled by the deception we were engaged in. I suppose I should apologize, Gran, but your letter, arriving when it did, made it impossible for me to come down here to see you unless I was already married."

"You never considered agreeing to my desire that you marry Miss Winward?"

"Never. I more or less accepted that Belhaven was lost to me. The marriage bargain with Claire was born out of frustration and retaliation, at least at first." Egon stopped abruptly and pinned his grandmother's gaze. "I had better make it clear right now, Gran, that though I can live without Belhaven, I have no intention of living without Claire. She may have been an actress, but she is far and away too good for me, and I am prepared to move heaven and earth to get her back. I'll make her love me."

Lady Hollister permitted a little smile to cross her lips at this fierce and undutiful speech. "I should say you have already done that," she replied encouragingly. She added with a straight face and a touch of malicious enjoyment in the telling, "What you failed to do was convince Claire that *you* love her. I understand you fell asleep instead."

Egon's jaw sagged. "That woman takes a lot of convincing," he said weakly, but the hard, anxious look about him had faded somewhat.

The anxiety had returned to his face in full measure five days later as he prowled the streets of London's theatre districts at all hours, hoping in vain for a glimpse of the woman who had been his wife for so brief a time. For lack of better information, he had started his search at Drury Lane Theatre, but Claire had not sought to renew her stage career. Neither had she been in contact with any of the cast of players as far as he could determine after haunting the green room for the first two nights after his return to the city. The theatre management denied all knowledge of her past direction or present whereabouts. He cudgelled his brain to recall the name of the woman who had witnessed their marriage and came up with it at last, only to be told that Mrs. Mullins was no longer employed at the theatre as a dresser. Another trip to the green room after a performance gained him the information from a garrulous young actress that Lord Mostyn had been making inquiries about Clairisse Deschamps during the previous week.

Egon's big-eared intelligencer reported an acrimonious interview between Mrs. Mullins and the earl, which had resulted in the dismissal of the dresser from her employment. A nagging fear that Mostyn might have learned Claire's direction from the dresser was only partially put to rest by gossip going around the clubs that the earl had departed recently to join a hunting party at Lord Esterby's shooting box in Leicestershire.

The only thing that enabled Egon to hang on to his sanity was the knowledge passed on to him by his grandmother just before he left Belhaven that Claire had faithfully promised to send her direction to Lady Hollister within a sennight of her departure. Seven days had seemed an eternity at that moment when his confidence in his ability to track her down himself was running high. Now he found himself keeping the promised limit to his suffering in the front of his mind the way a child kept his approaching birthday fixed in his head as he plodded through the days that stood as obstacles to his delight. As he went about a daily routine to pass the hours that remained before his life could begin again, he often longed for a drug or a spell that would render him unconscious until word arrived of his wife's whereabouts. And always there existed the fear he could not entirely subdue that Claire might really intend to disappear from his life forever, though he would have sworn less than a week ago that she returned his love. Late at night this subterranean dread would bob to the surface of his mind to torment him and rob him of the blessed oblivion of sleep. He was staying out of his bed longer each night in the hope of exhausting himself to the point where his brain would cease functioning so that no thoughts could push their way into his mind to torture him.

The sleepless nights were beginning to be reflected in the lines of his face, which had deepened, giving him a haggard look that his man Henley commented on as he dressed for yet another trip to the theatre.

"I'm not sleeping as well as I might lately," he replied. "It's nothing."

"I hope her ladyship's brother, the one she's nursing, hasn't taken worse?" Henley said, handing his master his black silk hat.

"Not worse," Egon denied, keeping up the fiction his grandmother had set about to account for Claire's sudden departure from Belhaven, "but no better yet either."

"Sometimes it goes like that for a while, and then they ups and dies sudden-like."

This ghoulish pronouncement could not be allowed to stand. "Nonsense, he's a young man," Egon protested.

"Sometimes it hits the young ones the hardest," the determined Job's-comforter insisted, and he was allowed the last word as his master made his hasty escape into the evening.

Some blind instinct kept Egon returning to Drury Lane each evening, perhaps because it was his only connection, however remote, with Claire. These days he watched the audience, not the play, however, in the faint hope of spotting her in the crowd, not acknowledging to himself that if she were really determined to deny herself to him, this would be the last place she would frequent.

Tonight was no different from the ones that had preceded it. There was no sign of Claire in any of the boxes. In the first interval he remained in his seat in the pit, scanning the crowd through his opera glasses, but after that he joined those milling about. There were the usual roisterous groups of young bucks who came to ogle the ladies on and off the stage. He found himself behind one such assemblage before the farce came on. From their conversation, if such it could be called, he gathered that they were bank clerks and law clerks aping the young bloods' dress to the extent they were able. He was about to push his way through when a voice to his left said, "Give this to Yelland. I owe it to him."

Egon spun around, searching for the speaker, but there were a half-dozen very young cubs within earshot, and he was too late to see anything change hands. They were all talking at once, verbal scraps that meant nothing to him, but he kept close to them, his eyes examining each face he could see in the shifting group for some resemblance to Claire. She had said she had a brother, and his grandmother, who had learned much more about his wife's background in a few hours than he had been able to pull out of her, had told him this Jeremy was apprenticed to a London bank. He fought to stay abreast of the party of young men in the jostling crowd and finally elbowed his way near enough to tap one on the shoulder.

"Which one is Yelland?" he asked, raising his voice to be heard above the lowing of the herd.

"The tall one in the middle," the vacant-faced youth responded, pointing to three aspiring dandies ahead of him.

Egon muttered his thanks and shouldered his way forward, clapping a hand on the upper arm of a youth with light brown hair, who turned a questioning face dominated by black-fringed light-brown eyes toward him.

"Are you Jeremy Yelland?"

The youth nodded, his eyes appraising the other's exquisitely tied cravat.

"I'd like to speak to you for a moment."

"But the farce is just about to begin," the young man protested. "And who are you, anyway?"

"My name is Hollister and I'm your brother-in-law," Egon said, watching a wary look leap into the other's eyes. He tightened his grip on Jeremy's arm. "Let's go outside, where we can hear each other without shouting."

"It's all right," Jeremy said to his friends, who had noticed the stranger's hold on his arm and were trying to decide if assistance would be needed. "You go ahead; I'll be right back."

When the group had walked on, however, he turned to Egon and said with a fair assumption of maturity, "If you are looking for Claire, you've come to the wrong person. She doesn't wish to see you."

"Did she tell you that?" Egon demanded.

"She told me she had left you, and since you planned to divorce her after the marriage had served your purpose, there is no need for you to see her again. Your lawyer can handle the matter from now on."

They were standing outside the theatre under a clear starry sky. Egon studied the youth in the light of the building's flambeaux, noting the strong facial resemblance to his sister and the stubborn set to his jaw. He curbed his natural impatience now that he had found his conduit to Claire, but said in silky tones, "I want Claire's direction. I could beat it out of you, but I'd rather you told me willingly."

"You could probably mill me down eventually," the young man conceded, his eyes measuring the other's superior bulk, "but you won't find it as easy as you might suppose, nor will you succeed in getting Claire's direction from me. It is all my fault that she is in this mess, and I'll not have her made more unhappy by your bullying tactics."

"How is it your fault that your sister is in a 'mess,' as you so delicately phrase it?" Egon released his brother-in-law's arm but kept him pinned with his back to the building to discourage any sudden attempt to run away.

"Claire made that disgusting bargain with you solely because I was in trouble and needed a lot of money quickly. I let her throw away her chance to establish herself respectably to save my skin. I may be as weak and selfish as Sadie says, but at least I can protect my sister from your harassment."

"Very admirable sentiments, though a little belated," Egon said approvingly, "but you will be doing your sister a very great disservice by concealing her whereabouts from me. I would like to turn our 'disgusting bargain' into a respectable marriage, and I believe I can speak for Claire when I assure you that this is what she would like also."

Jeremy's eyes had been fixed on the older man's face during this earnest speech, trying to gauge his sincerity. Now he said slowly, "I would like to believe you. I will go to see Claire tomorrow at lunchtime and tell her what you have said. If she agrees to see you, I'll send a messenger to you with her direction."

Egon's teeth clicked together at this reasonable suggestion. "My God, man, I've been going out of my mind for the past five days! I want to see my wife now! I'm not threatening you, Jeremy, I'm begging you for her direction."

Jeremy read the desperation in his brother-in-law's haggard face and at once decided to give him the information he sought.

Egon wrung his hand and strode off without another word.

The door was opened to him by the comely woman he recalled from his wedding day. "Good evening, Mrs. Mullins, I've come to see my wife."

Her fine hazel eyes registered no surprise, but she remained planted in the doorway. "You have chosen a late hour to call, Sir Egon. Claire has already retired for the night."

"I apologize for the hour, but I just this moment discovered her whereabouts."

"How?"

"I've been haunting the theatre for days. I just met her brother there by the sheerest chance. Please, Mrs. Mullins," he added quietly, "I need to see Claire."

She nodded and stepped back. "Come in. If you'll wait in the parlour, I'll tell her you are here."

Egon paced relentlessly about the tidy room, seeing nothing, for long moments that stretched his nerves, though he tried to talk himself into a calmer state. It was over — the separation, the search, the misery — all was done with. He would persuade Claire of his sincerity even if he could not give her the eloquence of the speeches she was used to hearing on the stage.

She came into the room light-footed while he was pacing away from the door, and he turned to behold her, a lovely vision in the green velvet wrapper, with her tawny hair spilling over the shoulders and her eyes huge and questioning.

All ideas of fine speeches fled his brain and he burst out with the one thought that had tortured him endlessly. "How could you do it, Claire? How could you leave me like that?"

Claire responded instantly to the raw pain in his voice. She fairly flew across the room, flinging herself into arms that closed about her with a force that threatened her ribs, though she could feel him shaking underneath. "I couldn't trap you into a marriage you never wanted, Egon," she pleaded in extenuation of her crime.

He put her away from him firmly and stared down into eyes shimmering with unshed tears. "I want this marriage and you more than I have ever wanted anything in my life. Believe that, Claire, and believe that I love you, because it's true now and it was true last week and it will always be the most important truth in my life, and, I hope, in yours."

Claire flung her arms around her husband's neck and dragged his head down to hers. Light blazed in Egon's dark eyes as he complied with this wordless demand by kissing her breathless.

"And now, young woman," he murmured after a very satisfying interval, "I believe it is more than time that I heard a similar declaration from you. As a matter of fact, I had determined to demand just that when I got back from looking over Hollister Place that afternoon and got the shock of my life when I opened the bedroom door and found you gone."

"Oh, darling, I am so sorry, but, you see, you were so casual the ... the night before, and then you fell asleep, and I thought ... I feared..." Her eyes pleaded with him for forgiveness. "Of course I love you. I fell a little bit in love with you in the green room when Geoffrey introduced us, despite the disapproval that fairly oozed from your pores, and though I fought it with my mind, I fell more deeply in love each day, until I was afraid the whole world must know my secret."

"I call that an *amende honorable*," Egon said with a smile. "I misjudged you in the beginning, and that influenced our subsequent exchanges. I struggled against loving you too, and contributed my share to the confusion. But as for being casual and falling asleep, I can honestly plead total exhaustion at that point after four wretched nights on that hellish cot in the dressing room. Knowing you were so close, yet out of my reach, was an unholy exercise in frustration."

Claire's marvellous black-fringed eyes had grown wider as her husband made his rueful confession, and now she startled him by loosing a delicious trill of soft laughter, raising her chin, and exposing the long length of creamy throat to his voracious eyes.

Egon's lips followed where his eyes had been. He felt her quiver in response and reined in his own leaping senses as the incongruity of their present position struck him. "Claire, come with me, darling, now, tonight," he urged.

"But … but where? It's the middle of the night."

"It's scarcely eleven. I can testify that Miss Clairisse Deschamps has been abroad at an even later hour upon occasion and promise that Lady Hollister will be much better escorted. My lodgings will have to do for tonight. We could go back to Belhaven tomorrow, but I want to have you all to myself for a while, I don't care where. Is there any place you'd like to go?"

"It doesn't matter to me either," Claire said, her eyes shining with excitement. "I've always thought I'd like to visit Bath."

"Then Bath it shall be. You may drink the waters with the octogenarians. While you are getting dressed, I'll go out and find us a hackney carriage. Just pack what you'll need for tonight. We'll come back here tomorrow for the rest, and so that I may properly meet and thank the Mullins family for their loving care of my lovely girl."

Claire just stood there blinking at the rapidity with which things happened when Egon took charge — another trait inherited from his grandmother.

"One thing more before you go upstairs to dress, darling. This is the most important item to put on." Egon took the emerald ring from an inner pocket of his coat and slipped it over her finger to join her wedding ring. "This time I'll do it in proper fashion," he said, kissing her fingers, "and this time it will stay there, yes?"

Soft luminous eyes met intense dark ones as Claire gave her husband the pledge he demanded. "Forever," she promised.

A NOTE TO THE READER

Dear Reader,

If you have enjoyed the novel enough to leave a review on **Amazon** and **Goodreads**, then we would be truly grateful.

Sapere Books is an exciting new publisher of brilliant fiction and popular history.

To find out more about our latest releases and our monthly bargain books visit our website: **saperebooks.com**

Printed in Great Britain
by Amazon